Barbara,
Wishing you Merry Christmas
Blessings,
Bonnie

D1593424

THE TREES WILL CLAP

Bonnie Evans' Lacey is wonderfully reminiscent of Harper Lee's Scout, with a freshness that is all her own. Be prepared to be deeply moved by this story of innocence in the midst of a world that is not.

—*Nancy Rue, award-winning American Christian novelist and author of more than 120 books for adults, teens, and tweens*

Bonnie Evans' new novel, *The Trees Will Clap*, traces a young girl's journey through insecurity, loss, and redemption. The story deals with the essential issues of identity and family—both natural and spiritual—and with questions of the mysterious nature of God's will and the experience of healing for body and soul. In the process, the tale evokes childhood memories and images of an "American heartland" that many of us remember vividly and love dearly, even as it seems to be vanishing before our very eyes. *The Trees Will Clap* engages the imagination, warms the heart, and inspires hope for the fulfillment of God's promises. I heartily recommend it to readers everywhere, both young and old.

—*"Russ" Mason (a.k.a. R. L. Mason III) University of Delaware English Language Institute Assistant Professor, retired*

As years go by, our minds can readily slip in memory of the ways things used to be. We often talk of the good ol' days, and yet how few of us truly remember all the specifics of the past. As we forget the past, we may also forget how the past forges a way for our future. Bonnie Evans has captured both very succinctly in her new book, *The Trees Will Clap*. You will find yourself reminiscing, meditating, and looking ahead. Her ability to bring you right into the scene will hold you. But far greater will be the promises of God and His faithfulness when we don't really have all the answers. Sit by the fire and enjoy the pages of this book. You won't be disappointed.

—*Dr. H. Wallace Webster Senior Pastor for 30 years at Mt. Airy Bible Church Author of* Christ Will Build His Church, I Heart Parenting, *and* Graced to Grace

The Trees Will Clap

Bonnie Mae Evans

THE TREES WILL CLAP

Copyright © 2016 Bonnie Mae Evans
ISBN 978-1-938796-15-9
Library of Congress Control Number: 2016955153
Fiction • Cultural Heritage

Nancy Rue, Content Editor
Fran D. Lowe, Copy Editor

Cover design by Jessica Bastidas

Published by Fruitbearer Publishing, LLC
P.O. Box 777 • Georgetown, DE 19947
302.856.6649 • FAX 302.856.7742
www.fruitbearer.com • info@fruitbearer.com

To my mother
with love

For you will go out with joy,
And be led forth with peace;
The mountains and the hills
will break forth into shouts of joy before you,
And all the trees of the field will clap their hands.
Isaiah 55:12 (NASB)

"A few minutes ago every tree was excited,
bowing to the roaring storm, waving, swirling,
tossing their branches in glorious enthusiasm like worship.
But though to the outer ear these trees are now silent,
Their songs never cease."
John Muir

To him who overcomes,
I will give some of the hidden manna,
and I will give him a white stone,
and a new name written on the stone
which no one knows but he who receives it.
Revelation 2:17 (NKJV)

Chapter One

I remember the events of that day as clearly as if it had happened this morning. It's like an engraving on the innermost part of my brain: the sounds, the smells, the colors, and most of all—the feelings. The feelings of a five-and-a-half-year-old little girl, who, in a few ticks of the second hand—accompanied by the deliberate, dark strokes of a fountain pen—had her entire cosmos taken apart, shuffled around, and put back together, this time with two integral pieces in strangely different places.

"Yer name ain't no longer gonna be Yvonnah Elizabeth Lewis, ya understand?" commanded my new dad. "Now yer Lacey Joan Millford. We're startin' from scratch, like the day you was born. From here on out, that's who you'll be. You just remember that, and hold your head up high." He jutted out his chin. "You're a Millford now, and that's a good name. We ain't got much but that good name, and now I'm giving it to you, just like your mother. We'll all have the same last name 'cause that's what family is. It's all in the name and what pops up in people's heads when they hear that name. You be a hard worker and good for yer word, and you'll live up to that name someday, ya hear?" He shoved his hands deep into the pockets of his khaki pants.

The pants I would come to know as his work pants. Every morning he put them on with a clean, pressed cotton shirt of the same color that smelled of fresh air and Cheer. Since he wasn't much on cuddling little girls, I only knew this by catching a whiff of him on the rushing air pushed out of his way as he raced out the door to another odd job someone had called him to.

He took his work as seriously as a brain surgeon who had just gotten a call about a terrible accident and some poor soul's brain was swelling to the point of exploding and only he could save them. Every night, long after I was in bed, he would come home and drop the pants in a heap by his side of the bed and fall in beside Mother, exhausted.

He was exhausted from a compulsion that drove him on from the pinky-black hours of morning to the dark, sulking hours after midnight, leaving less than enough rest for any normal man. But then again, he wasn't any normal man. He was a Millford! And darn proud of it. Although it did seem to me that on many occasions he didn't seem all that proud of it, more like he was willing it to be true.

I caught sight of the wavy reflection of our new family of three in a storefront window as we hurried by that day. My name—as well as my life—was changed forever. Khaki Dad was bent forward with his Shoal Bank work hat pulled far down on his forehead, taking wide, impatient strides on his long legs as we crossed the street. Mother was wobbling along a few steps behind on her spindly-heeled, pointiest-toed high heels. She was reaching out her hand and wiggling it impatiently to pull me closer in line.

This scene reminded me of the times I had stood in the yard with my grandfather—Grandy, I called him—and watched with fascination as stray snow geese would wing their way faster and faster across the grey-blue blanket stretched out above us to catch up with the last goose in line and with relief, find their place at the end of the flying arrow. Grandy would pause from his work, resting his arm on the top of his rake handle. He'd push his straw hat back on his head with his pointer finger to get a full window of this miracle of togetherness that took place every autumn as the geese blasted their hoarse greetings back and forth to each other.

"Where do you think they're headed, Grandy?" I'd ask.

"Don't know, Son. Some place warm, I 'magine."

Even though I was a girl, he called me "Son" most times. I liked that term of endearment because it made me special to him, like the son he never had. The other times he called me "Sweetheart." I guess that would make him exempt from having to remember to call me by my new name. I liked that. It felt like quiet reassurance that nothing was ever going to change between my Grandy and me.

"Straighten out that dress in the front, Yvonnah." When Mother said my name, it was with a "Ya" at the beginning of it, so it sounded like this: Ya-vonnah.

"I mean Lacey, and stand up straight! Put those shoulders back. I don't know why you got to always slump, slump, slump. It's exasperatin'! That's what it is, tryin' to get you to look like a lady. Now, smile," drilled my mother. "Get that wupped hound-dog look off your face. We want Mr. Jackson to think you're happy 'bout this, don't we? If he don't think you're happy, he might not let you be a Millford. Then where would you be, huh? Mr. Jackson's a very important man here in town. He decides a whole lotta important things for people."

I had already figured out that he must be pretty important because she was out to impress him with the lavish use of Wild Rose cologne, which she saved for only the most special times: weddings, funerals, doctor's appointments —and later on, the all-important PTA meetings. Her voice nagged on and on, fading into the background. My attention was gratefully distracted from the uneasy feeling starting to creep in my stomach as we entered the Ben Franklin store.

Greeting us were high dark wooden counters with glass-fronted bins filled three-quarters to the top with yummy chocolate, vanilla, and strawberry-coated coconut balls; sugary orange slices; and spearmint leaves. The very sight of them made my mouth water to the point I almost drooled down the front of my dressy dress. Thank goodness I was able to catch it and swallow quickly before I did. That would have finished me off with my mother for the day.

Just last night she had stood hunched over my yellow Sunday dress spread across the ironing board, determinedly pressing out every wrinkle with the help of Argo starch and a silver clothes sprinkler stuck in the mouth of a green glass Coke bottle. She ironed as if she were trying to eradicate all evil from the known world. When finished, my dress was as stiff as one of the red-coated Queen's guards at the palace, hanging there at attention until called upon in the morning to its task of making me look presentable to Mr. Jackson.

The age-worn wooden floors gleamed invitingly as we passed by rows and rows of miniature bottles of Ben Hur and Evening in Paris colognes and Mavis silky white powder in red tin boxes. Sitting alongside them were neat piles of rattail combs and beaded hairnets, all separated with long, narrow glass dividers.

Then came the crowning jewel of womanhood, the forbidden fruit of a little girl's desire. The perfecting touch to make one who is oh, so plain, beautiful—someone acceptable to gaze upon; someone who could be lovely, even likeable. Makeup! All shades of lipstick stood in gold tin push-up tubes that had the aroma of waxy roses. Little clear plastic cylinders held six different sticky colors of eye shadow. Each fit neatly into the bottom of the other to form a tube. In flat red rectangle cases, small cakes of black mascara and tiny brushes were nestled side by side.

You had to spit on the narrow block of hard, dry mascara and smear it around with the brush before you could put it on your eyelashes while staring straight ahead in the mirror and steadily blinking with every stroke of the brush. Don't ask me how I knew such things. Lord knows, decent people like my mother and grandmother didn't use that paint-on sin. Nothing could surpass the wholesome look of a face washed fresh with Sweetheart soap.

As much as I loved that sweet scent, I knew deep in my heart that the minute I was able to, I would join the ranks of those cheap but beautiful women who dared to wear makeup. Someday I would, and I'd be a better person for it. I could almost hear those beauty products calling my name, but not clearly enough to distinguish which name—my old name or my new, improved name.

To be completely honest (although I would never dare to say it out loud, for fear of hurting Khaki Dad's feelings), I was sorta attached to my old name. I knew who people were talking to the first time when they said it, and I didn't get caught off guard quite as much with that name as I did with my new one.

Of course, I was marched right past all of those alluring products and their promises as I felt the hard pressure of a knuckle between my shoulder blades propelling me up the creaky wooden staircase on the left of the store.

Those old steps were so worn out in the middle, they gave the appearance of sagging under the weight of all those years. Footworn. Worn out by the travel of life. As I climbed, I marveled at the thought of how many people had trudged up those very same stairs before me to get their names changed. It must have been hundreds, for hundreds of years, to wear the wood out in the middle like that.

Amazing. And I had never heard of even one single other person besides myself who had to get a new name unless, of course, they were getting married. Just like my mother and Khaki Dad did a few weeks before this very important day. But these new-named people must be all over the place.

I guess it's something you just don't talk about. I'm not quite sure why. Maybe it was something to be ashamed of, or maybe it was something that if some poor children in an orphanage somewhere got wind of, it would break their poor little hearts in two. To think that some other little girl who had a perfectly good name and a Nana and Grandy who loved and took good care of her just for no good reason got to have a new home and a new name.

All this, while they were sitting there staring out of the upstairs window of a paintless, gray-shingled orphanage in hopes of being the first to catch a glimpse of a nice car coming around the bend of the gravel driveway to take one of them to a new home with parents who wanted them and would love them forever—and even give them a new name like theirs.

Adoption, or lack of it. Oh, the pain was too much to think about. For I had a tender heart for those less fortunate than myself and would gladly have let them have my new name and spooky new house.

Up until now I had only stayed there for a few short visits, and that had been quite enough. But, believe you me, something about that house was spooky. It may have been the hundred-or-so-year-old dining room that everything else was built new around. Maybe ghosts lived in the old wood or something. Then there was that secret door built right into the walnut paneling that opened into a forgotten little room under the stairs. Looking at the walls, no one would even notice a door. There were no handles or hinges to give away its presence, but there it was just the same, the edges corresponding exactly with the grooves in the panels. Hidden but in plain view, defying one to find the depths of its secrets.

An innocent enough painting hung over the door. Its subject was a flock of sheep wandering around aimlessly in a brown grass meadow beside a colorless, shallow stream under a plain blue sky. They were hemmed in by an equally boring, plain wooden frame—nothing to arouse suspicion, not interesting enough to even look at twice.

The door was opened by carefully removing the picture and leaning on one side of the paneling. Of course, if you leaned on it too forcefully or quickly, you went flying into the little hidden space and skinned your knee on the bare floor in there. Something I had learned from experience. Once inside the door, it swung quickly behind you, swallowing you up just like the great gaping mouth of a monster, shutting out all light except what slithered in between the tiny cracks around the edges—leaving you scrambling around, waving your hands frantically in the dark air, feeling for the string to switch on the light bulb, wondering if you would be able to find it before something else found you.

I quickly switched my mind away from that scary thinking to more pleasant thoughts of just a few weeks prior, to my mother's wedding day. Early that morning I heard her giggle when she was in the kitchen with Nana. The sound of her laugh was nice but unfamiliar. I smiled, remembering. Laughter was not something I usually associated with Mother. Most of the time she was too busy going to work and being worried.

The afternoon was filled with the swoosh-swish sounds of her blue lace wedding gown and the sweet cloud smell of her creamy roses. Ribbons and angel-white lace held the roses together that were poised in her hands, held at her waist just so, as she walked up the wine-red carpet in the aisle of the little country church to stand beside my new dad and me. Wearing a white wedding gown was taboo if a woman had been previously married—or Heaven forbid—she had a baby without being married.

The sun presided over the ceremony through the brightly colored Bible scenes picturing Jesus and His disciples on the ancient stained glass windows. It added its own special gift to the beauty of the day by reflecting see-through rainbows from the windows across the upturned faces of all of the friends and family who had come to share this special occasion with us.

I had stood there gazing into so many faces that I didn't yet know, family and friends of Khaki Dad. There were faces that would now become a part of my everyday life. Faces that would try their best to replace the old, familiar loving faces that I clung to in my mind's eye and whole heart with frightened determination. There were those precious faces that would eventually become near and dear to me. I would seek them out for reassurance and understanding that was beyond my years. Those were times when the faces I loved and needed so much were withheld from me for reasons that I could not comprehend. There were faces that never would totally accept an alien, an adopted one. Yet, other faces would become friends to me, delighting me with their funny ways and easy friendship. And, of course, there were those I didn't see, who would on no account be caught darkening the doorway of a church for fear of being struck by lightning cast directly from the hand of God.

Then, with sudden relief, on the periphery of that suffocating blanket of unfamiliar people, my search ended in the comfort of the two beloved faces that I had gazed up into since my newborn eyes first began to focus. Gentle faces mirroring back at me the deep, abiding love I felt for them.

Hidden in their lines and wrinkles was wisdom, knowing of my beginnings, my hopes, and my fears—along with their reassurance that all would be well. Taking special note of a perfect wishbone-shaped rainbow that had fallen across Grandy's cheek, I smiled and took it as a sign that my earlier wish had been granted.

Mother's wedding day. As I recall, I thought my mother looked beautiful that afternoon, exactly like the blue fairy in *Pinocchio*, if only she had held the crystal star-topped wand in her hand. While she was walking toward us, smiling behind her glistening rosy-red lipstick, I had a little daydream that I oh, so wished could have been real. She came to me and extended her glittering magic wand and lightly touched the top of my head with it and said, "Whatever you wish for, little girl, I have the power to grant you."

I knew right off what I would wish for without any hesitation. It was the same thing I had wished for when Grandy and I had pulled opposite ends of the greasy pulley bone (or wishbone, as most people knew it) from the buttery golden hen that we had just eaten for dinner. This was right before I was supposed to follow my small tan suitcase gripped by Khaki Dad down our steps and out the door of our cozy pink-shingled home to his old, made-new house. I knew as we pulled opposite ends of that upside down "V," gazing deep into each other's eyes, when it began to bend and crack a little, that it really didn't matter who got the long side with the knob on top. We were both wishing for the same thing.

Nana always made sure that I got that piece of chicken—the wishbone—in hopes that I would think I had to eat the tender white strands of meat first, before I could pull it and have a special wish come true.

She always worried about my lack of interest in eating and constantly tried new recipes and ideas that she thought would spur my poor appetite. Once, she made "ants on a log" to entice me. It was peanut butter spread in the groove of a crunchy piece of celery with raisins on the top. I liked that a lot—to play with, mostly. The ants were too nice to eat. After you played with them awhile, they became like friends. How could you *possibly* eat a friend?

Then there were her special brown-lace eggs. We would go out to the henhouse together and slip our hands under each fat hen and feel around in the warmth underneath for her offering of the day. Nana would always check under Nessie, Lily, and Gertie since they were the most excitable and likely to make a fuss. Walking silently and taking in the sweet feathery scent of their dwelling, I went straight for Lucy and Mildred's boxes. Gently sliding my small hands between their soft feathers and the warm straw, I extracted the perfectly formed warm eggs, carefully placing them in the woven basket. While I petted and coaxed Mildred, she would turn her head away as if it was a conspiracy between us to let me steal hers.

Having known these particular hens from the biddy stage and watching them grow into full-time laying hens, I had developed a special attachment to them. Love. Yes, it was actually love that I felt for them. Chicken love. Although

I knew very well that wasn't a heart-safe thing to feel for farm animals, I just couldn't help myself.

Going back into our kitchen, Nana would then quickly spoon a good-sized blob of bacon grease from the grease can into the cast-iron frying pan already heating on the front burner of the stove. As soon as there was the first sizzle in the now liquid grease, she would crack open in perfect halves one of our fresh eggs into the pan, followed by one and then another for our breakfast. She cooked them quickly, generous with the salt and pepper. She didn't turn them over but instead let the yellows cook from the bottom up. The delicious brown lace would appear around the edges, perfectly hemming in each egg. Although I was loving the idea that she cooked special for me, at the time none of those recipes was the magic solution to my grieving appetite.

This left a raw spot in Nana's heart. She so loved to feed and nourish people and animals alike. After all, how long could one go on living without proper nourishment? It was like the bread of God's Word to her, unfathomable to think of going a day without it. Your soul and body alike would surely perish. I mean, wasn't that one of the last things that Jesus had done for His disciples? He had prepared a nice dinner of good bread and the best wine for them all together. Next, He fed them while they talked about important things. Then later on He washed their feet. If it was that important to Jesus, then it was that important to Nana. She had a gift for good cooking, but if one just couldn't take it in, she felt a sense of personal failure.

I tried and tried to please her by eating some of her love-cooked dishes, but I just couldn't always force it to stay down. Sometimes after taking a bite, it would grow bigger and more liquidy in my mouth and start to gag me. I would chew and chew. Then my eyes would suddenly roll back, and that dreaded retching would spasm up from my stomach, determined to expel not only that bite but anything else that had escaped it and actually made it into my stomach.

I would have to jump up from my place at the table and run out the screen door to the cement step. Oftentimes, there was barely enough time to lean over in the grass before my indistinguishably chewed-up dinner would come flying out of my tightly held white lips. Instantly, I would feel better except for the shaking in my knees and sour, stinging taste in my mouth and throat. Sometimes one of my ears—deep inside, the part close to my brain—would sting a smidge too. I could picture a miniscule piece of barley that I had swallowed, lodged there deep in the "station tube" I had heard of, between my brain and ear hole.

I always stared at the offending multi-colored wad of slimy food for a few minutes as it laid there in the grass, and on occasion broke off a switch from a forsythia on the side of the house and poked at it a little to see if I might find the cause of the sudden repulsion that it had stirred up in my belly. Then I could have found the reason behind this. Something I could blame it on, something that would clear Nana's cooking and myself as the cause.

I could march back into the dining room and proudly hold out the offending object and say, "See, it was this old penny that I swallowed that made me throw up." We would all laugh together, and Grandy would say, "Come on, Son, let's go throw it in the well and make a wish." But, of course, I could never find the cause of that blasted throwing-up problem.

After a while I would come sheepishly back to the table, knowing that once again I had failed Nana and set the furrows deeper into her forehead. Her worry lines of concern and love for me started long before I was born to my too young mother and first dad. Those lines would continue to deepen the better part of her life. I think they most likely went so deep, they went right down to her heart and creased that as well.

By now we had reached the door of the great Mr. Jackson's office. The memories as they flood back tend to make me wander, and I just like to sorta float on them as I recollect. It's almost like moshing with my mind. Anyhow, we were on the way to get my name changed. Not just last but first and middle, too.

Looming ahead was a black wooden door. Khaki Dad boomed on it three times with his balled-up fist. The sudden noise jarred me back to the present and echoed back down the steps. The door opened abruptly as if Mr. Jackson had been waiting there behind it, listening to us as we climbed the stairs.

He was a huge man in a black suit and black tie with equally black hair. He shook hands with Khaki Dad and nodded in the direction of my pretty, young mother. She had worn her new purple-flowered dress, tight in the waist, full and flowing from the hips. With a loud bang to let everyone below know that important business was now taking place, Mr. Jackson closed the door and stepped behind his huge black desk. Mother sat ramrod straight, while Khaki Dad sorta lounged to one side in the big black vinyl chairs as I stood self-consciously in the middle, in front of the desk.

So this was the all-powerful Mr. Jack Jackson, who from this moment on in my mind would be remembered as Black Jackson because everything around him was so black except his face, hands, shirt, and the papers in front of him. But I *did* happen to notice that even his face had a dark, ominous shadow that started at his cheekbones and kept on going right down into his chokingly tight white collar. It was like the darkness of that office was bent on taking over all that was light. I sorta figured he was going to be like the Wizard of Oz, with lots of white smoke and clouds all around him. I thought all mighty and powerful people blew smoke.

"Well, young lady, do you want to have your name changed to Lacey Joan Millford?"

Paralyzed with the shock of being addressed directly by "The Great Oz," my mouth dropped open. I felt as if my breath had just been sucked out of the big vent over there in the side wall housing a huge, round silver fan.

Eons passed, it seemed, and then I felt a finger in my side jab me back from the brink of nothingness as I heard myself squeak yes in a way too quiet voice.

And that was that. They signed the papers, shook hands again, and we turned and left. Back down the creaky stairs, right past all those future promises of beauty and allure that the Ben Franklin store held.

Again I thought I heard them beckoning. I glanced over my shoulder and gave a nod with my bouncing brown curls, promising to return someday in the not too distant future. I'd return to get to know them personally and be made beautiful like those Hollywood actresses I'd heard about. Yessiree. I'd be back one day. I'd buy one of each kind, maybe even two.

Out the doors we sailed, the same way we came in. Well, not exactly the same. Some things would never be the same. We crossed the street and went directly back to Khaki Dad's truck.

Just then a big, booming but friendly voice came from the sidewalk outside of Vernon Lotwell's very fine clothing store, and of course, it belonged to Mr. Lotwell himself.

"How ya been, Howard?" But the way he and most people around here said it was, "Haird." No need to waste time on syllables. "See you brought the little woman into town. How's things goin' for you?" To which Khaki Dad raised two fingers up to the side of his head as if to salute.

Yanking the truck door open, he dove into the cab and slammed it behind him, faster than I could say hoot. My mother and I walked around to the other side of the truck right past the man on the sidewalk, opened our door, and got in.

Now, I might have only been five-and-a-half, but I felt a little embarrassed at having left that nice man standing there on the sidewalk without answering his question. I know my Nana and Grandy would have gone right over and stood beside him and talked to him. They probably would've struck up a meaningful conversation with him, asking him how his family was doing—that is, if he had one. Of course, Nana and Grandy would have known that because people and families were very important to them.

They genuinely cared about everybody and how their lives were going. Not for gossiping purposes later on, because they were very quiet about what they knew about other people and especially what they did to help other people out in times of need. And they were always doing something to help out somebody.

I remember when our neighbors across two fields on the closest farm to us had a near disaster when Mr. Rhodie— "Rossie," as we knew him—fell out of his barn loft and broke his leg so bad, he had to be rigged up with ropes and pulleys in his bed to pull that leg bone in the right position so it would heal properly. That was even after he had already had an operation on it at the hospital, Seacoast General in the city of Salsten, some twenty miles away.

Usually farmers tried to handle their injuries at home or with the help and wisdom of the country doctor, the beloved Dr. Gabe. If they had to go to the hospital, it was serious indeed. There just wasn't enough time or money available for farmers to go to the hospital. That was reserved for the very most serious of accidents and life-threatening illnesses or for people in town who could afford such a luxury. Although why they would want to go there even if they could afford it was beyond me.

One time my Nana snuck me in to see a dear old friend of hers, hoping to boost her sagging spirits by merely gazing upon my cherubic freckled face. You see, my grandmother thought that I was the most gorgeous little girl this side of the Mississippi. To her and Grandy, I was the cat's meow. Surely the mere sight of me would help her friend recover more quickly.

It was a dreadful place—all full of white sheets, long dirty-looking beige curtains pulled around the metal beds, and tubes hanging down from some of the bedsides, draining from those poor people the most sickening-looking colors of fluids I had ever before seen in my short lifetime. Colors that must be reserved on a special gruesome palette to be used just for those pathetic times when the ordinary colors of life could not begin to describe the agony and desperation of the situation. Colors that carried within them the power to convey to the seer the preciousness of their own sweet life. The place had strong antiseptic and disinfectant smells that didn't seem to take away or cover up the odor of real bad sickness and even death that hung heavily in your hair long after you had escaped into the bright sunlight and cool, fresh air outside.

Anyhow, Rossie was to be laid up for a long time with that leg a-healing. Tomato season was in full swing, and the Rhodies, as did a lot of farmers in Cedarton, depended mightily on the cash made off of tomatoes. So what did my Nana and Grandy do? Nothing but step up everything they had to do on their farm to a faster pace and even more backbreaking schedule to help out Rossie and his wife and two sons. They rose even earlier than their usual before-the-rooster rising time to milk the cows and get over to the Rhodie farm to start picking those tomatoes in those quiet, cool hours of early morn.

Grandy drove "Old Bucket," as we lovingly referred to it, his reliable but ancient farm truck with the flatbed, over there—right up into the field. Now, a farm truck was a totally different vehicle than the pick-up truck the three of us were riding in right now on our way to Khaki Dad's house. A farm truck was put together with muscle and steel and became a cherished member of the family.

With the precision of a surgeon, Grandy drove down those rows of tomato plants, wheels straddling two full rows of precious green vines and juicy, ripe red tomatoes at a time. Not one tomato was squashed or vine damaged in the maneuvers. He came to a stop at the other end of the field, where we started picking the tomatoes. We carefully but quickly put them in the baskets used to take them to the cannery.

When we began our work in the field, we could barely see the tomatoes in the dim transition of the moon relinquishing its place over the Rhodie farm to the waking sun. Nonetheless, Grandy told me to feel all around the skin of the tomato for any soft, slimy spots that would indicate rottenness. Rottenness was one thing that couldn't be tolerated in vegetables or people. Nana, Grandy, and I carefully plucked those red globes from the vines. Just like they had taught me, I held the stem in one hand firmly, giving the tomato a twist and tug to separate it with the other. This way, no plants would be damaged in the process.

Farmers knew and respected the importance of all living things, plants and animals alike. I had inherited this love of living things, which was evident on that morning as I took in the glistening dampness of dew sprinkled on the red skins and breathed the distinctive stinging aroma that could only be tomato vines, reveling in the cool sensation of the rich black soil as it sifted between my toes as I worked. I didn't even mind too much the itchiness caused by the little prickles on the leaves as they brushed against my forearms in the process of parting with their gift to this family in need.

Here, I was in my element with the people I loved and I knew loved me. Hard work didn't matter. I was at peace with the world and secure in the fact that God was also smiling down on me for helping out His people in need. I let myself be bathed in the innocence of this moment of feeling that this would always be the way it was. It was good that none of us could have known the future. It would have spoiled the day.

We hadn't been in the field but about a quarter of an hour when Mrs. Rhodie, whose first name was Aidleen, and her sons appeared. They were more than grateful to see us already hard at work. It was not something that had been previously discussed or planned—just doing for your neighbor what you knew they would do for you, if needed.

The boys were dressed in their ragged cutoff jeans and oldest short-sleeved shirts. Webster's outfit was looking a little more worn out and faded than Jerimiah's since he was the youngest of the two and got his older-by-eleven-months brother's hand-me-downs. Nothing could afford to be wasted.

Now, it may have seemed to some more learned people that Mrs. Rhodie had been mistaken in her spelling of Jerimiah's name, but in fact it was well thought out and inspired by her love for the Lord Jesus. She had spelled it out very slowly and distinctly for Dr. Gabe when he filled out the birth certificate after Jerimiah's very difficult emergence into the world. And then she elaborated on the spelling for his benefit and anyone else's in the future who might question it. "I want my boy to grow up knowing that there is two sets of eyes watching over him. There's mine and the good Lord's. Lest he ever forget that fact, I put them in his name."

We all worked with the urgency of ones who knew firsthand the intensity of the baking sun in just a few short hours. Now that there were three more of us to pick, the baskets were filling quicker. Grandy was a very strong man from all those years of hard physical labor on the farm, despite his age. So he began hoisting those heavy tomato-laden baskets up on to the flatbed, jumping up on the back from time to time to arrange the baskets so that they wouldn't shift and tip over during the trip to the cannery. Then, when the walk to the truck took more time than it needed to, he'd move Old Bucket down the rows farther to gather up more brimming full baskets.

By the time the sun was streaking peachy orange and lilac across the sky over the big hill on the farm, we were almost ready to haul that load to the cannery. The tomato cannery was a few miles up the road. It sat on the edge of the railroad tracks, not far from the main road that led into town.

Grandy drove the truck slowly and carefully so as not to spill our hard work and efforts, not to mention Mr. Rhodie's profits, onto the bumpy road to the tomato cannery. Jerimiah and Webster rode along with him to help unload when they got there. One rode on the back of the truck to be sure that no basket spilled, and the other got the pride and pleasure of riding in the truck with Grandy. Of course, there would be no bickerin' about who would ride in the front with Grandy since both brothers knew there would be many more trips to the cannery that day and for several more days after that. Naturally, they would alternate positions each time because fairness was a virtue and there was never any question of character among the boys.

I say pleasure because my Grandy was a very pleasant man to be around and respected by all who knew him. First off, he was just plain pleasant to look at with his farm-healthy tanned face surrounding his light crystal-blue eyes. His eyes seemed almost magical to me, like prisms with mirrors hidden inside that somehow beheld the wonders of the universe.

There were crinkles at the outside edges that ran deep down into his cheeks, crinkles of joy when he looked at me. Those eyes beamed out love and acceptance to me. They were my resting place from the time our eyes first locked when I was a tiny frightened baby placed in his arms for safekeeping, away from the screaming circumstances surrounding my very young mother and me. This thought gave me a sharp pang. I wondered how I'd fare living in a new house, not being able to see myself reflected in his blue love every day.

Under his wide-brimmed straw hat, he had a blizzard of white hair. His stature that some may have found intimidating was balanced with a gentleness that told everyone they were safe with him, safe to be who they were and express their feelings as they felt them without fear of being judged or looked down upon. And without saying anything, they knew their words and thoughts were as safe with Grandy as if they had been locked away in a big steel chest and thrown into the deepest sea, never to be recovered and examined at a later time. Never, never was Grandy heard to be repeating anything someone had told him. Never had anyone ever recalled hearing him say an unkind thing about anyone.

One time after a discussion with a man at the bank, the man said, "Rayford, I don't believe you'd say a bad thing about the Devil himself," to which my Grandy quietly replied without missing a step, "Well, Harland, he *is* an awful hard worker."

Partly because he was a man of great confidence but also because he was a man of few words, when he did speak, his words were listened to and always seemed to have otherworldly wisdom.

Nana filled the gaps with conversations, reasonings, plans, and oftentimes arguments for the good of others. Being quite a bit younger than Grandy, she had chestnut brown hair with not a streak of gray. Her warm brown eyes saw straight to the heart of a matter, not distracted by the superficial. Softly blushed cheeks sported dimples but no wrinkles, which added to her sprightly appearance.

She kept the two of us in the present and real, or I do believe that Grandy and I might have slipped over the edge to another world entirely where total peace and contentment reigned all the time, that place where there were no problems, misunderstandings, separations, or sadness. We hated unpleasantness of all kinds. We were old souls bound together with the knowledge that we shared the same manner of spirit. We were most comfortable there.

So, we made that little place for ourselves in the evenings in the slow creaking of the porch swing that Grandy had hung from a sturdy branch of Grandfather Oak. So great was his love for this tree that the porch had been built to include part of this huge branch that entered on the left side, held our swing, and exited out the opposite side in a flurry of leaves.

Slowly we swung back and forth, listening to the shrill hum of mosquitoes just outside the screen. They wanted our blood, our very lifeblood—to inflict misery on us and disturb our peacefulness. Bothersome. They resembled other souls we knew that didn't understand how to relax into happiness and appreciate the love that surrounded all of us. What a relief it would be to them if they could only realize it was there for the taking.

Chapter Two

I mentioned pride at being with Grandy as he drove Old
Bucket to the canning factory. You see, mostly poor black
folks who were migrant workers for the season worked at
the cannery, and as I didn't mention this before you couldn't
possibly have known that the Rhodie family were colored
folks also. That's how they were referred to back then, and
no one took offense to it. 'Course, Nana liked to call them
"brownies" to me because that, she said, described the way
God made them—"extra-special and good."

They were our nearest neighbors and friends. In our
piece of the country, which we had carved out to our liking
to please us and God, skin didn't matter. What did was what
was under it—red blood that God gave us all and a good
heart. Being seen riding with one as respected as Grandy was
indeed an honor for anyone, colored or non-colored, which I
guess would make *us* near invisible, but probably made as
much sense as calling them colored folks since brown skin

was definitely not colored like the pages when you finished with Crayolas in your coloring book.

Today Grandy was there to work for them as a friend. As they went up to the check-in shed, my Grandy announced for all to hear that these earnings belonged to the Rhodie Farm and Jerimiah, being the oldest and in charge while his father was infirmed, would do the signing for it. He wanted to be sure that no assumptions were made to the contrary.

Grandy, also being a very humble man, never would have accepted credit for something that didn't belong to him. It even seemed difficult for him to accept what was rightfully his, preferring to let his good deeds go unacknowledged here and get his "reward in Heaven," as he put it.

Their ideal for good deed-doing was, as Nana often quoted from the Bible, "Don't let your right hand know what your left hand is doing." Meaning, of course, don't go around bragging about what you do for others. God apparently didn't like that and would make sure that the angel in charge of your list of good deeds would cross that one out.

Well, getting in the tomatoes for the Rhodie family went on for the better part of the next two weeks. Not every day went as smoothly as that first one I described. There was that morning when we awoke to the rain steadily coming down like bazillions of thin, silvery liquid streamers from Heaven. But that didn't keep us away from our duties in the tomato field. We didn't mind the rain since it was a gentle, soaking rain—the kind that farmers welcome.

We put on our slickers but got so sweaty in them that by the end of the day, all of us had taken them off at different places along the field and left them hanging on a fence post here and a tree branch there. One was even draped on the old scarecrow. It reminded me of how cicadas shed their shells, abandoning them on tree trunks, fences, or even the old outhouse door.

Grandy said the rain would serve to keep the mosquitoes off of us, as a few had discovered us in the field the morning before and sent word out to their minions to come join in the feast of our aggravation and discomfort. Grandy said the Lord saw our plight and took care of it for us, and that the animals needed a drink since it hadn't rained for a spell and the pond was getting low.

When the hours started to get longer and harder and we were beginning to show signs of weariness, Nana entertained us with stories she had known of woodland creatures. I always loved hearing these stories, and I noticed that Jerimiah and Webster were listening to her too with their heads bent in our direction, although they didn't want it to seem that they were. Listening to stories would have made them look like little boys and not the young men given responsibilities whom they had become.

This day she was telling the story that I had heard before but could never hear too many times. It was about the summer that they had planted a large watermelon patch and were looking forward to the day they could begin picking them and taking them to the Hungry Man's Market to sell.

She described in detail the day they went into town to Ingersoll's Field and Pasture store to buy the seeds. She and Grandy (she always lovingly referred to him as "Grandy" in her stories as well as in life) had looked at all the packages to decide what kind of watermelon they would grow, which basically boiled down to three suitable varieties. They decided on a globe-shaped, deep green-skinned melon instead of the traditional long, Hindenburg-shaped lighter-in-color watermelon. This special kind of seed promised to produce the sugary sweet red insides that everyone so loved on hot summer nights. Nana thought they would get more attention at the market because they were not the usual ones sold, and by mid-summer everyone needed something out of the ordinary to share and wonder about with each other late in the evenings on the porch.

It was a wondrous mystery how God had made so many different kinds of all things to give us a delicious, tempting taste of the wonderful treats He had in store for us. If Heaven held promises of things we had never seen or heard or tasted before, better than these watermelons, now that was something to look forward to! Nana's stories 'most always brought it back to God in one way or another.

Prepared ahead of time, deep, rich furrows of soil awaited the teardrop-shaped black and cream stippled seeds. Backs bent over their task, they stooped along down the rows, carefully depositing a seed into a depression in the soil made with the circle of their fists. She told how they carefully palmed the soil over it at just the prescribed depth to protect the seed from washing away or being plucked out and eaten by birds, but not so deep as to hinder the progress of the fragile sprout as it inched its way through the soil in search of the sun.

Suddenly, like being sucked out in the ocean by a riptide, I was snatched away from my watermelon patch memory. I was jarred back to the approaching certainty of my new home as Khaki Dad said, "Na' listen, best you know where yer allowed to roam. Don't you be puttin' one foot on that stone road out front or you'll get killed by a truck. You can play 'round the yard, the barns and fields, but look out for snakes. Don't be venturin' on crosswise the back field where it meets the woods, 'cuz that's Bad Otis's property and he's con-trary on a good day. He'd jest soon shoot you as look at you. You understand?"

With that admonishment the cloud of dread darkened, and I simply said yes as a shiver shook me all the way down to my toenails. I wasn't entirely sure, but I thought that might mean he cared a little about what happened to me or maybe he just didn't want me being a nuisance. I couldn't decipher which, but I would heed his warnings for sure. And, as if I needed one for good measure, I shook as another shudder ran back up my body and tingled in my hair roots.

Pleasant thoughts, quick! Back to the watermelon patch. Now where did I leave off?

Oh yeah, sweet respite as I remembered Nana's story. She and Grandy saw the little green beginnings of leaves start to appear. My mind gratefully drifted back. There were good, gentle rains that nourished them that season. This saved Grandy the extra work of having to water them by hand as he had to do some years when the clouds were especially stingy. They watched over all the needs of those plants, carefully pulling out any weeds that would suddenly spring up to compete for the nutrients and water of the soil, along with providing a light dusting of bug powder when a few mooching caterpillars were noted hungrily chewing on the leaves.

After a time, here and there a curly little tendril appeared and then a bud, which eventually opened into a golden yellow flower to attract the fancies of the bumblebees. The bees came and hummed merrily right down into the center of the flowers, where their hairy little legs picked up the necessary particles of yellow powder and continued on their way to other flowers for what Nana described as pollination, a necessary step in the making of watermelons or any fruit or vegetable.

"Even these tomatoes had to have been pollinated by bees," she said, "or there would have been none for us to pick."

Here she paused for a moment and looked around to see where Grandy was in his loading of the tomato baskets. Old Bucket's bed was once again almost full with the baskets of our hard work.

She continued on with her story. "Not long after that, the blossom would shrivel up and fall off, and a small, hard green knot appeared where it had been. That knot would grow and swell . . . and swell some more, until one day you realized this was the beginning of a baby watermelon. In that tiny knot from the very first day, it had all of the makings of something pure and good. All it needed was a watchful eye and care along the way to be what God intended it to be." Here she looked around at each one of us and said, "Much like the way that chil'ern grow into the people God wants them to be— each for His own special purposes.

"After that, the rest of the growing was up to the good Lord, as it had been all along. But then you suddenly realized your work was done until picking time. And grow they did!" (She was a terrific storyteller and always carried you through each detail with such expression that you felt you had received a gift just in the hearing of her tale.)

"Bigger and bigger, a little more each day. Grandy would go down the rows, gently giving one here and there a thump with his knuckle," demonstrating with her hand just how he did it.

"'They sound good and ready,'" Grandy said. ("Little did we know that nature was listening also," Nana whispered.) "'Nice and full sounding. I think tomorrow we'll need to start picking them.'" So, that night we went to bed with the big full moon watching over the farm and the activities of the night. Grandy rose early in the bleary, soft hours of morning and went out to the barn to milk the cows. I got up and went downstairs to get the coffee pot on and start the biscuits for breakfast. Grandy came in, and we had our breakfast of hot biscuits and elderberry jam.

"Then we went out together to pick the watermelons." Here, her voice became very low and suspenseful. "When we came to the patch, nothing seemed any different than any other morning. The mist of night was still hanging in the air, and the sweet smell of the farm was all around, quietly awaiting our arrival. There might have been the slightest scent of furry wildness on the air, but it went unrecognized by us.

"When Grandy cut the stem and gave the first big watermelon a heave, he cried, 'Whoa!' and stumbled backwards." Here, her voice suddenly became louder. "The expression on his face was one of puzzlement and surprise.

The watermelon that just yesterday had been so heavy and ripe for market was now as light as a bag of feathers! I went over to where he was holding it up in his hands, looking at it from all angles. He gave it a hearty shake just to be sure of what he was feeling. Then our eyes fell on a big pile of shiny watermelon seeds right beside the fresh indentation where the heavy melon had been growing these past weeks.

"Grandy turned the melon over in his hands, and there on the side down close to where it had lain on the ground was a hole the size of a silver dollar," continued Nana. By this time Jerimiah and Webster were both looking right at her—listening, not making any attempt to hide their curiosity to find out what had happened to the watermelon.

"Grandy handed it to me while he got out his pocketknife and opened it up. Then he made a long cut down the side of the green rind and split it open. We couldn't believe what we saw! It was clean as a whistle mostly, all except one side, the far end from the hole, which had a few shreds of red flesh left hanging on the white rind inside. There were deep scratches all around in little rows of five.

"After a few moments we began to realize we had been the victims of a burglary by nature. We went down our rows and found melon after melon had been cleaned out. Not until then had we noticed the many busy tracks of mischievous little feet all around the vines and the pile of seeds left tucked neatly beside each one. No doubt the work of a crew of very energetic, ingenious watermelon-loving raccoons."

At the completion of Nana's story, Webster jumped up and clapped his hands. We all stood up, stretched our backs, and laughed together, Aidleen and Grandy included. We were all probably picturing in our own minds the chubby, little black-masked bandits that had outsmarted the farmer by the light of the moon.

As we looked around, we realized that Nana's story had carried us through the last loading of Old Bucket for the day. We hardly remembered picking those last few rows of tomatoes. As often happened, Nana shared her stories at just the right time to transport the sick, the weary, the frightened, or lonely to another place in time—a place of rest and lightheartedness. This was one of the many gifts that she was happy to share as needed.

Remembering her story had served its purpose once more. Now I returned to the veracity of my journey. We were still beating the road in that dusty white pick-up truck. Mother, Khaki Dad, and me, all three of us, sat side by side on the high-up bench seat, none of us saying a word to the other since my territory warnings were issued. My now official dad took out his pack of Kents from his shirt pocket and gave it a sharp rap on the back of his driving hand. Sure enough, two cigarettes popped their golden tobacco heads part way out of the pack like soldiers volunteering for duty. He pushed one down and then pulled the other one out. He then extracted a pack of matches from the same pocket, opened it up, tore one off, and struck it, lighting the end of his cigarette while breathing in deeply.

The smell of that match when it was first struck was very pleasing to me, sharp and sulfuric. Later, I liked it so much that I found myself stuck in the disgusting habit of licking ashes from the many ashtrays that were suddenly part of my new life. The ashes tasted the way the just-struck match smelled, and for whatever reason, I had developed a compulsion to lick them. Regardless of how many spankings and talkings-to I got, it didn't matter. I had to do it. I couldn't help myself.

Sometimes my mother would eye an ashtray with a fresh, damp streak down the middle, and she'd call me before her, grab me by the chin, and say, "Open your mouth!" There would be the telltale wide charcoal-colored line down the center of my tongue. Although caught yet another time, it was worth the punishment. I'd had my ash fix for the day.

As we drove past, I looked longingly at the faded ocean-green awnings and through the windows at the hunched-over backs of customers at the counter of the Cozy Cove soda fountain. Since my name change seemed like such a monumental occasion, they should have said it called for a celebration of an ice cream cone or at least a vanilla zip served with that crunchy kind of ice made with zillions of air bubbles trapped inside. The kind the waitress would scoop out of a large rectangle chest with sliding doors using a silver metal scooper, making a loud *crrrunch* followed by a *crrrink* as it was shoveled into the glass.

The glass was shaped wide on the top and came narrowing down so that it was easy for a small hand to hold. It said "Coke" on it and always had a straw sticking out, which would rise slowly up in the glass trying to make itself look taller. Magic straws. You could push them back down with your pointer finger, and back up they would rise, slowly but surely up, up, up. Drinks tasted so much better icy cold and quenched your thirst better too when they were set down in front of you like that.

Well, maybe they had my best interest at heart, not wanting to spoil my appetite for lunch with chocolate ice cream. But I could've had vanilla. That was my favorite flavor anyhow, but then again they might not really have known that, like Nana and Grandy did. My Nana and Grandy knew every little detail about me, and I knew them pretty good, too. Like right about now, they were missing me real bad.

We drove along the five miles outside of town, silently— like we had done this every day for a hundred or so years. Nothing special here. I watched buzzards circling above a field on my right and briefly wondered what had met its fate out there in the middle of that cornfield. I knew the buzzards were just doing their buzzard thing, but still I didn't like the sight of these big black birds with the naked red heads and necks. They always looked so chapped and sore from the wind and cold in the wintertime, and in the summer I imagined that they were blistered and raw from the sun.

The very sight of them usually sent a shiver up my spine because they told of death, and death really, really scared me. The thought of having to die or losing my Nana or Grandy to the Grim Reaper with that razor-sharp scythe was enough to keep me awake with the tremblin' sweats half the night. I wondered what he used that sharp thing for, anyhow. There were never any big cuts or slices on people they found dead, or everybody would know about it. It must be to cut away the final ties with earth as you are swept away to the outer atmosphere on your way to the final judgment.

Then there were the already dead people who roamed around after dark. Sometimes at night I could almost feel them breathing down the back of my neck. But I would snuggle even tighter against my Grandy's back and tug real urgent-like on his T-shirt sleeve.

"Grandy! Grandy!" I'd say. "I think something's looking at me. I'm scared!"

Grandy would always reassure me that I was perfectly safe and the only ones looking at me were the Good Lord Himself and His angels, and they were smiling.

I always slept in the twin bed with my Grandy because I knew that nobody was stronger than he and he would never let anything happen to me. I had tried to sleep with Nana, but she wasn't as strong as Grandy. Matter of fact, she was little. Besides, she was a very light sleeper, when she slept at all, and had tender legs that I had nearly kicked to pieces one night trying to escape a bad dream. The next morning told the tale by the bruises on her legs. That was the end of that (at least for sleeping), but I did like to crawl in with her sometimes to hear a special made-up, just-for-me story, and then I would cross the squeaky wooden floor back to my bed.

The beds were very high for me, so I had to step up on a little stool to crawl in each night. Then I'd scoot over to my side, which had been pushed tightly against the wall so that I wouldn't fall out on the wooden floor in the middle of the night and break my arm or get a concussion of the brain.

Every detail of that wallpaper was painted indelibly on my memory. I had fallen asleep and awakened to that same paper as long as I could remember. There were great big white and pale-pink water lilies and lily pads with light blue ripples of water flowing gently all around, set on a grayish-lilac background. A small dragonfly hovered over one of them just before the pictures started to repeat themselves. Nothing too exciting. After all, it was supposed to be a peaceful scene to lull your mind to sleep. Soon I would long for the smell of that old wallpaper—that warm, accustomed smell.

We drove past a large white farm house that sat way down the end of a long dirt road. Big orangey-looking mud puddles scattered here and there, all the way up to the house. A boy stood peeing right there in the yard around the side of the house. A black dog was just lying there in the dirt circle drive, watching him. He reminded me of the stone boys in the funeral home fountain who just stood there frozen, peeing night and day. Perpetual pee-ers.

My cousin, John Lloyd, had told me their story. About a hundred years ago, those boys were there at a funeral. It was the viewing of a peculiar old man who had lived a few miles outside of town, all alone. Mysterious things were always happening when he was about. These things could never be explained satisfactorily, so they were just pushed in the back of everyone's mind—until something else strange happened.

Anyhow, the boys went outside and decided to relieve themselves in the fountain. There was a huge crash of thunder and a flash of lightning that struck that fountain with an unearthly, blinding shade of blue, and those boys are there to this day to pee for all eternity for everyone to see. Now, that's embarrassing. The moral of the story, I guess, is this: never, ever, dishonor the dead, especially the strange ones, or be prepared to suffer the consequences forever and ever.

The road made a sharp curve to the left. It curved and curved and seemed extremely dangerous should we happen to meet someone who was coming a little too fast. It could be very deadly and, at the least, quite dangerous. I bet someone had even died on this curve before. Their ghost was probably still wandering around, wondering what the heck happened. It seemed like we might be going all the way back toward town, but just then it straightened out and kept on going past a dilapidated white house with crooked, faded blue shutters.

In the front was an irregularly shaped, green algae-covered pond. That pond looked like anything could have been lurking deep down in the depths of it. *Creeeepy!* I shook off a shudder that crept up from my toenails and went clean to my eyebrows. I sure hoped there were a lot more miles to go between that pond and my mother's new house.

At Nana and Grandy's we had a beautiful oval pond in the front yard. Although it was twice again the size of this one, there was no green slime on the top of it. There were pretty creeping phlox that came back every year. Nana and Grandy and I planted them early one spring. They circled the whole pond with alternating pink and white flowers. The pond, pretending to be a mirror, reflected them perfectly, creating a double ring of color with the bright blue sky shimmering in the center—a picture straight out of the Garden of Eden, I'm sure. Everybody who came to our home admired it. Some even came all dressed up after church on Sunday to have their pictures taken in front of it with their Brownie cameras.

People were always welcome at our house. When we heard a car come crunching up the long peach-colored gravel lane, we'd go out and stand at the end of the sidewalk and wait for them to get out. When the time came for them to leave, we would go back out there with them and stand and wave until they turned back out on the black-topped road and were out of sight, past Rossie and Aidleen's house.

Boy, things sure did look unfriendly on the drive to my new home. And that was the daytime. I hated to see what it was like after dark and hoped it got better soon. No, sooner than soon.

My attention now was drawn to a huge brown horsefly buzzing upside down in the corner of the dash of the truck. It was spinning round and round on its back. Scattered all around it were parts of other insects—dead, dried up, and crunchy. There was a ladybug that had been there so long, the once cheerful red of her shell was now a faded orange. And there were other horseflies, although not the exact variety of this one. These were the green-headed ones, the ones that wouldn't hesitate to inflict a painful bite on a human, unlike this pitiful one that only bothered horses and cows. He must be horrified staring eyeball to dead eyeball with them, and you know, bugs have many, many eyes, so that must have made it even more terrible for him, looking his own mortality directly in the eyes.

All of a sudden, I lurched forward on the seat and strained to reach him. My arm was almost long enough. Just a little more, stretch, *strrreeetchh*—got him!

"Yvonnah! I mean Lacey! Leave that nasty old thing alone!" yelled my mother.

With a quick flick of the wrist, he was free, but not so quick that I didn't feel a sharp slap on the forearm first. Out the open window he went, hopefully to find some nice horse's behind to nurse himself back to health on. He'd probably tell that tale to all his squiggly maggot grandchildren for years to come.

Well, great. Just great. What could be even more welcoming than a bunch of buzzards, a dead man's curve, and a slime-possessed pond? Coming up on the right side of the road was the most fearsome-looking house you could even imagine. It was small, only one story, with a door that resembled a gaping mouth, smack in the middle of the front between two grotesque-looking windows. What was left of the curtains hung in ragged pieces, gray behind the grimy, greasy glass. There was the faintest eerie yellow in the background, not quite light—too weary to be that—just something breathing there, but barely.

The house had the appearance of a tormented gray face, the eyes jaundiced and half closed but not even. It was sorta like one eyelid was drooping more than the other where the used-to-be curtains hung. But that wasn't the really scary part. *That* was on the side of the house face, up too close, closer than death should reside by life. It was a graveyard. It was small, only two or three crooked headstones at best that I could count riding by. I thought that I saw a smallish one. It was different than the rest. It had a shape on top, some type of figure, but I couldn't make it out.

There were weeds growing every which way in there. You would think out of respect that at least a few of them would have been flower weeds but no, not one blossom could be seen. A poor little rickety fence stretched out around it, falling down in places, defenseless to do a thing about the rude trespassing weeds.

Now, I had been coming to my new dad's house quite a bit lately since the wedding, spending more and more time there, even a few nights lying there with eyes wide open in the dark, all alone in my "own room" waiting for daylight and the moment that I would be able to see Nana and Grandy again.

But prior to this day, I had always been brought from the other direction, coming from Nana and Grandy's and my house. It didn't look half as ominous coming from there. I couldn't be sure, but it seemed to me that the sun wasn't even as bright on this side. I leaned across Mother to look out the window, up at the sky. Yup, I was right. Not a single cloud in the sky, and yet it seemed gloomy here.

Coming up on the right was a small pasture. The weeds were cropped short in it, obviously the work of some farm animals, but none were in sight. Along came another sagging building, innocent enough, which looked like it could have been a small barn at one time. It was sad now without the company of its animals.

Directly beside it, two very old, very big, gnarly-looking trees grew. Black walnut trees, judging by the pattern of their leaves. I had appreciated many trees over the years with my Grandy. Nana had read me a lot of Bible verses, but my favorite of all was in the Book of Isaiah about how all the trees of the field will clap their hands with joy at the presence of Jesus. Sometimes when a stiff breeze shook a nearby tree, I tried to imagine the sound of *whole forests* of trees getting so happy and excited that they just started to clap with hands I didn't even know they had. That would be the loudest applause ever. Now, that would be a time. I didn't want to miss that.

Trees so comforted me—something about their strength and steadfastness, their silence as their mighty roots pushed deeper and deeper into the soil in their search for stability and nourishment. Occasionally one would make way for an obstacle such as a stubborn rock, wise in recognizing that the rock was indeed a rock by nature, created hard and immovable that way. And then patiently, wisely, the tree shaped its course slightly around one side or the other to allow the rock to be a rock, but not allowing its rockness to wither its own roots or hamper its own growth on its journey to becoming its own unique tree.

Oh, there were plenty of rocks on this path of life, both below the ground and above it. The stone kind and the flesh kind. Sometimes the flesh ones were the hardest of all.

Chapter Three

Ohhh no! What was he doing? He slowed down and eased his work boot up from the accelerator. He flicked his cigarette out the window and put on the right-side blinker light. Click . . . click . . . click . . . click. It couldn't be. It was. We were turning onto the oyster-shell driveway that I suddenly recognized in a panic. *Wait a minute, or a lifetime!* my thoughts yelled. I couldn't have to live just one building and a small pasture away from the creepiest house on earth, not to mention the bone yard. I looked out the side truck window to see if I could see it from here.

My mind was racing. *Oh heavens, I'm done for!* I had just disrespected the dead! I meant cemetery. Ce-Me-Te-Ry! I meant no harm. *Please,* I deliberated silently, *if there are any ghosts around, if you can hear my thoughts, what I said was a mistake, just a silly slip of the lip. Forgive me! Please! Believe you, me!* The last thing I wanted to do was to make enemies with anything or anybody in that new place. I was actually pretty friendly and easy to get along with and very, very respectful of dead people and animals. Why, I even had respect for dead trees.

Nana always said to put your best foot forward, especially in new situations. I wasn't real sure which was my best foot, so I stuck both of them out straight in front of me, just to be sure I had the right one.

Eeeeerrrht! The brakes on the truck came to a screechy and quick stop. All of our heads bobbed forward and back quickly at the sudden stop. *Boom!* Khaki Dad's truck door slammed shut as I saw him round the front of the bumper heading toward his shop on the end of the garage. A gritty cloud from the tires sliding on the driveway caught up with him there. My mother got out too and glanced in his direction as if she were about to say something, but realizing he was already absorbed in what he had to do, she just let the thought die in her head.

Over her shoulder, she said, "Come on, I'll fix some lunch."

I climbed out the cab of the truck, jumping down on the sharp pieces of crushed-up shells in the driveway. I could feel the sharp edges even through my shoes. Good thing I had on my hard-soled Sunday patents. I'd have to put a string around my memory finger: *Do not forget to have shoes on when I run out in this driveway.* Unlike the smooth peachy-colored gravel and sand driveway at Nana and Grandy's and my house (which we didn't call a driveway at all, instead it was a lane), this stuff would have no mercy on my tender heels.

I followed my mother across the maroon-painted cement patio, up two steps and into the house. The spring, tight on the screen door, banged it shut on my heel. Again, a good thing I had on my Sunday shoes. My mother went straight into the kitchen and began fixing our lunch. She pulled the loaf of Holsum bread out of the breadbox, which was in the far corner of the counter. From the cupboard above it, she extracted a can of potted meat. Next, she opened the big new refrigerator and removed a jar of dill pickles.

"You go on up to your room and take off that dress before you get it messed up. Be sure you hang it up on a hanger, too. So it doesn't get any more wrinkled than it already is. There's shorts and a top you can put on in that bottom drawer." With a sudden turn she added, "Here, let me unbutton you."

Turning back into the kitchen, I banged my head on the corner of the bar and rubbed away the sharp pain that reminded me this wasn't my familiar old kitchen at Nana and Grandy's and my house.

I turned and looked up the stairs, dreading the trip up there alone. Even though it was daytime, I didn't like to be up there by myself. Honestly, I felt like something was always hiding behind the door or in the closet or perhaps under the bed. Whenever I went in *my room*, I always looked behind the door, prepared to take flight back down the steps should anything be there.

Then, that being deemed safe, I knelt by the bed and looked under. But I never looked in the closet except at night 'cause I guess I felt like I would see the door slide open in the daylight if someone was about to grab me. It wasn't worth the fear of having to open it in the first place. I had to check in there at night, though, since when I stayed here I had to sleep all alone. Not that it was likely to happen, but just in case I fell asleep, I might miss it sliding open in the middle of the night. So, holding my breath, I'd quickly slide the door all the way to the right, peering into the darkness at the back for anything lurking there. And then, just as quickly I'd slam it back shut and wheel around to be sure nothing flew out into the room past me.

I was generally terrified anyplace indoors without someone with me. Outside was another thing completely. There, aloneness was good. I loved to wander and daydream and appreciate the quietness of my own thoughts. Although who can say they've truly ever been alone outside with all of God's fascinating little creatures everywhere? Even plants had personalities. Just to not have my thoughts and observations interrupted by a human voice or manmade sound as I communed with nature was familiar and reassuring to me.

So, my ritual completed upon arriving in my room, I proceeded to slip off my dress and itchy crinoline, black patent leather shoes and white lace-cuffed socks. There was a hanger lying on my bed, which I slipped my dress over just the way Nana had taught me to do.

The problem came after I'd gotten up nerve enough to sling open the closet door. Stretch as tall as I could, there was no way to reach the pole that held the clothes. Nothing to do but jump up and try to hook the hanger over it. First jump— missed. Three more jumps. Success. Finally. Like Grandy always says, "If at first you don't succeed, try and try again." That's when I heard my mother yell.

"Are you jumpin' up there? You know better. There's no jumpin' allowed in this house, young lady. Now get on down here and eat this sandwich."

I quickly yanked open the bottom dresser drawer, which in turn fell out on the tops of my feet. No time to rub them, but ouch, ouch, OUCH! I hope I remembered not to pull so hard next time.

I grabbed the first top in sight, yellow daisies on green background. Now, shorts . . . shorts. Found them, and green too. Good. They sorta matched. Downstairs, holding the banister as I went, so as not to fall and inflict another whelp somewhere on my body. At my old house I would have hopped on and slid down the banister the way Grandy taught me, but that wasn't allowed here.

Climbing up on the bar stool, I took a nibble of the crust of the sandwich. I never ate the crust, even when Grandy told me it would make my hair curly. It was too dry and brown. Nana cut it off ahead of time and added it to Grandy's plate. His hair was only a little wavy. Must only work on children.

I tried another bite and got some of the spread and pickle—not too gaggy, mostly salty tasting. We almost never had stuff out of a can at home. My other home, that is. I swallowed it and tried a few more tiny bites. Taking a drink of the Dr. Pepper in front of me, I put it down and examined the condensation collected on the bottle. I drew a heart in it and watched the trickle go down onto the turquoise and orange-speckled countertop and circle the bottom of the bottle all by itself.

Mother's back was to me as she was busy washing some dishes at the sink. Seizing the opportunity, I quickly said, "After this, can I go outside and play?"

She replied without looking around, "Yeah, but be sure you're back here for supper when it's ready."

Waiting one more half minute, I scooped up the rest of the sandwich. At the same time, I slipped down off the stool and scurried out of the kitchen and house as quick as a mouse can disappear when you suddenly turn a corner and startle it.

Quicksilver, I thought, *I'm slippery and quick as quicksilver*, having recently been acquainted with it after dropping a thermometer and trying to pick up the tiny balls of silver. Each attempt showed me its delightful quality of being able to divide into even tinier little balls each time and elude my grasp. I had been mesmerized by it for the longest time, amazed at its almost magical properties.

Finally, I was able to trick it into rolling onto a folded piece of paper where it formed one larger ball. With it laying unsuspectingly within the fold of paper, I expertly tipped it over an empty Avon cream sachet jar and screwed the lid on tightly, hiding it in my special secret spot to be played with later. Then I threw away what was left of the thermometer, the broken glass pieces that had once been a prison for the cunning silvery balls.

Once outside I ran to the side of the yard, close up next to the house, in between the shrubberies, and hurriedly buried the sandwich. Undetected, I crawled out and looked around. *Let's see . . . what to do first?*

Deciding to go spend a little time under the shade of the two walnut trees on the other side of the house, I started off in that direction, being very careful not to let even one toe touch on the blacktop of the road that ran in front of my mother and new dad's house, remembering my serious warning of the dangers of the high-speed thoroughfare.

I certainly didn't want to end up scattered all over the road, or worse, flattened like some of the frogs I had seen. They were so flat and dried out, I had considered possibly using one as a bookmark rather than having its life simply float away in the air as it turned back to dust. It would be something like a memorial to its short life, saying you were and still are appreciated by someone. But this idea had not come to fruition, simply due to the fact that as of yet I had not figured out a way to retrieve one without the danger of becoming flattened myself.

As I walked along the grassy edge of the road, I noticed how much hotter the sun felt on the side of my body next to the blacktop than it did on the yard side. I could almost feel the road breathing out hot, deadly breath.

My eye caught sight of a shadow floating along ahead of me.

"Hey, Patsy, how'd you know where to find me?" I called.

No answer. She was silent as usual. Sometimes I made up words for her, pretending she was a real playmate.

She was always fun when she was around. Except for the fact she didn't talk, of course. That left me to wonder what she might say if she could talk and what her voice would sound like—a soft wind blowing maybe, or the high notes on a penny whistle.

At times her silhouette was short and stout, and I teased her about having too much cotton candy and ice cream. Other times she appeared long and lean. Then I called her "Spaghetti Legs." Hope I didn't hurt her feelings, if shadow people had feelings, I mean. She danced just ahead or behind me, sometimes off to the side. Once, I caught a glimpse of her on a full-moon night when I was out walking quietly in the meadow beside my Grandy. And wouldn't you know it, she brought along her shadow Grandy for a walk too.

Crouching down and taking a big hop, I tried to play leapfrog with her. She jumped ahead of me instead. Next, I tried running away suddenly and leaving her behind. Glancing back at my heels, I saw that she was still attached and running with me. As I approached the tree couple, she waited patiently for me, a shadow hiding within a bigger shadow. She was awfully good at hide-and-seek under a tree. Try as hard as I could, I never was able to find her there. Instantly, when I emerged from the cool grayness, she was back at my side. Sometimes when I was tired or plain ol' wanting to be alone, I ignored her completely. She seemed to understand those feelings and followed along, assuming my mood within her own gray sulkiness.

Honk-a-dee-honnnk-honk! Snatched abruptly from my shadow game by the sudden blaring of a horn, I looked up to see my new Uncle Donnie in Pop Jazz's pick-up with a huge load of trash in the back. He was my new dad's younger brother. Pop Jazz was his dad and my new grandpop.

Donnie graduated from high school recently. He was worried about getting drafted and having to go off and fight in the jungles of Vietnam. I heard him say it would near 'bout kill his mom, who was my new grandmother. Him and every other young fella it seems had the same thing on their mind. I saw little bits of the news some nights. There was a lot of yelling between the hippie people in their flowered vans and soldiers. One night after the news, Nana said, "It's a turrible time in our country." That made me feel uneasy for some reason.

Uncle Donnie was gone most of the time. But when he was around, I think he liked me and I liked him okay too. He played loud music on his car radio while he waxed it, and when he was finished, he'd pull out his comb and carefully rake it through his hair while using the side of his fender like a mirror. He smoked cigarettes like my new dad and Pop Jazz did. But instead of keeping his in the front pocket of his shirt, he preferred to roll it up in the sleeve of his white T-shirt. That was a right clever idea.

With one arm hanging out the truck window, he yelled over to me.

"Hey, Li'l Toot, you want to ride to the dump with me?"

"Okay!"

Running to the truck, I stopped short, realizing my side of the truck was on the road.

"What's wrong?" he asked.

"I can't get in."

"Come 'ere, I'll lift you up."

"It's not that. I'm not allowed on the road."

"Oh, for Pete's sake! Here, get in this side." He spit in the grass as he jumped out, and then slung me in the driver's side of the pick-up. On the short trip to the dump, I asked Uncle Donnie if he was mad at me.

"Naw, now why'd you think that?" he asked.

"It sounded like it . . . about, you know, not being allowed to step on the road."

"That? Oh, I see. Naw. It's just, well, we ain't never had no little kids around much before you," he said, fiddling with the gear shift knob. "Jes' kinda seems like a whole lotta rules to remember. But I reckon you're worth it."

We drove along the rest of the way quiet, just taking in the warm breeze whipping in the open truck windows. Sitting with my neck stretched to see out the windshield where we were going provided a view of still another direction from my new house. We passed a couple of corn fields, a small bungalow farm house at the end of a curved dirt lane, and some wide, deep ditches with cattails growing out of them.

All of a sudden, Uncle Donnie turned the big steering wheel sharply to the right, hardly slowing down at all, sliding me across the seat right next to him. Embarrassed, I straightened myself up as we bounced over some big ruts in the dirt road and headed directly up to a humongous pile of junk.

There was the usual old tires and oily rags, crumpled-up newspapers, tin cans, boxes that once held sweet cereals, a worn-out broom with the few remaining broom straws all bent over to one side (funny how that happens, as if trying to assume the right- or left-handed traits of its owner), cans of hardened paint with buckled lids, a broken-down and rusted swing set, a stained and flabby-looking mattress—nothing of real interest at first glance.

But as we pulled closer, my eyes began to separate things out of the heap. Salvageable things. Things with possibilities. That is, if the smell had not soaked deep into them yet. Fly-drawing smells, sticky and rank, pee-yucky smells from the leftovers of people's lives. This was a place they could get rid of the old and start over new with fresh. These were things they no longer wanted around or had use for—things that held within them the ability to haunt lives with the past. Better off dumped in a heap down a dirt road far, far away.

Uncle Donnie jammed his foot down on the brake and stopped just short of the pile. Opening the door and starting around the back of the truck to unload, he said, "Hop out and look around. Jes' don't step on any rusty nails or cut yourself on anything."

Jumping out, moving cautiously at first, I moved closer to the heap, watching the ground before each step. There was a rusty red tricycle lying on its side. When I pulled it up on the three wheels, how grateful it looked. The angle of the handlebars gave it a smiling look. As I sat down on the bent seat, legs too big for it, I banged my kneecap on the handlebar and quickly examined it for bleeding. None. Good, I was obeying Uncle Donnie so far.

That was a new word I had just learned the meaning of from my new dad: Obedience. To do what you are told by an adult with no questions asked. The first time. Or else. Mother said the Bible said to obey your mother and father and respect them or you would make God very mad and have to go to hell forever. Plus, get punished by your parents right here and now.

To the right, my eyes caught onto something else of interest. Could it be? Yes! It was a pocketbook. Lucky day! How I would love a pocketbook of my own. Grabbing the handles, I yanked it up out of the clutter. It was large and round with a zipper and tassel hanging from it. The color was cream with long tan and brown diamond shapes on the front, the back a solid cream vinyl. I pulled the zipper back and forth a few times to see if it worked. Perfect. Hanging inside was a faint aroma of Juicy Fruit chewing gum, along with a few bobby pins, ink stains, and foil gum wrappers that I shook out on the ground.

Then my hopes were popped like a bubble as I realized it was written all over the back with a pen. "Uncle Donnie, what's this say?"

"Let's see. Oh yeah, they broke up last week." He pointed his finger as he read, "Helene and Lee. Lee and Helene. Helene Loves Lee (*inside a heart*). Lee Loves Helene. Mr. and Mrs. Lee Bruenn. Love is Forever."

"Apparently not," he added.

"True love" (*inside a pair of lopsided lips*).

"She musta been more tore up about it than she looked in school if she had to go and throw her pockybook away 'cuz his name was all over it. Must be purty sure it's over for good this time. Looks like ol' Lee Boy ain't the only rooster in the henhouse anymore. Maybe *I'll* just ask her out Friday night."

"Is she pretty, Uncle Donnie?" I asked, suddenly feeling a little jealous of this pocketbook person, Helene. "Does she wear makeup?"

"Oh yeah. She's pretty all right—got sorta chocolate brown hair, wears it in a pageboy," he went on dreamily, as if she were a walking mirage right there in the middle of the dump in front of us. "Wears those tight pink sweaters with a ribbon around her head to match, and the lips on that girl, I swear! I could eat them right off her sweet face!" At that statement, my sudden gasp snatched him back to the dump and his job at hand.

"Here," he said abruptly, "I gotta get this truck unloaded."

"Well, can I keep it?" I said, holding up the pocketbook.

"Yeah, but I don't know why you'd want it, all written over as it is."

"Maybe I can scrub it off with Comet," I said hopefully.

"Nah, that won't do it. But maybe I could spray paint it for you and cover it up," he offered. "Put it in the truck."

"Okey dokey, Uncle Oakey," I responded happily and immediately wished I hadn't. I looked over at my new uncle, but he was already throwing things out of the truck onto the side of the junk heap and hadn't heard me. *Thank goodness*, I thought, not wanting him to think I was a baby or something. Silly rhyming was a game that Grandy and I enjoyed together. I never felt dumb with him. Sometimes Grandy's rhymes were the silliest of all, and I giggled until I almost wet my pants.

Now, back to the exploration of the dump. Seeing some rather colorful rags sticking out of a cardboard box, I began to dig through it. There were some old dresses that had seen a lot of wear—extra, extra-large kind of wear—and the lady must have been still growing because every one of the seams was either busted out or straining with all the might their tiny threads could muster just to hold together. Wonder if Uncle knew this big lady also.

Well now, lookie here. She must have dropped her glasses in the box and not been able to see well enough to find them, 'cause here they were. Black and silver frames that came to a point on the outside edges. They were called cat eye glasses and looked quite businesslike. I bet she was a secretary or a telephone operator. Putting them on and looking around, I started to prance with one hand on my hip and the other in the air holding a mock cigarette.

"Operator. Operator! Can I help you?"

All of a sudden, I felt dizzy and like I might throw up. Too strong. They were way too strong for me. Pulling them off, I closed my eyes for a minute to stop the queasy feeling.

Opening them again, I was fine, ready for more exploring. If I could bang the glass out with a hammer, they would be fun to pretend with. I dropped them into my purse.

Let's see what have we here. Some pill bottles with labels and more writing. I bet it was the name of this big lady that outgrew her dresses, lost her glasses in the throwaway box, and needed pills to keep her alive. These would be fun to play with also. I dropped them in my pocketbook with the glasses . . . spectacles. I would call them spectacles. *("Just a minute . . . let me find my spectacles," I would say when I played secretary. "There. I have them now. Let me just put your name in the appointment book.")*

"Lacey, let's go," Uncle Donnie yelled. "Find anything good?"

"Sorta," I said, holding up my pocketbook for him to see in.

"What's this? Pills! Why the tarnation did ya put these in here, girl? Don't you know pills could kill a kid like you if you ate them? Didn't nobody ever tell you that before? Man! Ya gotta watch a kid like a hawk every second, or they're doin' sumpin' deadly."

"I thought they would be fun to just, you know, make believe with—like a grownup," I replied, voice quivering as I felt the sharp prickle of tears behind my eyes. "Please don't tell my mother. She'll get real mad at me. I didn't know."

"Well, how can you get in trouble if you didn't know?" he answered more gently.

"I just will, that's all. I will. She'll say I should have known."

"Well, I got a good idea of what we can do with these bottles. Come on over here. No need to get your eyes all red and drippy," he said walking toward a big mud puddle. I followed sniffing, close on his heels to see what he was about to do.

He unscrewed the lids on the bottles one at a time. Then he tossed the contents deep into the weeds at the edge of the trees that surrounded the dump. I heard them hitting the ground like little hailstones. Leaning down, he dunked the first bottle in the puddle and scooted it all around in the water, stirring up the mud and making it cloudy as he went.

"Gotcha!" he said, as he quickly scooped his hand in an arc out of the now muddy water. Droplets fell off his knuckles and back into the puddle.

"Here you go, Li'l Toot," he said, presenting me with the largest of the bottles. In it were several little tadpoles. They didn't even have the buds that would become jumping legs yet. These were teeny frog babies.

"Wow! This is great, Uncle Donnie! You're the best! I can watch them grow legs and everything!"

"Just promise one thing."

"Anything."

"You'll never even think of playing with anything dangerous like that again."

"Promise, Thomas!" I answered too quickly to think first, and then I felt the heat of red on my cheeks.

"It's a deal, Lucille," laughed my new uncle. All embarrassment dissipated into the stinky air above the dump. We left it there as we drove off side by side.

As we pulled into the driveway, my heart took a leap as I saw Nana and Grandy's car there. I grabbed the handle and jerked the truck door open, clutching my pocketbook full of treasures.

"'Bye, Uncle Donnie, and thanks for the tadpoles," I yelled behind me, jumping down into the crushed shells. My bottom hit the ground a second after my feet 'cause the truck was so high up. I recoiled and flew into the house, oblivious to the stinging shell cuts on my backside.

I shrieked with joy, "Nana! Grandy! I knew you'd come!" Although before this moment, it had only been an unspoken wish.

I hugged Nana's neck and jumped into Grandy's lap for a big bunny kiss. I wasn't disappointed. Grandy puckered up his lips and wiggled them like a rabbit and pressed an Aqua Velva-scented kiss on my forehead. I loved that smell. Sometimes I would hoist myself up on the edge of the tub to reach his bottle of after shave on the shelf over the sink just to get a sniff. I would close my eyes and breathe it in deeply—'*mmmm*, my Grandy.

There on the table was one of Nana's famous creations, a beautiful pink and yellow and white cake. It had a heart on the top with writing inside. The round edges of the heart were decorated with pink flowers, and pale blue birds with yellow ribbons in their mouths hovered, forming the lower sides and point of the heart. The centers of the flowers and the bird's eyes were silver shots. I thought they were very pretty, but if I ever tried to eat them, they always put the silver fillings in my mouth on edge—a feeling that I hated. So, I avoided them altogether.

"What does it say? What does it say?" I said excitedly.

"It says, 'Happy New Name Day,'" Nana read, pointing at the first line and then the second, "Lacey Joan Millford."

I stuck my finger in one of the white sugary scallops on the bottom edge close to the plate and licked my finger. Instantly, I was cracked across the top of the head with a wooden spoon my mother had been stirring a pitcher of iced tea with.

"Don't you dare! Not one bite until after dinner." My mother's sharp tone meant business.

I saw a dark shadow pass over the moment and Nana's face. Grandy's jaw muscle tightened almost imperceptibly, but I knew my Grandy too well not to notice. *Ow-wee!* The welt on my scalp smarted, but I didn't dare rub it for fear of making too big a deal of it. Excusing myself to the bathroom, I shut the door behind me and rubbed it gingerly. Running some cold water on my fingers, I then held them on the stinging spot.

Through the hollow wooden door came quiet but angry words. "Don't see why it was necessary to do that. She was excited," Nana said. "It's a day of memory-making for her, and it should be a happy occasion."

"Rules are rules, Mother. You know how hard it is to get her to eat anything," blared my mother.

"Judy Faye, I know all about that child, every detail, and I know she doesn't need to be hit," Nana's voice met hers.

"You are not in charge of her care anymore, Mother. I am!" snapped my mother.

"Enough." Grandy's voice—not raised, just level—cut through the tension in the air and commanded attention. Both mothers were hushed at once.

Counting to five before opening the bathroom door, I walked out into the kitchen. Grandy said we should go outside for a walk until dinner was ready. Grabbing his hand, glad for the escape, I pulled him toward the door.

"Look, Grandy! Look what I got at the dump." I grabbed up the pocketbook with my treasures in it and unzipped it to show him. "A pocketbook, spectacles to play grown-up lady with, and these baby tadpoles!" Grandy looked at them carefully in the pill bottles and said, "They're nice ones, but I reckon we'd better find a jar a bit bigger to give them room to grow."

So we went out back to the trash barrel and found a big dill pickle jar, which we rinsed out with the hose and filled up with water. Grandy pulled up a few sprigs of grass with the roots from the ditch and put that in for them to hide in and feed off of. Next, he carefully poured them into their new home. *It must be a lot different for them here in this jar rather than their mud puddle,* I thought. *But just like me, they would need time to get used to it.* Suddenly, I had the urge to return them to their mud hole at the dump as soon as possible.

The next morning I awoke alone in my new room, flat on my back because I was too afraid of the dark to turn on my stomach or either side to sleep. My eyes felt swollen and sticky from crying myself to sleep when Nana and Grandy had to leave without me. After throwing a genuine hissy fit to go home with them and clinging to my Grandy's legs for dear life, I was pried off by my mother and sent to my room after a few mighty whacks on the backside and bare legs with a yardstick. My nose was stuffy, and a thick, crusty smear went up into the side of my hair and matted it together there.

I listened for sounds downstairs and heard some murmurings that I couldn't decipher. I had to tinkle but not as bad as usual when I woke up. Probably 'cause I had cried all the pee out my eyes last night when they ran out of tears. I would think a thing like that could be downright dangerous to your health. I'd have to ask Nana about that.

Downstairs I snuck into the bathroom unnoticed and tried to wash out some of last night's crusties from my nose and hair. When I emerged from the bathroom, my mother was sitting on the little telephone seat at the end of the counter talking on the phone.

"I know just what you mean. If she hikes up them prices over there one more cent, I'll just have to do my shopping in town, even for the little things. Everything is high as quinine as it is. Well, listen, I have to hang up now. She just woke up and's standing here looking at me. Gotta fix her some cereal. Okay. You too. 'Bye now."

Putting the phone back on the hook, she turned to me. "I certainly hope you're in better spirits this morning. I don't expect that kind of behavior out of you again. Do you understand me, young lady?"

Looking down at my feet, I replied, "Yes, Mother."

"Good. Things is hard enough without you deliberately making it worse. I'm your mother. You belong to me, and I want you here with me. It takes time, but we all got to adjust, and you cain't do it if you're running back to the farm every whipstitch, ya hear?" I nodded in agreement, but I still didn't like it.

After breakfast I was free to go outside. The grass was still cool and damp under my feet as I made my way out to the shed where I had left my tadpole jar. I watched them at close range for a while with my nose almost on the glass. Their bellies were decorated all happy looking with little swirls and squiggles on them. Grandy said it was their guts. "Intestines" was the doctor word for them. I wondered if my guts were as cute as theirs. That was doubtful, and I hoped I never had the occasion to find out! They were darting up and down, gulping water with their little round mouths and wiggling their tails.

So funny that I wished I could take them out and play with them a while, but I knew better than try that. They breathed water just like I breathed air and would die quickly if they were taken out it. Funny thing was, in a few weeks they would breathe air and be just fine, whereas I would never be able to breathe water and live. The thought of turning them loose after they got their jumping legs made me feel better about taking them from their mud hole home at the dump. At least *they'd* be free to hop back to their Grandma and Grandpa frogs.

Chapter Four

Looking way across the yard at the old, rundown house next door, I saw a girl with blonde hair come out. She stretched out a hand behind her, careful to ease the door back so it wouldn't bang. With the sun coming over her shoulder, it lit up her hair, giving her the look of an angel my age with a glowing halo circling her head. She ambled across the backyard, choosing her steps with great care—some short and quick, others long and stretching—so as not to step on a bee, I supposed.

I noticed her glancing in my direction a couple of times. She went over to the crab apple tree with the double trunk and sat in its big crook, facing me. I thought to myself, *She looks as lonely as I feel. Wonder if she'd wanna see my tadpoles, or if she was one of those "prissy, missy girls" who would think they were disgustingly yucky. Well, only one way to find out. Here goes.*

Starting to walk across the driveway into the side yard, I raised my hand and gave a flutter in her direction. The jar almost slipped out of my hand. I quickly grabbed it again with both hands, causing some water to slosh out the top and down the front of my shirt. I looked back over at her just in time to see her wave back, a quick, bashful little wave but friendly just the same. That felt encouraging. If I had to live here, it would make it somewhat more sufferable if I had a friend.

She sat there watching me cross the yard a few more seconds just like she was deciding something. Then she eased up, straight with her body first, and then her legs sorta stiff as she pushed out of her tree seat and walked slowly to meet me. It seemed like our steps were measured exactly the same. Reminded me of a cowboy movie I saw on television with Grandy, where two gunslingers stood back to back and paced away from each other step by step. Enemies. But we were pacing toward each other step by step. Could I dare hope . . . friends?

"What's in the jar?" Just like that. No "My name is . . ." No "Howdy-do." Just straight to the matter at hand—"What are you bringing over here to show me?" I liked that.

"Tadpoles."

"Where'd you get 'em?" She and I came to a stop, bare toes to bare toes.

"At the dump with my new Uncle Donnie."

"How's he new?"

So I told her as we ambled over and sat down on a tickly clover patch in the shade of what I soon found out was her favorite tree. The morning hours melted away faster than an ice cube dropped on a hot sidewalk as we shared everything and anything that jumped into our heads. One idea flowing into another, sparking conversation back and forth between us.

Her name was Lyddie, short for Lydia Adele Magistorm. Thinking that it was the most beautiful name I had ever heard, I was incredibly surprised to hear that she didn't like it. Even more was her surprise when she heard that I had a name that I actually had liked a lot but my mother and new dad had just changed it to suit them. Like me, she had never heard of such a thing and promised to never mention it to anyone else but to just call me by my new name so that it wouldn't hurt Khaki Dad's feelings and make Mother mad.

"Lyd-die," a rather high singsong voice called from the open screen door. Holding it ajar was a tall, thin woman with blonde hair that matched Lyddie's. Well, not exactly. Hers was a more yellow color and looked real dark near her scalp. (My mother called the color "bleach-bottle blonde." "Cheap" is what she called it.) But this lady didn't look cheap to me. She was smiling out the door at Lyddie like she was brimming over with love for her. She looked like a mother whom I would like to get to know more.

Lyddie got up stiffly again, I noticed and thought it peculiar for someone our age. Now, sometimes Nana or Grandy would get stiff, especially when the air felt heavy with rain or when it was cold out or they had been sitting too long. But they were up in years, so that was to be expected. "Up in years" was the nice way to say "old." Nana had taught me the kind, considerate way to talk so as not to hurt people's feelings or make them feel bad.

"I gotta go take my medicine and try to blow up the balloon again," Lyddie said nonchalantly as she started across the yard. Then, over her shoulder in my direction, "You can come too if you want."

I jumped up at the invitation and skipped to catch up with her. I glanced back at the jar of tadpoles. *They'll be fine*, I thought as I followed her into the house.

Once in the kitchen, the warm air that enfolded us smelled like buttered toast. I liked it instantly. Lyddie went up to the old, rust-stained sink and rested her arm on the edge, waiting patiently while her mother poured some kind of reddish, thick syrup from a brown drugstore bottle into a spoon. Leaning forward, she opened her mouth extra wide while her mother quickly stuck the about-to-drip spoon into her mouth. Lyddie then swallowed quickly without even making a face.

Turning to find me still standing just inside the screen door beside a green-painted table, Lyddie announced, "Momma, this is my new friend, Lacey," There. Just like that. She and I were friends.

"Well, very nice to meet you, Lacey. What a pretty name!"

Lyddie and I turned and looked right directly into each other's eyes. Her blue sought the depths of my brown, sky to earth. We both knew and thought the same. Our first secret. I felt goose bumps tingle up my arms. Wow! She really was my friend. We could already read each other's minds. That was the good kind of spooky.

Lyddie picked up a red balloon that was laying on the plastic lace placemat. She stretched it several times, pulling it out between her hands. Next, she put it between her lips.

Taking a big breath in between her teeth, she blew hard—but hardly blowing up the balloon at all. I noticed she winced as if something hurt. The balloon deflated and hung limply against her chin. Taking in another big gulp of toasty scented air and puffing out her cheeks, she blew again. More air filled her cheeks than the balloon. Her face turned bright pink, except around her mouth, which was white from holding the balloon so tight with her lips.

"Thatta girl, keep goin' . . . a little more . . . hold it . . . one . . . two . . . three."

Each word spoken by her mother was sounded into two syllables, going up in pitch on the last. She stood softly cheering Lyddie from the other side of the kitchen as she peeled an apple. Its red and white curl growing longer danced to the rhythm of her paring knife, reminding me of how Grandy peeled apples for me. When he was done, how we each took a dangling end in our mouths and raced to the center as we ate it, ending up nose to nose, lip to lip, laughing and loving. Lyddie's face became an alarming darker shade of pink, sorta purply. She struggled so hard.

"I can help! I'd be happy to! I'm really good at blowing up balloons!" I blurted out. With that, Lyddie let all of the air from her lungs and balloon come rushing out at the same time, making an alarming snorting and whooshing sound. Much to my relief, it was quickly followed by husky laughing that sounded too deep to come from Lyddie. I looked from her to her mother. She was also chuckling and looking at Lyddie as a look of deeper knowing passed between them.

There was obviously something more to know than I was aware of. They both turned to me at the same time, almost as if their heads were connected by the secret they held.

Lyddie said sweetly, "Thanks for the offer, Lacey, but that won't really help me none. You see, I've got to do this by myself three times a day, *at least*, to strengthen up my lungs."

With that, she hoisted up her shirt and showed me her chest. I stood there for I don't know how long, staring. It seemed like time took a deep breath and held it in as I tried to comprehend what I saw. Straight down from the hollow spot at the bottom of my otherwise perfect friend's neck, running down the middle of her chest was a raised, mean-looking scar.

It followed the curve of her ribs on the left side like a deep, purply-pink railroad track going around all the way to her back. It looked so sore . . . so very scary. No wonder she got up and down real stiff-like. *No wonder the balloon was so hard for her to blow up*, I thought, as I began to realize there was a lot more to Lyddie than I knew. There would have to be many more clover-patch talks to share everything there was to know about each other. But all I could manage to utter was a weak, "Ooohhh," as if all of the air in my whole body had just leaked out between my lips, leaving *me* deflated.

Lyddie's mom came to the rescue with a quick and simple explanation of how Lyddie's ribs were weak and needed strengthening, so the doctors put a special metal bar right in the center of her chest to help her lungs have enough room to grow and expand properly. The surgery hadn't been too long ago, so that's why the scar still looked so pink. But it would soon fade. That was also why Lyddie had to do the breathing exercises herself to strengthen up her lungs. But it sure was very sweet of me to offer to help her.

"I can see right now that you two are going to be the best of friends. Now, who would like a nice bite of this scrumptious apple?" she asked us in the high-pitched, whiny voice of the wicked, old witch in *Snow White* as she held it out, perfectly balanced on her palm.

With that, Lyddie and I looked back at each other and giggled with relief to change the subject as we reached for the apple halves. We automatically held them up to each other's piece, making a whole.

"Just like us. Both of us together make good friends!" Lyddie said aloud—my exact thoughts!

"What's in that jar under your tree that's got Misty Maple so interested?" Mrs. Magistorm asked, looking out the kitchen window over the sink.

"Oh, Sugar! Nooo, Misty Maple!" shouted Lyddie as she ran gingerly out into the yard with me hot on her heels. Apparently, Misty Maple was a rather large orange, yellow, and mostly grey cat with a white neck and paws. She looked up, pulled her paw out of the jar and licked off the tadpole-flavored water, not the least bit concerned as we raced toward her. The tadpoles were swimming around vigorously, but no worse for the stirring as far as we could tell.

The rest of the afternoon was spent luxuriating in the shade of the tree and in each other's friendship. Misty Maple, I found out, was named for her colors that resembled a nearby maple tree drenched in morning mist the day she showed up at Lyddie's door. She hung out with us for most of the day, rolling from side to side and purring loudly as we rubbed her fat belly and neck. It turned out that she was really gentle and wouldn't hurt a fly. Maybe stir things up a little, but that was just her curious kitty nature. After all, she had to give everything new a careful inspection to see if there was any fun in it.

I told Lyddie what my Nana always said about cats: "Curiosity killed the cat, satisfaction brought it back." She thought that was pretty comical, a new word I had recently been introduced to by Big Mom, my new grandmother.

As we laid flat on our backs with Lyddie's mimosa tree draped overhead, laughing and looking up at the blue sky-shapes peeking through the tiny leaves, it occurred to me that I was really, truly happy, something I thought I would never feel again apart from my house with Nana and Grandy.

That evening at supper when my mother, Khaki Dad, and I sat down at the big dark wood table, my mother announced that she would be leaving me alone with Khaki Dad right after we ate. She had to go to her new job at the hospital and would be back in the morning. I looked across the table at him. He didn't look mean or anything. He just didn't look at me, period.

I suddenly missed the warmth and familiarity of our tiger oak table at Nana and Grandy's house. The ache went so deep that I knew I wouldn't be able to squeeze down one bite of that meatloaf, liquidy mashed potatoes covered in brown chunky-looking gravy, or peas sitting in front of me. I wondered if maybe it would actually work better if Mother tried pouring her potatoes over the gravy instead. Didn't she know I liked my mashed potatoes and gravy shaped into a bird's nest with the peas in the middle like little eggs? Inside my head I was screaming. "I WANT TO GO HOME! I *NEED* TO GO HOME! I CAN'T STAY HERE ANYMORE!"

But on the outside my face showed nothing, nothing at all. Nothing to set that yardstick in motion again. Glancing down at my plate, I gagged at the sight of the food, and dread made my stomach hurt and head swim.

"Don't you dare even think of startin' that retchin' business with me, young lady. It might work on your grandmother, but it's not workin' with me. You can just sit there all night long if you want to. But that's supper and you're eatin' it. Do you have any idear how many kids would be happy to have that tonight?" *Blah . . . blah . . . blah.*

While she fussed on about my ungratefulness, I began thinking of innovative ways to get rid of the mess on my plate. Taking a big gulp of water, I began to move some peas around with my fork. After they stopped glaring at me and continued on with their conversation about how much Khaki Dad had to charge Widow Wells to make a profit on unclogging her sink, I got busy pushing the peas under the glob of potatoes. Next, I dumped some in my hand and shoved them into the pocket of my shorts. And so forth and so on until most of them were gone. Stealthily, I began to work on the potatoes to make them appear half eaten by spreading them out a little, careful though so as not to expose the hidden peas. What I really needed was a dog.

There was absolutely no way I could make that chunk of meatloaf disappear without putting some in my mouth, and *that* was out of the question. I would have to volunteer to wash the dishes and linger over my plate until they had left me alone there at the table. Then I would quickly hide it in the bottom of the trash can. Out of sight, that's where things like that belonged.

As it turned out, dumping the remainder of food from my plate down the toilet unnoticed wasn't any problem at all. Mother had glanced up at the sunburst wall clock and quickly disappeared into their bedroom to change for work.

She emerged minutes later, a working woman, yelling behind her as she rushed out the door. "Haird! Haird! Did you fill the car up with gas last night?" To which I never heard a reply, only the rumble of the car starting and crunching of tires against driveway as she took off. Silence. Then, the tinny tenck . . . tenck . . . tenck of the second hand of the sunburst clock on the wall.

I turned to the dishes left on the table, wondering where Khaki Dad was and when he had disappeared. His plate was empty and water glass drained. In the orange beanbag ashtray beside his plate, his cigarette, though crumpled and bent sideways, was still sending up little smoke signals. Those ashes did look tempting, but instead I tiptoed soundlessly to the front of the house where his den was. Yep. I guessed right. There he was, with his back to me in the big brown chair on wheels, ticking on his adding machine—"figurin'," that's what he called it. He was figurin'.

Quietly, one foot carefully placed behind the other, I backed away until I was safely down the hall. Then I turned around and quickly disappeared from his line of vision should he turn around. Excellent detective work. Maybe I would go to work for Perry Mason someday. Della should be about ready to retire by the time I was grown up. Oh well, dishes waited.

Finally, chores done and back to the freedom of the yard. Wonder if Lyddie was outside? Lightning bugs. Hurray, lightning bugs, my little lanterns on wings! Running out into the center of the yard, I swirled around and around among them.

"I'm so glad to see you. I didn't know you would be *here* too, or did you just come for a visit?"

I heard giggles coming from very close. I swung around to see Lyddie dancing among the tiny yellow lights also. My heart took a picture. I moved in her direction as I continued to twirl round and round. Finally, we bumped hard into each other, knocking each other down in the dewy grass. Giggling together, we laid as we had fallen, staring up at the tiny lights going higher and higher over our heads. Lyddie was the first to break the silence.

"Where do you think they're going?"

"Maybe Australia," I replied, recalling a magazine I had recently seen.

"Why would they be going there?"

"Maybe to hitch a ride in a kangaroo's pouch."

"Well, I think they're going to keep on going straight up until they reach Heaven," Lyddie said in a whisper. "And then God will turn them into twinkle stars where they will never, ever have to die."

"Oh, Lyddie! I think you're exactly right. That's where they're heading, Heaven."

"Lacey! Git yerself up outta that wet grass. What're you doing out here anyhow in the dark? Git in that bathroom and git yer bath and into bed straightaway." For once he was looking at me, and I wished he wasn't.

The wonder of the moment was snuffed out like a cigarette under his work boots as Khaki Dad scolded me all the way into the house. I glanced over my shoulder, a little embarrassed, meeting Lyddie's eyes directly and promising without words that I would see her tomorrow.

I disappeared behind the bathroom door that came in from the dining room. Closing it, I turned around and found the other two doors into the bathroom wide open. Privacy had to be worked for around here, and Heaven forbid if you had to *really* go. You had to decide if you wanted to just go straight to the hopper and sit down and possibly be caught sitting there in plain view of anybody that happened by, or if you wanted to risk peeing your pants—*or worse*—while you went about shutting all three doors first.

Since a bath called for being naked as a jaybird, complete privacy was a necessity. Deciding this, I closed the door coming in from the utility room. The last of the three was the one that opened into my mother and new dad's room. Closing that one also, I peeked in.

Unlike Nana and Grandy, they had one big bed that they shared. Mother slept on the left side and he slept on the right. I knew this because Mother had a favorite little blue-flowered pillow that was always on her pillow when the bed was made, just like it had always been at Nana and Grandy's house. He had an amber-colored glass ashtray on his side on the headboard. Their headboard was pretty neat, really. He had made it with sliding doors on each end that made a fascinating little hiding place for things. I wished my headboard had those. The one he made for my room just had a shelf for my knick knacks, all two of them.

One was a light-blue cat with pink stripes with a pretty collar and two little chains hanging from it that held onto two little kittens identical to her. The other one was a gray elephant with pink ears sitting back on her rump with her trunk curled in the air. Her collar also had chains that led to two fat baby elephants assuming the same pose as their mommy. Both of them had been won at the games on the boardwalk in Oceanside and presented to me as gifts. One was from my uncle, and the other one—the cats—I couldn't remember from who or even when I had gotten it. It had just always been there and was my favorite of the two.

Being very good at making things out of wood, *Haird* made a lot of things for the new house. Nana described him as being extremely industrious. Unlike the furniture in my other house, this was made from new wood. It had no history with me or anybody else, for that matter. Yellow and glaring, it just stood there smelling all varnishy and uncured green with nothing to add to the room of its own, depending totally on us to make memories for it to be a part of.

What would those memories be? Sometimes I wondered what the future would be, and when and if I would ever be able to return home to live with Nana and Grandy again. I had to look for my gold-speckled Treasure Trove gift box that I had stowed away in the bottom of my new dresser drawer under my shorts. In it was my half of the pulley bone that Grandy and I had pulled apart when we made our most recent and most sacred wish together. Feeling the need to see it again and hold onto it for a while, I decided to hurry up and get this bath done.

Now, I had never been told to go get my bath before. I had always had help to run the water to the right temperature and add a capful of Soaky to make lots of bubbles. *Soaky soaks you clean, in an ocean full of fun. Mmm-humm-mmm. Mmm-humm-mmm. Clean before you're done!* That catchy little commercial song always ran through my mind at bath time.

A hand was especially needed to get over the side of Nana's big oval tub, which stood on its own four feet. It was too tall for me to step into by myself, way too easy to slip and hit my you-know-what as I straddled the curved side trying to get in. Believe me, I had learned that the hard way once when my cousin Bethie Lou was at Nana and Grandy's to spend the night and I had tried to race her into the tub.

Stripping off my shorts, shirt, and underpants, I looked at the knobs on this legless rectangle of a tub and gave the nearest one to me a big twist. Eggy-smelling water came blasting out. Within seconds it seemed, as I stood there stunned, a thick steam rose from the water that was already too hot for me to deal with. It fogged up both mirrors on the medicine cabinets behind me. Turning the handle didn't slow the geyser in the least. Nor could I reach the cold-water faucet on the other side to make it cooler. I turned and cranked on the "H" handle, not really knowing which way to slow it down. Finally, the now scalding water slowed down as I cranked and cranked, my face red and sweaty from the hot steam.

Next, it occurred to me that I didn't even know how to stop the water from steadily running down the drain. There was no rubber plug hanging from a beaded silver chain anywhere. The lever thing below the spigot was strange to me. I moved the lever this way and that, and still the water ran out.

Right then and there I made a decision. If this was the way it was, I could do without a bath tonight and every other night if I had to. I let the smaller stream of still scalding water continue to run while I brushed my teeth with Dr. Lyon's tooth powder and then, sitting down beside the tub, I inspected my toenails.

After what seemed to be enough time to take a bath, I reached in once more and cranked the hot-water faucet the rest of the way closed. Grabbing the rough yellow towel from the rack, I quickly tucked it under my arms and around myself. Sneaky like, I opened the door leading into the dining room, glanced around for him, and dashed quietly through the dining room and up the stairs, where I dropped the towel. Then I grabbed my jammies from under my pillow, and put them on as quickly as I could.

Yanking open my bureau drawer with one hand instead of using both with the handles, I jammed it sideways. So then I had to pound on one side to get them even again in order to get it open enough to run my hand under my shorts and feel around for my treasure box. Aaah, here it was, with the sea-green rubber band around it. Inside was comfort as I gently removed the pulley bone half and pressed it up against my heart.

I carefully inspected it, turning it over and over in the palm of my hand. It looked like any ordinary chicken bone, but this one was definitely different, definitely special—as within its hard, brittle little exterior, down in the brown marrow part where wishes are sent, there laid the possibility that this situation was temporary and soon I could go back to where I had help with my bath and someone to say prayers with and tuck me in and stay until I fell asleep. Someone to paint my face with the tip of his finger, saying the colors out loud . . . *sunflower yella* . . . *soft bunny brown* . . . to help chase away all of the scary, bad feelings that darkness brought with it . . . *violet purple* . . . *sky-blue pink* . . . *periwinkle* . . . curling up on the rug with my back securely against the wall and the precious pulley bone pressed between my palm and cheek . . . *cottontail white* . . . *buttercup gold* . . . *cloverleaf green* . . . drifting on warm, fuzzy, silver-edged, dove-gray clouds . . . floating . . . floating back home.

Early next morning in the yard biding time 'til Lyddie came out, I watched Misty Maple carefully covering up her business on the edge of the shrubs. She stretched her paw way across it, scraping sand over it, and then crossed over from the other direction, scraping some more. She raised her nose in the air, sniffing. Scrape. Scrape.

Uncle Donnie pulled up in the driveway, stopping next to me, left arm hanging down the side of the car door. Blowing cigarette smoke out the window in my direction, he said, "Better git on over to Mom's. She's baking her 'east rolls.

Cottage cheese is outta the oven a'ready, pineapple's goin' in, then it's prune."

"I'll have to ask my mother first. I'm not s'posed to wake her up 'cause she worked all last night at her new job. And I can't cross the road by myself."

"Well, let's just go in there and leave her a note, nice and quiet, tellin' her you're over at Big Mom's."

Big Mom was the name we had agreed on for me to call my new grandmother to distinguish from Nana, who had always been described as "not big as a minute." I would never have suggested such a name for fear of hurting her feelings, but she had offered it up herself, laughing at the idea of her first grandchild calling her by a special made-up name. "'Big Mom,'" she had said, chuckling to herself. "Yes, indeedy, that suits me to a 'T'. 'Big Mom' it is!"

That day I felt like she was genuinely happy to have me around, even though she hadn't known me very long and didn't cater much to the idea of "adaptions," as she called them. I had overheard her and her friend Iris over a cup of coffee talking about how nothin' good ever came out of them.

"You take Sid Farnsley, jes' for example. There he took that girl in, raised her jes' like she was one of his own, and what'd she do but turn tail and take off with that no-account Fuller Brush man. Near 'bout broke Sid and Ella Belle's hearts in two! No sirree, nothin' good comes from 'daptin'," said Big Mom, crossing her arms across her humongous breasts. "It jes' ain't natural."

And the matter was settled. Iris agreed with tight lips and a downward jerk of her head.

Of course, that did leave the question of just how I had come into her family at the not hardly newborn age of five-and-a-half. Evidently, it was understood *that* was untreadable ground and *I*, quite obviously, *was* the exception to that rule.

Big Mom was tall and straight and had big bosoms and belly that seemed even bigger with the bright colors she liked to cover them with. When we first met, she looked me up and down and then grabbed me into a big hug against her, smooshing my face into her breasts. She smelled warm and cinnamony. Her forehead was real tan and shiny, all the way up into her blue-gray hair that had a pure white wave running straight back from her right temple. It was striking and made her look high-fashion. When she wasn't in the kitchen cooking up something, she was out in the garden. Always in one of her boldly-colored flowered dresses, working up a steam wherever she was.

She had several different dresses, all of which were my favorite. They were so friendly and cheerful looking, and she made all of them herself on her old black sewing machine with the black treadle that she pushed back and forth with her foot, fast as lightning up, down, up, down. *Cchhh, cchhh, cchhh, cchhh*, faster and faster, all up and down those long seams of her dresses. "Shifts," she called them. Simplicity was her pattern of choice. Nana made her dresses and mine too, but she always used Butterick patterns. After being carefully removed from the pattern envelope, they all looked the same to me. Each new fashion creation began as thin, crinkly paper with dark lines to cut on and long, skinny teepees for darts to make the garment shapelier.

Walking into Big Mom's kitchen was an experience like no other. The warm yeast fragrance wrapped itself 'round me, pulling me deeper into the heart of her kitchen. The heat from the oven was welcoming, unlike the sticky heat of the morning building outside her kitchen door. The table was laid out with row after row of square golden pastries. The counter was cluttered with flour and bowls covered with tea towels, canned pineapple, and boxes of prunes. On the end was her broomstick she used for a rolling pin. It was made of golden-colored wood worn smooth as silk. She could roll dumplin's thin as paper with it. Big Mom greeted us with a swipe of flour across her cheek and down the side of her sunflower-printed apron. As always, she was hard at work. Whatever she did, she went at it with her whole heart and body.

"Mornin', 'Tunia," she crowed cheerfully. 'Tunia was shortened from Petunia, I gathered. Why not add one more name to the growing list of new names I was acquiring. "He'p yourself. Those on the table coolin' are cottage cheese. Eat up. Lord knows you could use a little plumpin'. You ain't nothin' but gristle and bones."

"Mornin', Big Mom," I said as I reached for a roll. Who ever heard of cottage cheese rolls? But the aroma was so wonderful, they had to be good. It was warm and soft in my fingers as I pulled off a piece and shoved it in my mouth. *Mmm*, heavenly. It melted away as I chewed one bite and then another, licking my fingers when it was suddenly gone. The flavor was a comforting mixture of creamy vanilla, nutmeg, and old-fashioned love.

"Can I have another?"

"Of course, and you need'un ask. Yer welcome to whatever I got. What's mine is yorn. Does my heart good to see you eat sumpin'. Skinny as you are, a good stiff breeze come along and blow you to kingdom come."

Uncle Donnie was sitting in the corner chair, slurping on a milky-looking cup of coffee with a roll balanced on the knee of his pants. Above his head were a whole lot of phone numbers and names scribbled right on the wall—in ink pen, no less. Nana would have never allowed a wall to be written on like that. But it didn't seem to bother Big Mom in the least. I looked up and wondered how many of those names were girlfriends of his, and if Helene, whose purse I now owned, had been added to the jumble of names.

"Whyn't ya pull up that chair over there and he'p me roll out this dough?" offered Big Mom.

Surprised by the offer, I looked up at the expectant lump of dough. "I don't know how to roll a broomstick like you do. I might make a mess of it," I answered while scraping a silver-legged chair across the floor up close by her side.

"Well, there's no way to learn without doin'. Cain't mess nothin' up with dough. Worst happens, you roll it all up in a ball and start over again. Here, lemme wrap this here tea towel 'round you to keep the flour offen yer clothes. Don't wanna get Judy Faye aggravated first thing in the mornin' after workin' all night."

With that, she sprinkled some flour on the countertop in front of me just like fairy dust and plopped a big, yeasty-smelling lump of dough on top of that. Next, she scooped some more fairy dust out of the sack on the counter and ran it smoothly up and down her broomstick. It reminded me of watching baseball with Grandy, when a batter rubbed dirt up and down his bat. In baseball this meant business. I guess in baking it meant business too.

Then she laid the broomstick down in the middle of the dough, placed my hands carefully in just the right position, and placed her hands over the top of mine. Gently, she pushed down and forward and backward and to the left side and to the right side, working the dough into a shiny, smooth circle. Then quick as a wink, she picked it up and smooshed it back into a ball between her hands. I gasped, having fallen in love with what we were creating together. Big Mom just laughed and said, "Here now, it's your turn by yourself. Don't be bashful. Do 'xactly as I showed you."

Somewhere during that time, Khaki Dad had come in for a break from his work and was eating a pineapple danish with a cup of coffee mingled with Pet milk. I didn't even realize he was there until I heard my name.

"Every single time Judy Faye's parents shows up, she goes to squallin' to go home with them and makes a turrible ruckus, like we ain't givin' her a good 'nuff home or nothin'. It don't look good," said Khaki Dad. It was like I wasn't even in the room. Right then, I wished I wasn't. I felt like a trapped mouse. No, I felt like a rat.

Uncle Donnie piped in, "I think she just needs sumpin' to take care of. You know sumpin' to love on here at this house."

"What the Sam Henry do you know? You're still wet behind the ears yerself. Heck, she cain't hardly blow her own nose. She jes' a kid. Humph, take care of sumpin'. You mean another mouth for me to feed."

"Well, Mr. Dang know-it-all, I guess I'm old enough to fight in this stupid Vietnam War, and I know this much too—everybody has to be loved and needed to feel at home."

The argument ended when Big Mom said, "You two gettin' a bit riled up for bein' in my kitchen. Jes' ca'm yourselves right down. You gonna cause my 'east not to rise with all that loud talk."

Khaki Dad took the last big gulp from his mug and put it down a little too hard on his way out the door.

After that, the morning hours just slipped away without my notice as did Uncle Donnie at some point in my lessons on baking Gram's Bulgarian 'east rolls, a cherished recipe passed down to Big Mom when she had married. Today it was just for fun and to pass the time, but in years to follow I would come to realize the significance of that recipe being shared with me on this special day.

By lunchtime Mother had called, worried and angry, to see if Big Mom had seen me anywhere. She hadn't noticed the note Uncle Donnie had scribbled down by the telephone on the counter in the kitchen. Big Mom soothed her over with the offer of fresh sweet rolls and coffee. It seemed like she showed up at the kitchen screen door before she hung up the phone.

"Mornin'," she mumbled as she took one each of the pineapple and prune delicacies and poured herself a big, steaming cup of coffee. Black, that's the way she drank her coffee. Black with no sugar. Just like Grandy, but sometimes he put a spoonful of molasses in his. She took a seat at the table, drinking her coffee and eating her roll, mood improving with each bite. Big Mom was quiet, letting her rolls work their magic. Till finally on the last bite Mother actually offered up some conversation with Big Mom. Not much, just enough to let us know she had returned to the land of the living.

Within a few minutes two more ladies had come in and sat down around Big Mom's table. One was another good friend of hers, I learned. Beulah, whom she had met years ago while working at the shirt factory. She was tall and slender and a lot more fixey about her hair than Big Mom was. Hers was mousey brown and sprayed stiff as starch. "Bet a strand wouldn't blow in the eye of a hurricane," Big Mom said. They must have been good friends a long time, by the way they squabbled back and forth at each other without getting mad.

The other I remembered from a brief previous encounter. She was Elzie, the older sister of Pop Jazz, and probably one of the fattest people I had ever seen. I tried very hard not to stare at the sheer size of her, but I couldn't help noticing how the kitchen chair made pitiful, groaning noises as it disappeared from sight under her. She was pleasant enough, and when she spoke there was something beautiful about the way her words came out all fancy. I hadn't had the occasion to meet many people who had a foreign accent and was absolutely fascinated by it. I caught myself staring at her mouth as she talked. As she ate one after another of our sweet rolls, it seemed that her accent made the food taste even better. She appeared to be savoring even more delicious flavor than we of ordinary weight and tongue could ever imagine.

I recalled from our first meeting that their parents had come here from Bulgaria when she was a little girl. Hard to imagine that she had started out as a *little* girl. Pop had been born in this country shortly after they arrived, in the very same bed that was in Big Mom's and his bedroom right now. It was the same bed that apparently his mother had died in!

There was something terrifying about that fact to me. I wished that Big Mom would keep that bedroom door pulled tightly shut when I was here. Whenever I had to go past that doorway, I glanced in at the cool darkness and felt a shiver tingle up my back. Before I was privy to that piece of my new family history, I had enjoyed being in that room and lying down on the white bumpy chenille bedspread, tracing my fingers along its swirling pattern, feeling sleepy as I watched the summer breeze draw the lacey curtains back and forth.

On those occasions, in the background I had overheard muffled conversations of people stopping by for a visit on a Sunday afternoon. They discussed the weather and how the rain was affecting the corn and soybean crops, who was and wasn't in church this morning, what the preacher had to say about eternal damnation, that new hat with the golden pheasant feathers that must have cost a fortune and worn by a city lady who recently moved in the railroad track house. And then in more hushed tones, the latest scandal—the distant cousin of someone named Ruthie who had come to stay with her from Minnesota because she was PG. I wasn't sure what that meant, but I knew it couldn't be good, just by the way it was spoken of . . . "army boy" . . . "disgraceful" . . . "shotgun wedding"—were just some of the words that escaped the whispering circle of ladies.

Big Mom went over now and picked up the telephone on the end of the counter. When the operator came on, she said,

"Marge, stop on over after work. I'm savin' some prune rolls for you and Walter. And give me 176, will ya'?"

Within minutes she was connected to her very best friend, Iris. "You comin'? Stories 'bout to start. I'll pour your coffee." As she spoke, she was adding a hefty dose of Pet milk from the can to a cup she had just poured.

The stories she was referring to were the afternoon soap operas, *The Edge of Night* and *Secret Storm*. When they came on, all else stopped except for eating and drinking. This was serious stuff. A sad day on the stories could bring on a heavy spirit among the ladies in the neighborhood. Big Mom swore these were real people with all these problems, mostly brought on by themselves because they lived in that big city. "Cities are that way, dangerous to one's soul," she said. Although she had never been farther away from home than Salsten, which was hardly a big city. It was something she just knew in her heart.

Next, all of the ladies gathered around the kitchen table moved into the living room. They took their places on the sofa and in the upholstered chairs with lace doilies on the backs and arms.

Iris had created these delicate lace patterns for Big Mom years ago. Just like a spider spinning a web, her hands moved quickly, flashing the needle with quick little motions. She could do it without even looking at it as she talked, never missing a word or a stitch. I think she was part spider, you know—way, way back in her family tree. Her glasses were so thick they gave her the appearance of having more than the normal amount of human eye power, which supported my theory.

Everyone faced the television that sat on a gold-colored metal stand. On the wall above it were three large oil-on-velvet pictures of John F. Kennedy, Jesus, and Elvis Presley in that order, from left to right. The picture of Jesus hung slightly higher than the other two. They were Big Mom's holy trinity. The picture on the television was in black and white, and all of the people looked as if they were forever caught in a snowstorm. Occasionally, the picture would begin to roll and someone would stomp their foot real hard to make it stop. But once, Big Mom had to get up and whack the top of it good and adjust the tin foil on the rabbit ears.

I had never been allowed to watch soap operas. They were considered an evil waste of our precious time by Nana. So naturally, as guilty as I felt, I still followed the other ladies in and sat down for my initiation. I simply could not believe that I was being allowed to join them.

I sat mesmerized and a little terrified as the story unfolded in front of me. There was a strikingly beautiful lady who appeared to be in some grave danger, but before I found out just what type of danger, another story began with a man and woman kissing real hard. She began to cry a flood of tears because they couldn't marry each other because one of them, or maybe it was both of them, was already married to someone else. For the life of me, I could not understand how they came about kissing if they belonged to someone else. But there they were just the same, heads swiveling back and forth, eyes tightly shut, and their lips definitely touching.

Next, within the blink of an eye, even though I'm quite sure I didn't blink even once, another man was driving in a car on a rainy road and skidded off, hitting his head, causing blood to run down his forehead but not mess up his perfectly combed hair. The show ended with him falling over in the seat, leaving us to worry if he was dead or merely in a coma.

I was absolutely exhausted from what I had just witnessed. My mind felt a little muddled and soiled, like I needed some fresh air or maybe a nap or possibly a drink of water. Yes, that was it—a cold, clear drink of Nana and Grandy's well water. That's exactly what I needed to cleanse the images of those poor people and all of their turmoil away. I wondered what Nana and Grandy were doing right now. My chest ached for them.

Not anxious to see any more soap operas for a while, my attention was drawn past the flowing sheers draping the picture window. Across the road I could see Lyddie's house. Oh, doggone it! I forgot all about meeting Lyddie to play. There she was now, swinging slowly back and forth on the old tractor tire swing that hung from the outstretched arm of the ancient maple tree in her front yard. She looked lonely and bored. How long had she been there? Baking day at Big Mom's had flown by, and now it was almost supper time. Did I dare to ask Mother to walk me back across the road so I could play with Lyddie? I glanced over at her and took a chance.

"Mother, could I please go back and play with Lyddie?"

All heads snapped in my direction as I realized to my dismay that the next show had just begun. I would most likely have to occupy myself with other things until it was over, and Lyddie would have to swing alone a while longer. Little did

I know that Lyddie was used to playing alone since most kids shunned her, their parents suspicious that the problem in her chest might actually be tuberculosis. Gossip caused her family unnecessary pain and isolation.

Chapter Five

By the time Mother and I finally crossed the road to go back home, Lyddie was nowhere in sight. Moping around the yard, I hoped she would see me and come back outside. The thick afternoon air over my head gave evidence of someone's supper cooking, heavy with fried meat and onions.

Flopping down on the grass and flipping onto my stomach, I laid there looking deep down into the dirt between the dry blades of grass and dandelion leaves. Watching carefully, I spied an ant on the way to its anthill and followed it on my hands and knees. It was carrying a whitish-beige oval that I knew instinctively was an egg. Approaching the hole, down it went out of sight. Within seconds it reappeared, or maybe it was a different ant altogether. They *are* exactly identical, you know. Back through the grass it traveled, as if on an urgent assignment. The blades of grass must have seemed like skyscrapers to this busy little creature, but it hardly seemed to notice.

I had recently learned of these incredibly tall buildings in New York City. The thought of being so high up in the sky, held up only by lumber and bricks that mere men had put together, was a scary one. Not something I longed to experience.

The ant went straight to another egg laying on a blade of grass, which, until that moment I would never have noticed. It picked it up effortlessly and hurried back to the anthill. Down it went again. I watched this ritual of nature take place over and over. I pondered what the meaning of all this was.

I had learned from Nana and Grandy that everything in nature is done with purpose. Nothing is wasted, not even the energy of tiny bugs. They must put the eggs out in the sunlight during the day and bring them in again before night. I would have to mark this spot in the yard and watch for them again in the morning. Getting up, I glanced around for something to put there. But before I could do that, I was distracted from the ants and their tasks.

Lyddie came skipping across the yard after she had eaten. It must have been her dinner I had smelled cooking because the greasy aroma wafted from her hair and dress.

While wandering past the perimeters of the yard to the ditch that ran between my new house and the soybean field, our conversation convened as if we had never been apart at all. As it turned out, Lyddie had a big brother named Tony that I had not met yet because he was visiting cousins in Philadelphia, wherever that was. Apparently, he was a pain in her big toenail.

As we talked, we ran our hands over the fuzzy brown cattails growing out of the ditch. We had so much in common; we both just loved cattails and their sharp, reed-like leaves. I told Lyddie how they reminded me of the Bible story of Moses in the bulrushes. Lyddie didn't know much about the Bible, but she really liked hearing the story. We pondered if we could have put our own little baby in a basket to float on a river surrounded by crocodiles.

At the thought of crocodiles, a shiver ran up my body as I looked into the muddy water we were standing in with bare feet. I knew it was silly. No crocodiles lived around here, I was sure. I wasn't *that* far away from Nana and Grandy's farm, and I *knew* none lived there. The most dangerous thing I knew of there was the rare occurrence of wild dogs—which I had never witnessed, only heard stories about.

My mind took me back to a hot day walking with Grandy on the trail that wound through the acres and acres of home, Sanctuary Oak Farm. "Don't move, Son!" Calm and steady as anything. He raised his old shotgun up to his shoulder and aimed, I thought, right at the center of me. But I didn't move the teeniest fraction of a hair, hardly a muscle to breathe, because the tone of my Grandy's voice told me he knew what he was doing. And he was serious. My eyes locked onto his for a split second, and then he looked slightly behind me to my left. I had a thought float across my mind as I stood there motionless, looking at my Grandy, shotgun leveled at me. There was absolutely no fear in this situation with Grandy and me.

This was like when Abraham had taken Isaac up to the mountain to sacrifice, just like God told him to do. Isaac didn't understand what his father was about to do, and it must have looked pretty bleak to him too. But right then and right there while standing on that ridge, I knew what Isaac had felt—complete trust in someone who loved you more than life itself. Someone who also loved and trusted God in the same way that you loved and trusted them right in this moment when time stood still. Trusted with your very life.

There was love and trust just beaming down on the two of us from all sides and from the ancient ones who observed from above. Of course, it didn't hurt one single bit that I also knew the end of that Bible story, how God had provided a ram stuck in the thicket to be sacrificed in Isaac's place. He just wanted Abraham to put Him first, trusting Him enough to be obedient even though he didn't understand. So, I stood dead still and waited for whatever was to come, listening for the bleat of a ram or a lamb in the bushes. I heard nothing.

As I watched Grandy's pointer finger, steady as anything, slowly pulling back on that old metal trigger, I saw the glint of sunlight off the barrel of that old gun as the sun shuddered. BOOM! The sound of the blast ripped through the forest and the hills surrounding us and echoed over and over again, each time getting a bit fainter as the sound died into shocked silence. In slow motion, I watched as a flock of blackbirds, startled, flew up into the paling blue sky from a grove of pecan trees where we gathered nuts in the fall.

In that split second, Grandy dropped his gun on the ground from where he had stood stock still and fired. He snatched me up in his big, strong arms, hugging me to his chest, squeezing the living breath right out of me. He had moved with the speed of lightning, so fast that I couldn't even comprehend what had happened until it was all over. He stroked the back of my sun-warmed brown curls, saying, "Good, Son. You did real good, not moving one bit. You listened to ol' Grandy."

Then he turned me around to see, not a ram, but a great big old copperhead blown into two pieces, both of which were writhing and twisting around on that huge flat rock where it had been sunning. The very same rock that I always liked to jump up on and sing to hear my voice come back to me in echoes that sounded like backup singers, as I belted it out for the whole forest to hear.

I stared at the size of its head, at the copper-penny shield covering it, the beautiful orangey-tan markings circling its now slowing-down long body. I felt sadness that I had caused the death of one of God's magnificent creatures, even if he would have tried to kill me for surprising him if Grandy hadn't got him first. With my arms tightly around his neck, I looked back into Grandy's face, and only then did I realize the real danger I had been in, punctuated by the beads of sweat on his brow.

"Boy, Grandy! That was a big old snake, wasn't he?"

"He sure was, Son, and contrary too. 'Specially this time of year when it's mating season. He was all drawn back in striking position, just waiting for you to take one more step in his direction."

We both stared at the now still body, remembering the story of Newbie Metner, who had not had his Grandy there to save him a few summers ago as he apparently had jumped over a log, landing right square on a cantankerous old copperhead. He was found there late that night lying face down in the moonlight after he didn't come home from a fishing expedition with a friend from a neighboring farm.

There he was, all bloated up and swollen around the face. They said his tongue was swelled bigger than his mouth. But the purplish-black swelling was the most hideous on his leg, where the snake had sunk his deadly fangs deep into his ankle. He hadn't any chance of making it back in time to get help, even if he had thought to take off his rope belt and use it for a tourniquet.

Judging by the space between the fang marks, Dr. Gabe had determined that it had been a real big snake with lots of venom stored up. It was his guess that, judging by Newbie's heel print where he had jumped over the log, the scuffed-up dirt immediately beside it, and then Newbie's body just a few steps away, its fang must have hit directly into a vein, sending the deadly poison straight to his heart and killing him practically in an instant.

He also knew that it wouldn't have been a cottonmouth because there wasn't any pond or stream close by. They liked to stay pretty close to some kind of fresh water. There were just those jagged rocks and fallen dead trees that copperheads like to slither up on and heat up in the sun.

Lyddie was quick to notice the shiver and sudden pause in our conversation as I stood remembering the snakes of my past. "What's wrong, Lacey?" she said quietly.

Not wanting to worry or frighten her, I looked up and saw the old hose hanging on the side of the faucet. Perfect timing.

"Let's go wash the mud off our toes and make rainbows with the hose!" I shrieked, splashing out of the ditch and running toward it, with Lyddie hot on my heels.

"Hey, you made a rhyme!" laughed Lyddie. "Let's wash the mud off our toes and make rainbows with the hose," she repeated, this time adding a happy-sounding little tune to it. I quickly took her cue, and we began singing it together over and over again.

We took turns pointing the hose toward the sky and holding our fingers over the opening to make just the right arc of spray to produce the brightest rainbows, while the other would run under squealing and trying not to get the cold water on her back. We made all kinds of wishes running under our rainbows, with fingers crossed and held high over our heads.

Our conversation naturally led to the monetary aspects of a rainbow, such as that ever elusive pot of gold that was supposed to be at the end of it. What would you do with gold anyhow? we decided. It didn't fit into bubble gum machines, and nobody would know how much change to give you if you tried to use it at the store. Plus, I had heard it was really heavy, 'specially when it was melted into those big gold egrets they were always talking about in movies. I never could figure out why they made them into a bird shape as opposed to some other animal, like a cat or a dog, who was supposed to be man's best friend.

And so the hot summer days rolled by, as our legs grew a little longer and our skin turned golden brown in the sun.

During the daylight hours, that pining deep in my heart was sometimes not so bad now. But frequently at night, I would be almost overcome with emotion from missing Nana and Grandy. With throat aching, looking out the window of my new bedroom up into the sky at Ursa Major and Ursa Minor, the Big Bear and Little Bear constellations that Grandy showed me, I found a teensy bit of comfort in the fact that the same stars were shining over Sanctuary Oak Farm not so very far away. Grandy might even be looking up at them right now too. But the distance that ached in my heart left me wishing all the same to be seeing it from the windows of my old house.

That's when Lyddie and I discovered that our bedroom windows faced each other. We began to blink our nightlights off and on each night to send silent messages across the yard long after dark. As one of us (usually Lyddie) got sleepy, the blinking light would gradually get slower and slower and the pauses in between longer and longer and then finally, just darkness.

"Good night, Lyddie," I would murmur sleepily. "Sleep tight. Don't let the bedbugs bite."

Now, this is when a strange and eerie thing happened—more than once I might add—as I was left lying there awake after Lyddie had fallen asleep. It's important to know it was not just one occurrence, or it might have been chalked up to being part of a dream, like maybe I had dozed off or something. I'd be lying there, and then I'd hear it. Wee quiet at first and then traveling louder and closer at the same time. Whistling. A haunting kind of tune, it sounded kinda mournful and sad, with a few notes of spooky thrown in. The sound raised every fine hair on my body. It would go right on by my window and keep on going 'til I could hear it no more. I would whip my sheet up over my head, pulling it tight and breaking out in the tremblin' sweats. Afraid to let the ghost or whatever it was hear me talk about it out loud, I never mentioned it to anyone, not even Lyddie. This is called "suffering in silence." I did a lot of that.

Shortly, a new peculiarity came to town. Khaki Dad owned a large shed perched on the corner lot at the edge of the soybean field. It was pretty dilapidated, with a few faded, broken green shingles left hanging here and there to try and cover its bareness. The big concrete steps had long since separated themselves from the door frame as if embarrassed, leaving a large gap.

With the help of a couple of carefully stacked wooden crates placed under the windows, you could see a collection of rusty, bent buckets hanging from nails, old saws, a chicken coop or two, and various pieces of odd furniture leaning beside old-fashioned-looking hoes. There was even a heavy ox yoke propped up against an iron wood stove in front of some old bales of hay. Lyddie and I knew all this first hand because by now we had almost explored every hole and corner of my new neighborhood.

Apparently, a preacher man came and asked Khaki Dad if he and his congregation could rent and renovate that old building into a God's Church meeting house. And since it wasn't being used for anything important and extra money was always welcome, he said okay. This was a surprise to most folks around, knowing that Khaki Dad didn't particularly like church or preachers.

Almost immediately, new trucks and cars began pouring into our previously undisturbed piece of country as men and women alike began working on the clean-up and restoration. When a car would pull up and the people got out, the ones who were already there greeted them with huge hugs like they were family that hadn't been seen in ages. This in itself was odd since we recognized the same automobiles day after day. As they worked, deep, booming voices singing all kinds of hymns echoed through the fields and yards nearby. Their laughter drifted into our yards and surrounded us like air. Happy, light air.

At dinner time they set up long tables covered with daisy-flowered cloths. Picnic hampers, cold pitchers of lemonade, and dishes heaped with food appeared as if from nowhere as they all gathered around to eat. That is, after a painfully long prayer was said over the food and workers by the loud little preacher man. It was sorta like that miracle Jesus did when He fed all those people on a hill. He multiplied the food out of practically nowhere.

He had introduced himself previously to my new dad as Sam Whitecap, although his hair was thick, black, and greasy like he had used too much pomade. Guess he didn't know *Brylceam, a little dab'll do you,* I thought, as the commercial tune played in my head. *The girls'll want to woo you.*

It seemed like no time at all before there were gleaming white shingles in place of the old, broken ones and a freshly painted red door. The concrete steps, scrubbed spotless, joined up to the door again like they were proud to be a part of what was happening. All of the windows glistened in the sunlight. Holiness seemed to settle in and around the building. A fly wouldn't have dared to put a speck on one pane of glass for fear of being struck dead. Last of all, a sign was planted on the front edge of the grass. It read,

THE ONE TRUE GOD'S CHURCH OF
PROPHECY AND HEALING
Samuel W. Whitecap, preaching
Services Saturday 7:00 PM
Everyone Welcome

Now, up to this point everything looked pretty good for the God's Church people—that is, until that sign went up. You see, the only religion most everybody around Burleyville had ever known was the reserved, predictable, meet-on-Sunday-morning kind. Immediately, suspicions started to rise. What was this foreign religion all about?

Next, a bent-up blue truck pulled up, and they started unloading. Upright piano first and then drums, hauling them into the church. Drums. Holy-moly! All we ever had was piano music. Now, this was starting to look real interesting.

Tongues began wagging, and there were speculations on what it could mean. Someone even brought up the idea that they might be snake handlers. Lyddie overheard someone at the store say that they might be bigamists. But all one had to do was take a look to see that wasn't true. None of them were exceptionally big people. As a matter of fact, the preacher was on the small side.

There was a big discussion about it in Big Mom's kitchen immediately before the soap operas started one afternoon. Quite naturally, Beulah and Big Mom had opposing opinions on the subject. Just to be sure they'd have something to quibble with each other about later.

So, that first Saturday night when the church doors were opened, nobody was out doing their usual Saturday night things. Everyone stayed at home and observed as the procession of vehicles began to pass by. Under the watchful eyes of the neighborhood, nothing appeared amiss. One by one they drove by, like any other ordinary family in an ordinary automobile on their way to church. The only extraordinary thing was, of course, the fact that it was a Saturday night.

The preacher man had arrived earlier than the rest of the flock, and now he waited by the steps with arms spread wide, smiling toward Heaven. Once everyone had filed out of their cars and up the steps—little children like baby ducklings following close behind their mothers, who followed close behind their husbands—he waited a few more minutes. With one long last dramatic look toward the sky, he clasped his hands together and followed up the steps and disappeared into the church. Now, I say "disappeared" only because the doorway was dark just beyond the entryway, for he had left the front door wide open.

Within minutes of his disappearance inside, loud music commenced to play. Drums beat a deep, erratic rhythm as the piano did its part to keep up. Boisterous singing rang out through the slowly darkening night air, the pitch growing louder and louder. Cymbals could be heard crashing every once in a while. I'm not entirely sure, but Lyddie and I thought we even heard a kazoo or two while we hid out in between the hedge across the road and watched with quivering excitement.

When the music quieted down, the little preacher's voice began to rise and fall like fiery flames in between loud shouts of, "Amen, brother! Glory! Hallelujah!"

Well, I had never heard the like in all my life. The music was one thing, but yelling things out loud while the preacher was preaching was quite another. If I had behaved like that in church, I would have got the switch on bare legs for sure. But it didn't seem to bother him one iota. As a matter of fact, it sounded like it fired him up all the more and encouraged him to preach faster and harder. I actually think he liked it.

Lyddie didn't know what was normal and what was not because her family didn't cater to church-going. But I could see by the small band of light stretching across from Ritter's Store that her eyes were wide with amazement. We looked at each other nose to nose and giggled behind hands clasped over our mouths.

It was a bit past closing time for the little country store that sat kitty-cornered across from our houses. On the porch was the usual Saturday night gathering of men. They met there after supper was eaten, propped their wooden chairs against the worn places in the shingles, smoked cigarettes, and talked until way into the night. I listened to the low murmurings of their voices, and from time to time one of them would let out a husky laugh and eventually, one by one, they would get into their trucks and disappear down the road to their homes.

Sometimes I laid propped up sideways on my bed at night and watched through the screen as their cigarettes flickered glowing-red dots when they drew in long breaths of smoke. First here on this side of the porch, then over there, and once in a while two or three would light up at a time. It was eye music, playing to the night. Sometimes when the wind was in my direction, I could catch a pungent whiff of burning tobacco on the air. I liked the smell. I had even practiced with a straw how to dangle a cigarette in its long holder from my fingertips and lips, just like those Hollywood actresses did. But the end of my paper straw soon got all soggy and ruined the effect.

Now, getting back to the goings-on inside that church. The sounds filling the night air around us became just too tempting to stay hidden in the hedgerow any longer. Creeping across the road, we sidled up to the side of the church. We were plastered on the side trying to be invisible, just in case anybody's eyes happened to look our way.

My swanney! I do believe I felt some peculiar vibration, some unseen force pushing out on the walls. Scary as that thought was, I just had to see what was going on inside. With finger to lips, I motioned Lyddie to follow me. Waddling like ducks, we found the two old crates that had been stashed underneath the building during renovation and soundlessly drug them out. I even endured without a whimper the sharp pain of an old, rotten splinter ripping into the soft, fleshy part between my thumb and pointy finger.

Of course, the being quiet was just for our benefit to make it more exciting because we were about to embark on an adventure that we probably shouldn't. There was no way on this green earth that anybody inside could have heard us even if we shouted, with all the ruckus going on in there.

Under the middle window, we carefully placed one crate on top of the other. Lyddie pushed down on the top one and wiggled it around just to be sure they were steady. Neither one of us wanted to have to explain how we came about breaking a leg or an arm if we fell off.

We both knew without words what we were about to do next as we crawled up shakily onto the top crate, first me and then Lyddie. Slowly, ever so slowly, hardly moving at all, holding our breath we inched up side by side to standing positions, Lyddie on the left and me on the right side of the window frame. Fingers gripping the window sill for dear life, we moved with the stealth of a cat stalking a mouse. It could hardly be called movement at all. Hair by hair, inchmeal, our heads reached the edge of the open window, bodies aching with the tension of it, until at last we had a view of the mysteries within. Mysteries that up to this very moment had been observed by no one else in our town.

As we peeked over the last millimeter of window frame, I was awestruck by what met my eyes and brain. Things were definitely out of order! Anything and everything but the ordinary seemed to be taking place. Ladies with churchy-looking hats on their heads were swaying back and forth in big, dramatic swoops with their white-gloved hands held high over their heads. Their eyes were squeezed closed. Some were bright faced and smiling while still others had tears streaming down their twisted and contorted faces.

Indistinguishable mumbling was rising up from all around, like fireflies from a soybean field at dusk. Voices joining together and floating overhead to God, I guess. In our church we knew that God knew everything and could hear thoughts before they were said out loud, so we kept quiet except for singing.

The men weren't behaving any better than the women. They held their hats in their hands and fanned them in big arcs over their heads. Men and ladies, boys and girls, were all in disarray, not standing in straight lines in their usual pews like we did. They were all over the place, standing in the aisles and dancing around wherever they felt like going. Yes, I saw dancing.

But that was not the most shocking discovery of all. That came when I looked up front and realized that the whole choir and the preacher himself had worked themselves up into near frenzies. These didn't even resemble the same people Lyddie and I had so closely observed quietly cleaning, carpentering, and eating together a few weeks back.

Before I could give it another thought, some people carrying a young boy who didn't look quite right—as Big Mom would say, *"He was titched in the head"*—came up to the altar. There they lay him right down, pitiful like, on the floor in front of Preacher Whitecap, who immediately looked up at the ceiling and prayed in a commanding voice.

"Gawd! You healed the lepers and you healed the blind man. You cast out the devils." His voice was shaking, and drops of sweat were soaking his white shirt as he continued. "This boy is brought before You tonight for a healing! We are asking You for a healing!"

With that, he dropped down on his knees beside the boy and pressed his hands down hard on the boy's head and shouted, "BE HEALED, BOY, AND BE WHOLE, BOY, IN THE LORD'S NAME! HALLELUJAH!"

With the last word, he shoved down on the poor boy's head and got up just as quickly, moving to the next person in line. The boy appeared to go to sleep instantly with his head drawn to one side. The thought ran through my mind that maybe the preacher had broken his neck by mistake.

The mother and father knelt down quickly where the preacher had been. The mother was shaking the boy's face and gently smacking his cheeks with her hands, calling over and over again, "Jeffy! Jeffy! Can you hear me, Jeffy? Can you see me, Jeffy? Do you know me, Jeffy?"

From hidden corners of the room, strange-sounding words joined with others to form languages neither Lyddie nor I had ever heard before. They raised higher and higher, following the air overhead past the frosted-glass cylinder lanterns that hung on chains casting long shadows across the ceiling and down the walls. *Tongues.* Now, I had heard about them in the Bible, but I had never heard them for real before; and the way I was feeling right now, I kinda wished they had stayed in the Bible.

The next in line was a lady in a pink seersucker dress. Her white straw hat had a sash of matching material around the crown. Placing her hand over her heart, she approached, stood up on tiptoe, and whispered something in the preacher's ear. He raised his hands over his head, swinging them back down in one swift motion, giving her a mighty push in the center of her chest, awfully close to her bosoms, I noticed.

"IN THE NAME OF JESUS, BE HEALED!" roared the mighty voice of the preacher.

She fell backwards instantly in what appeared to be a dead faint. At least I hoped it was a faint and not just dead. Instantly, there were two men, one on each side of her, who caught her ever so gently and laid her down, right there on the floor in a straight line with her hat placed over her chest.

Our attention was startled away from that lady by a piercing shriek of apparent joy from Jeffy's mother. We looked back just in time to see Jeffy sitting up, smiling, and—for all the world, looking as normal as pie.

Lyddie's and my eyes met and asked each other the same question. What the heck just happened to Jeffy? Could we possibly have just witnessed something that spooky? A supernatural miracle right here in Burleyville! My mouth was dry as a bone, but I swallowed hard like it was full of spit. Lyddie looked pale as milk in the light from the church. We turned away from each other, mesmerized.

The next person in front of the altar was a man we had seen earlier being hoisted up the steps in his wheelchair by some big, strong men dressed in dark pants and white shirts drawn tight like a noose around their necks with a tie. He was tipping back and forth. We thought at one point he might spill out of his chair, right on his head in the dirt below. But he didn't. He made it safely inside, and now here he was at the altar of strange occurrences.

We watched expectantly as the preacher man approached him. No words were exchanged between the two. Preacher Whitecap looked up. Oh boy! What now? Look out. In the blink of an eye, he had grabbed onto the man's legs, giving them a powerful shake. All at once, the man gave a loud yell and jumped up out of the wheelchair, waving his arms in the air. He started running down the aisle headed for the door. There were crazy drums and wild, happy shouting. Someone was banging on the piano. There was clapping. Sheer chaos broke out from all over the sanctuary.

With that, one, or maybe it was both of us, jerked backwards, causing the crates we were standing on to overturn. We fell onto the grass in a heap of legs and elbows and heads that smarted from being knocked against each other. Loud whooping and commotion was suddenly coming from the front yard of the church. We both ran like scared rabbits not away from the sounds, but directly toward them, terrified but unable to resist seeing what was happening now.

Wheelchair man came stumbling down the steps of the church. Straight out into the yard, where he fell down and began rolling around on the ground. He was laughing and rolling and praising the mighty Lord the whole time. He kept right on rolling, right up to the edge of the road. Someone else came running down the steps and grabbed him, rolling him back just in the nick of time before he rolled under the wheels of Ad Pettijohn's truck. I guess if he *had* got run over, they could have just scooped him up with all his parts and took him back inside the church for another healing.

That was enough for us for one night. We took off running across the soybean field, the leaves slapping at our bare legs as we went. We didn't slow down until our heels landed on the dewy, cool clover of Lyddie's backyard.

Giving one another a final glance in the moonlight, we each raced off toward our own back door, knowing full well we had tarried too long after dark. Fortunately for me, my mother was on the telephone with her friend Doris, the Avon Lady, already talking about the events of the evening.

I gathered from her end of the conversation that Big Mom had joined in their discussion on the party line, along with Elzie. I imagined telephones ringing off the hooks all over town, with all of the ladies sitting on their telephone seats and sofas with legs crossed, shaking them agitatedly as they spoke, adding to each story what they had heard from the previous caller. I overheard Mother say something about *sacrilegious*!

Preacher Whitecap's ears must be burning off his head! But that wouldn't bother him none because he had the power to HEAL. All he had to do was reach up and smack those burnt-up ears hard, and they would be good as new. I could see where that gift he had could come in awfully handy.

I fell asleep that night pondering how someone got the healing power. How I might have used it when Martha, our old gray and white cat at the farm, got a bad infection in her hind paw from a fight lost with a fox. There was little doubt that he'd been trying to steal another hen from the henhouse when feisty Martha tried to stop him. The germs from the bite festered and swelled despite Nana's soaking and treating it with Epsom salts. Martha suffered terribly until finally one day she just up and disappeared.

Oh, how I had cried and grieved over losing her. I knew animals often went off by themselves to die. Weeks went by, and I gradually adjusted to not having her around, when all of a sudden, one day while I was up on the hill picking cicada shells from the trunk of an old oak, I heard a familiar "mee-ow-ll," and here came Martha running up the dirt road to me on three legs. Upon examining her I found the stump completely healed. She had learned to run just as fast as before, and it didn't appear to bother her in the least. But if I could have touched her on the leg and had God heal her, it would have saved her a lot of suffering and a leg—and me a whole lot of tears and sadness.

Next morning was Sunday, the day church was meant to be on, and I couldn't wait to get there to see Nana and Grandy. Mother and I still went to our little church near Cedarton. Bowley's Methodist, so named after long-dead ancestors of my grandparents. Khaki Dad worked on Sundays, like he did all the other days of the week. This was a regular bone of contention between him and Mother that brought on a storm of loud arguments, followed by long, uncomfortable silences and tightened jaws.

The minister there, The Reverend Gladding as we called him, had just had a new baby girl—well, actually his wife had the baby. There are some things that only women can do, and that is one of them, for sure. They had named her Gloria Joy Gladding, and she surely lived up to her name. She had cornflower-blue eyes and bright orange hair that stood straight up on her head, looking just like a little sunburst peeking up over the horizon of her mother's shoulder. She was always grinning, apparently thrilled at just being alive.

I was all spit and polish from the top of my flower-embellished straw hat to the tips of my white lace-gloved fingers. No one would think of going to church without the proper coverings. I purposely put on my peach-colored dress with the big satiny sash that Nana had sewn for me. I knew she would be so proud of me picking it to wear.

When she made it, I had to stand for what seemed like hours on a wooden stool while she pinned up the hem to stitch at just the right "len'th." She made most of my clothes, summer and winter. To her liking, I might add. I didn't usually have much say in what she made. However, there was one particular winter coat that I absolutely adored. It had been made from one of Grandy's old suits. It felt like having his arms wrapped tightly around me. I could smell him lingering in the weave of the wool. Sometimes at night when I was lonely for him, I snuck it out of the closet and wore it as long as I could stand the heat of it and then took it off and held it beside me for comfort.

Mother and I took off for church, late as usual. I stood on the blue-carpeted hump of the axle behind the front seats and held on for dear life as we slung around the hairpin-curved back roads through the woods of Casket Switch. It was named that because a long time ago there was a casket factory on about the sixth curve. Rusty remains of the factory could still be seen peeking above the overgrown bramble like long giraffe necks. The place was said to be haunted, and some people swore they had seen strange lights floating around there. I tried not to look in that direction as we sped by.

On the next to the last curve, Mother swerved suddenly to miss a rabbit that ran across the road. She said she missed it, but I was sure I heard a sickening little thump. Losing my footing, I was thrown against the passenger side door, ripping some of my hair out on the ashtray mounted there. The lid had been left flipped open. When I regained my balance and extracted the clump of hairs caught there, I checked hopefully inside for ashes to see if I might have just one little lick, but— too bad—it had been carefully cleaned out. Oh well, better off to get my bunny kiss from Grandy without ash breath, although he would never complain.

Arriving at church during the opening hymn, I ran straight up the aisle to Nana and Grandy's usual pew and crawled up on it to stand between them. Grandy hugged me to him as I stood on the bench straining to reach him for my kiss. It was a song that I knew by heart and had sung many times while swinging. "I come to the garden alone, while the dew is still on the roses; and the voice I hear falling on my ear, the Son of God disclo-o-ses."

I sang out loud off key, my rendition of a joyful noise. For the next hour, my heart beat to a happy tune. Things felt right. I didn't really listen to the sermon as my thoughts were on other important issues at hand, such as thinking up the perfect reason to go home with Nana and Grandy.

Then it came to me. It made perfect sense. Next weekend was the grand family reunion. It was held at Sanctuary Oak Farm. About sixty or seventy family members came from all over, and there were tons of things to do to get ready for it. Nana would need my help, for sure. Rooms had to be made ready for the long-distance relatives who would spend a few nights. There was lots of cleaning in the house and around the yard, not to mention all of the food that had to be cooked ahead of time. There would be hustle and bustle and hoopla all week as Nana tried to think of everyone's favorite dishes and new games and entertainment.

Although we usually sang funny songs accompanied by Cousin Kenny on his accordion as he swayed back and forth, far to the left and then right, squeezing air in and out of it that somehow came out in tunes we knew. *She'll be comin' 'round the mountain when she comes, when she comes.* We all made up silly choruses to sing until we were breathless and tired.

This year, however, we'd have to get some other form of music because Aunt Louise said that Kenny had turned queer and moved off to the big city. I'm not quite sure what she meant or why that would stop him from coming home for the family reunion, but it did and everyone was satisfied with his not being there. Everyone except me. I would miss his teasing and funny jokes. Oh yeah, and the way he said,

"Well, bless your little pea-pickin' heart." He got that from *The Tennessee Ernie Ford Show*.

Nana was considering asking her second cousin, Florence, if she would play the piano once again—that is, if she could behave herself. A few years back she had near about disgraced herself right out of the family tree when she fell off the piano stool in the middle of Swanney River and broke her hip after she had snuck a few too many sips of Uncle Theodore's homemade blackberry brandy. He delighted in spicing things up a bit by sneaking it in to 'most any celebration. Generally, it was only a few wayward men in the family who would meet behind the corn crib and partake with him. But somehow that year Florence got lured in, like a moth to a flame. And so, now she had a limp to remember her peccadillo, as her schoolmarm, second cousin-once removed, labeled it.

Anyhow, church was over, and everyone was saying their howdy-dos and good-byes. I presented my case to Mother about the need for me to go home with Nana and Grandy to help. Nana agreed that I would be a big help and it would give Mother and my new dad some time alone together, too.

Reluctantly, Mother said okay, but added with a raised eyebrow in my direction, "Young lady, when I say it's time to come home, I mean it, and there's not gonna be any squallin' and bawlin', understand?"

"Yes, Mother, I promise," I said with big sincere eyes. My heart was shouting, "Yippee! Yippee! Hurray!"

It was all I could do to stand still. As soon as Mother's

back was turned, I gave Grandy's arm a big yank toward the car. I couldn't get there fast enough.

The ride there was wonderful with the honeysuckle smells and bird calls floating in the open windows as we cruised through the cool of the woods. I stretched out on the back seat and watched the rich green and blue dapple of leaf and sky splash by the rear car window. *How many hundreds of miles had I ridden in the back seat of this car?* I wondered. The left triangle-shaped back window had colorful, translucent decals of states we had been to. They made little rainbows of color on my legs.

Brrrrrrht, brrrrrrht came the sound of our tires as we crossed over the first wooden bridge on the way home. I knew the way home by heart without having to look. I could feel where I was going. Next came the clearing with no woods, just pure sunshine, which opened up to millions of tasseled rows of cornfields. Yes, there it was—the big curve to the left around Brentford's farm. I raised up to see which direction their big steel weather vane was pointing, even though I was pretty sure there wasn't enough of a breeze out today to change its direction.

Lying back down, I knew we were meeting another car by the sound of gravel under the wheels of the right side of the car. On just a small blacktop country road, everyone had to slow down and pull way over to the side of the road, and sometimes even in the weeds, in order to go by each other. As the cars passed, the occupants of both cars would usually look at each other in the eye and wave, kinda friendly-like. More times than not, we would know them and stop right there in the middle of the road and have a chat until someone else came along wanting to get by.

Within minutes we were in the shade of another woods, the branches stretching out overhead to form a green canopy of cool. Any minute now we would be crossing the second wooden bridge. One, two, three, four, *brrrrrrrrht*. There it was. That one was older and more rickety. I didn't like looking into the black water running under it. It always made me shiver at the thought of the bridge giving a big shudder and caving in as we went over it.

Just a few more minutes and we would be there. I could hardly wait to get there and run all over the farm and announce to all the animals and trees that I was home. We had to go past the tomato cannery next. Today there was not a whiff of the usual stinky tomato steam that engulfed the plant six days out of seven. It was closed on Sundays, like all businesses. A couple more miles and I felt the bump, bump of the railroad tracks. Now nothing but wide-open country road until we made the sharp turn right and another right into our lane.

By this time, I was standing up behind the front seat, steadying myself with arms wrapped around Grandy's neck. If I was about to choke him, he didn't complain. There it was, Sanctuary Oak Farm. It was a sight for sore eyes; I meant that in the most loving of ways. The pond was beautiful. The ducks' reflections gave them the look of having two heads. The willow trees swished their graceful greeting to me on the windshield as we drove up the lane. One after the other they swished by, twelve in all, six on each side. Nana jokingly called them "The Apostles." I couldn't imagine one of them being evil like Judas. Yes! I was home at last. I wouldn't think about for how long. All that mattered was this moment in time where everything was as it should be.

Chapter Six

There was Martha, peering over the side of the bucket that hung over the well. She liked to have her afternoon nap there. No need to be concerned about her falling down the well. Grandy had slid a heavy piece of thick metal over the opening so that none of us kids or Martha would fall in. Sometimes when my cousins were there, we pushed in unison to slide the metal to the side so we could toss pennies down and make wishes. Nana didn't like for us to throw things in the well because that's where our water came from.

We always had spigots in the house as far as I could remember, but a long time ago the well was used to draw up water for all their needs. Sometimes even now I helped Grandy lower the bucket slowly from the wheel at the top, way down the deep, dark hole, and crank up bucket after bucket of crystal-clear, icy-cold water for the animals, or if it had been very dry, to water the grapevines on that side of the house. When Martha saw me, she jumped from her perch and ran to meet me, leaving the bucket swinging wildly behind her.

I rubbed behind her ears, automatically lapsing into kitty talk. "Hey, wittle gi'l, did oos miff me, huh? Did oos miff me?" She seemed very pleased indeed to see me, purring loudly and rubbing hard against my legs. She was starting to show signs of age. As she let me preen her whiskers, I noticed her other canine tooth was missing. Martha was slowly disappearing piece by piece, first her leg, then a tooth here and another tooth there. I jiggled her tail to see if it was loose. No, still firmly attached. Good. I liked the way she held it straight up and slightly bent at the tip. Sometimes in the garden as she hunted, all I could see was the tip of her tail, like a little flag bobbing down the row.

"Come on in, sweetie. Let's go up and change our clothes first thing," said Nana, leading the way up the walk. We just opened the screen door to the house and walked right in. No one ever gave a thought to locking a door when they left. Just like no one ever gave a thought to coming in while you were gone, unless it was to leave you something fresh baked, fresh caught, or fresh picked. Quite frequently we came home to find a surprise left in the kitchen and would guess as to who had left it. We loved surprises but hated that we had missed a visit from a friend.

After we changed clothes, Nana quickly packed our picnic hamper with our lunch of salty country ham on baking powder biscuits, cheddar cheese sliced from the hunk kept under the glass dome on the counter, and my favorite—juicy yellow peaches. She had fresh-made lemonade, ice cold in a big Mason jar for us, and another jar with Grandy's sweet iced coffee. The three of us, with me in the middle, walked up the hill on the back of the farm, spread out our red and blue starburst quilt, and ate in the shade of the massive sycamore tree.

The breeze gently ruffled our hair and whispered in the leaves above us. *Shhh, rest. Be still and know that I am God. This is My day.* Grandy laid down with his head on his arm and soon fell asleep. An iridescent blue dragonfly buzzed by and briefly lighted on Grandy's elbow. Nana propped against the sycamore's smooth gray and tan mottled trunk and took out her wooden hoop of needlework and began to hum softly. It was Sunday, a day to rest and be peaceful. Sometimes we visited sick people and took them flowers or vegetables from our garden, but today we were blessed with a quiet day at home.

I set about poking around in the field looking for arrowheads. On the shelf in the settin' room, there was a nice collection of ones we had found. Turning a new one over and over in my hands, I wondered about how it had come to be right here on this plot of land. I daydreamed about the Indians who had lived on this land before us and fashioned these sharp arrows out of stone. Had it fallen from the bow of a boy my age, missing its mark and getting lost in the undergrowth of the forest? Or had it found its mark, piercing the heart of a deer and providing food and clothing for his family? Would we have been friends if I had lived then or he had lived now? Or would he have burned my house, stolen my horse, and rode off with my brown curls dangling from his deerskin belt? *Owiee!* At the thought of that misery, I stuck it in my pocket fast and rubbed my scalp hard in the front, abandoning the arrowhead hunt and taking off toward the verdant woods.

The lacey ferns that grew there were a special favorite of mine. Sometimes I even found Jack-in-the-Pulpits growing there—preaching to the salamanders, I imagined. The fragrance was so earthy and inviting, a whole different realm, green and magical. I honestly would not have been one bit surprised to catch a tiny fairy lounging under a toadstool. As a matter of fact, upon entering the forest sanctuary, I tread very softly for just that reason: I hoped desperately to see one.

Nana's humming was barely audible now as I dropped down on my knees and crept soundlessly into the lush forest glen. Ever so slowly and quietly, knees sinking into the moss carpet before me, I tried to become one with the essence of the forest. As the fallen log by the stream came into focus, there was an interruption of color. Yes, the russet and white splashes of a doe and her fawn lying nestled together against it. The stream bubbled music like a heavenly flute playing especially for this moment.

Time stood still in wonder of the gift of nature that God had laid before me. The doe saw me. We held each other in the warm embrace of our gaze. I crept closer, slowly, barely daring to breathe. Within a few feet of them, I could smell their wildness and see the dark pools of gentleness in Momma Deer's eyes. I saw something different in the fawn. Newness, inexperience, curiosity, but most of all, innocent trust in Momma Deer. Closer now, I put down one knee, one hand, then the other knee and hand, on all fours. I could almost touch them now. Inching forward slightly, I pressed my hand down on the sharp prickles of a pinecone and too quickly jerked it back. The doe gave a snort and jumped up, alerting the fawn as they both leapt in one motion over me in a flash of rust and white, spots and hooves, gone. Opportunity lost.

Spinning around, falling on my bottom, I stared into the open air after them. The swaying of low-lying branches of the pines was the only proof that they had passed by. Looking back to the spot where they were lying contented, merely seconds before, the soft ferns and moss remained pressed down with the imprint of their bodies. As I watched, one and then another of the tendrils sprang back up and straightened their stems. Crawling forward, I laid on the warmth where they had been. While I nestled down, the scent of deer enveloped me. As I was gazing up at a branch overhead, a red-winged blackbird perched in a tree looked down on me and turned his head from side to side, curious as to what I was doing there, and then he too vanished.

Drowsiness slipped over me like a blanket. I closed my eyes and immediately was swept away on the back of a large buck, my arms holding tightly around his neck. On my right, the doe was running beside us. We were gliding over the ground, hardly touching at all and then we weren't. The fields were small patches beneath us. I was ecstatic, laughing out loud, with my hair rippling out behind us in the wind. I waved my hand in a big arc, back and forth, as we passed over Sanctuary Oak Farm. Nana and Grandy were tiny dots in the garden. I wanted them to see me flying by over their heads. They looked up just as we passed by. I thought I heard them calling, quietly at first and then much louder. "Suh-un. Son!! Answer me, sweetheart! Where are you?"

Reluctantly, slowly, I released my grip on the buck's strong neck and let myself fall back, back, back, floating down over the meadow and gently landing back in the forest cradle where my adventure had begun. I opened my eyes and heard their voices nearby.

"Son!" Grandy's voice.

"Lacey girl, time to go up to the house. Come on now," Nana's voice sounding a little worried.

Jumping up, I ran out of the forest into the clearing to meet them. "Nana! Grandy! Here I come. You'll never believe it! It was great! Wait 'til I tell you . . . ."

Later that evening, we were settling in together as if I hadn't been gone at all. Ah, the hominess of the soothing Sunday night ritual of Nana and Grandy's. A warm, sudsy bath in the big tub. I appreciated its legs and smooth curviness more now, especially since I hadn't had a real bath in a while. Nana kneeling down on the fuzzy rug to help me, washing my back, oohing and clucking her tongue in regard to my scrapes and scratches. Then wrapping me up tight like a mummy in a rough, lined-dried towel to run across the hall to my room for my jammies. Everything felt just right. It was good to be in my very own room again, putting on my old, soft jammies that smelled like fresh-made air. The blue room with its silvery-winged butterflies. It was used for keeping my things in mostly, since I had always been too creeped out to sleep alone.

Had to get done double quick if I didn't want to miss the beginning of *Lassie*. Although I'm not sure why, I always wanted to see it so badly. More times than not, the story drove me to tears of worry over Lassie's getting lost or hurt, and Grandy had to reassure me that it wasn't real, only make-believe. I wasn't easily convinced. Once, she was lost for a very long time, the end of each story saying across the television screen, "To be continued." It kept me so upset that Nana said she thought it would be better if I didn't watch that show for a while.

"Don't know why in the world they wanna make a chil'ern's show so sad and worrisome. Why, even the song at the start of it sounds like someone whistling a funeral dirge. It's pert near enough to drive one into a state of melancholy. There's enough sadness in the world without inventing more."

Channel 16 was the only channel we had on our black-and-white television, as did most people around. My cousins in Salsten, however, could get two channels. I couldn't wait to see one of those new color televisions I had heard talk of. Even though Aunt Vi had seen one and declared it a big disappointment. She said the red lipstick that was supposed to be on Judy Garland's lips as she sang, "Somewhere over the Rainbow" was off on the side of her cheek, and the blue of her dress missed its mark and looked more like fresh paint that had been smeared.

Nana brought in a tray with three saucers of blueberry cobbler with a dollop of whipped cream on the top. Ed Sullivan was just introducing some new guys in a band. A lot of the singing acts on his show were sorta snoozy, but these guys sang a real catchy song and wore their hair longer than any boys I had *ever* seen. We ate and watched, mesmerized. The drummer kept shaking his head around all the while he played. He seemed to be thoroughly enjoying the feel of his hair whipping back and forth, almost as much as he liked walloping on his drum.

Our saucers were almost empty, and my stomach was feeling way too full, a bit queasy, when Topo Gigo suddenly appeared and took my mind off it, saying as he usually did, "Ed-die, kees me good night."

Imagine, a talking mouse. He would be fun to play with for a while, just to get a mouse's perspective on things, but he didn't really look much like the mice in the barn—not half as cute. He was an imposter, but I liked to play around with the idea anyhow. Wouldn't it be fun if animals really could talk? Nana said it would be way too noisy, and then they'd probably want to vote.

Bedtime had arrived, and we had a big day ahead of us tomorrow. We all knelt down beside the trunk at the foot of Nana's bed and said our prayers together, holding hands just like we had always done. When we were finished with out-loud prayers, we kept our heads bowed for silent prayers or to listen just in case God had something special on His mind that He wanted to say to one of us. Grandy said we needed to spend time listening for God.

"As powerful as He is, the Bible says He often speaks quiet, gentle like a breeze, and it would be a shame to miss what He had to say," said Grandy in a hushed tone.

"Like the time Elijah was running from Jezebel." Nana was quick to pick up his lead. "He needed help, so he stood on a mountain to talk to God. God came by causing all kinds of commotion. A mighty wind tossed around the rocks, an earthquake shook everything up, and next a terrible fire burnt up what was left."

According to Nana, God has that effect on nature because even creation recognizes Him. Continuing on, she said, "When God finally *did* speak, it was like *gentle stillness*. Mysterious. Good thing Elijah held on tight to himself and waited silently, or he would have missed what God wanted to tell him."

I probably woulda run away, scared rabbit-like when the first boulder came flying by. Those nature things reminded me of another verse that I liked a whole lot, about when Jesus comes back to earth. It says, "The mountains and hills will shout with joy. And the rocks will cry out." Keeping that in mind, whenever I found a neat rock for my collection, I'd look at it good, try to tell where its mouth will be, and then turn that side up on my shelf. You just never knew when He'd be coming back, and I didn't want to muffle a rock that was supposed to be celebrating. That would most likely be a sin.

I crawled in and snuggled next to Grandy. Within minutes it seemed, half dreaming, I heard clapping. Yes, it was definitely clapping, but not hands clapping. This was a gazillion million leaf-hands clapping. There were deep, booming hill voices chanting, "PRAISE HIM! PRAISE HIM!" from the back of the farm. High-pitched, excited hollers rang out from the shelf in my room. "Holy, Holy, Holy is the Lord God Almighty!" Trying to struggle free of the sleep that was washing over me, I wanted to get up and go see. Alas, sleep won.

Bright and early I woke up to the sound of crowing. Blackie, the barnyard king. He was the meanest old rooster. Just hateful. For some reason known only to him, he had taken a nasty disliking to me. Every time he got the chance, he chased me, trying to peck my legs.

That is, up until one day when Nana got fed up with me running in the house with bright red whelps on my legs, screaming. She looked out the screen door, and there on the step looking in was the big bully himself, feathers all ruffled out and ready to fight. That did it. Nana went and got the wire fly swatter outta the broom closet, stuck it in my hand, and shoved me out on the step with Blackie to fight it out.

My surprise was his advantage as he struck out to pierce my bare flesh. Swinging hard, I missed, fanning the air just in front of his beak. That just served to make him madder as he struck again, quick as lightning, landing a sharp stab on my thigh. In self-defense, this time I swatted him hard, right on the blood-red comb crowning his head, his pride and joy. His dignity wounded, he looked at me, stretched his wings out wide and shook them. Then he jumped down off the step and ran off to the barnyard, squawking furiously all the way. He never pecked at me after that, but I could tell he held a grudge. Good thing for him that he kept it under wraps, 'cause Nana said if the swatter didn't cure him, rooster salad would.

Anyhow, Nana and Grandy were up before me, and her bed looked like it had never been disturbed, complete with the rose-colored afghan across the bottom. They were probably out in the garden, already staying ahead of the sun. Rolling over, I could see a branch of the tree outside the window. There was a teeny little nest made mostly of horse hair pulled from the tail of Samson, our aging mule.

He didn't seem to mind when the birds were busily plucking long strands from his generous brown and white tail. But once in a while, when the parting hair especially pinched, he'd swish his tail, look around sharply at his hind quarters, and shift his weight from hoof to hoof.

Throwing off the sheet, I plunked off the bed onto the wooden floor. My stool wasn't needed for getting out of bed, only getting in, so it was neatly tucked out of the way underneath. Running to the other bedroom window across the hall that overlooked the vegetable garden, I saw Nana and Grandy.

His basket was almost full of cucumbers, and she was singing, filling a smaller leather-handled one with pole beans. Slipping my leg over the banister, I slid down, all the way to the curve at the end, coming to an abrupt stop when my backside bumped into the carved lion's head post. My jammies helped make it a super-fast ride.

Running to the pantry, I quickly pried the lid off the oatmeal tin to grab a handful to feed the goldfish in the pond on the side yard. This was a special made-out-of-cement pond, a deep rectangle filled with lily pads and sweet-smelling water lilies scattered among them. Big orange and white goldfish lived in there, summer and winter. They came to the surface to feast on sprinkled oatmeal, letting us rub their noses while they gulped it down. Well, not actually noses, but where their noses would have been if they had had them.

I hoped to be lucky this morning and catch a glimpse of Blue Boy and Greenfella, the beautiful bullfrogs that lived there. Nana dearly loved frogs, and these two were extraordinary frogs indeed. Besides their enormous size, their colors were exquisite, with Greenfella being an emerald shade of green with bright gold eyes and Blue Boy being an extremely rare turquoise color. Both sported creamy white bellies. At night, their loud croaking could be heard a long ways off. First one and then the other, deep into the night. Frog talk. If they went suddenly silent, Nana would say, "Lord, please don't let a snake get my frogs. You know how I love them." And so, they were spared, year after year.

One thing they weren't spared from was Nana's loving. Whenever she got a hold of them, she rubbed their bellies and stroked their backs and generally adored them at close range, I mean, nose to nose. Oh, how she fussed over those frogs. Someone visiting us one day told Nana that Blue Boy was a rare frog indeed and likely worth a mint. To which Nana replied rather indignantly, "Well, Mr. Rutherford, I wouldn't take a million dollars for my frog if somebody from the Smithsonian Institution came here today and put it right in my hand!"

They were nowhere to be seen this morning. So, after petting the goldfish briefly, I headed into the garden, stopping along the tall white fence to pick a few choice blackberries for breakfast. *Mmmm.* They were sweet and I loved the crunch of their tiny seeds.

I rounded the end of the fence just in time to hear Nana say, "As much as it hurts my heart to say it, we've got to wean her off us. It's for her own . . ." My tummy did a flip-flop.

"Nana. Grandy. Who has to be weaned off?" Feeling something dreaded and ominous hanging in the air, I decided I didn't really want to know after all and quickly changed the subject. "What're we doing today?"

Waving at a pesky sweat bee, Nana looked up. "Good morning. How's the blackberries?" The previous conversation was dropped and hopefully forgotten forever.

Smiling, she pointed at the big juice drip on the front of my jammies.

"They're yumalicious! Good thing we don't have any bears around. They would eat every last one of them."

"They sure would, but there's one thing they like even more than blackberries," growled Grandy, as he came running toward me, hands swatting the air like claws, "and that's tasty little girls! *Grrrrrr. Grrr-OWL!*"

His straw hat fell off behind him in the dirt. Squealing, I ran away as fast as I could and hid in between the bean poles, peeking through the leaves to see where he was. Grandy searched up and down the rows, pretending not to know where I was hiding, and then suddenly, sneaking up from behind, he reached through the jungle of beans and grabbed me, growling, pretending to eat my neck first. His morning whiskers were prickly and sharp.

"Help! Help! Nana, help me! A bear got me!" I shrieked, giggling all the while.

"All right now. Let's finish up so we can go to town. There's a few errands we have to do so we can get ready for our reunion," answered Nana, pulling us from our bear play, back to the garden.

Nana didn't like much clowning around when she had a lot on her mind to get done, which was almost always. Busier than a one-legged grasshopper constantly, she was a firm believer in the old saying, "Idle hands are the Devil's workshop."

"Hurray! Can we have lunch at Woolworth's?"

I loved going to Woolworth's lunch counter and sitting high up on the swivelly chrome stools. Nana usually sent Grandy and me on ahead while she finished up her shopping. They had balloons blown up and stuck around the mirror behind the counter. Customers could pick a balloon to see what price they would pay for a banana split. Grandy always let me pick the color. One time we got one for ten cents from a lucky blue balloon. Grandy and I shared. Nothing tasted better than when it was shared with my Grandy.

"Yes, if we can get ready to leave before too long, we'll have time."

"Let's go feed the bunnies and give them fresh water," said Grandy, lifting his basket to take to the house. "Misty should be having a new litter any day now."

"Oh boy! I hope it's today. Do you think it'll be today, Grandy?"

"There's no telling. She'll have 'em when she's good and ready and not a moment before. Didn't notice any fur pulled out this morning, though."

That was the surefire sign there would be babies soon. Bunnies always pulled out some of their chest fur and lined their nest with it right before they gave birth. That was the warmest welcome ever. The first thing their tiny bodies felt would be mommy soft. Sweet bunny love.

I quickly pulled up some carrots, shook them good to get off the remainder of soil, and then raced toward the hutches. Unhooking the door and sticking my head in, I felt around her nest in the corner. Just hay so far, no fur. Misty nuzzled my cheek, tickling it with her whiskers, wanting attention. Giggles followed by bunny rubs, right between her ears, the sweetest spot. It smelled warm and like meadow blossoms. Her furry tummy was round like she had swallowed a rubber ball.

"Hey there, little girl. Are you gonna have some sweet babies soon? How's my good little mommy bunny doing, huh? Have you missed me?"

Questions were left unanswered as always when talking to bunnies. They loved to be talked to and cuddled, but they never made a sound. Hearing a loud stomp rattle the cage to my right and turning, I saw Jack Bunny peeking out his hutch door. He wanted attention too, and of course he would get equal amounts. I was careful to divide my time evenly so no one felt sad or left out. Bunnies with hurt feelings would be unbearable to think of. They were just so innocent and dear. Not a bad bone in their little bodies. After pulling some chickweed nearby, I gave each a treat mixed with the freshly picked carrots. I filled their water bottles from the hose and left them munching happily as I ran to the house to get washed up and dressed to go to town.

The ride into town sitting between Nana and Grandy with the windows down was like a thousand times before. We passed familiar farms with long dirt lanes and the peach orchard on the left, followed by the silver towers and chutes of the feed mill. The hot summer air drew in the smells of everyday life being lived as we rode by. The peaceful green smell of timothy hay contrasted with the nostril-curling ammonia smell of chicken manure being spread on a field. Next, the pungent odor of tar as we passed a truck with perspiring workers repairing the road where there had been a washout. They waved and we waved back. Our life passing their life.

There was sparse conversation on the way. No need— our words would be swept out the open window unheard to fall by the roadside. We just rode on, looking and thinking for about three quarters of an hour. The heat from the road quivered ahead of us, looking forever like long, wiggling snakes disappearing into the dull gray road as we approached.

Then houses began to get closer together, yards got smaller, and the city smell, hot pavement, and gasoline exhaust began to surround us. Walking up the sidewalk to the cluster of stores where we needed to go, I felt invigorated by the pace of it all. Everything moved faster in the city.

In the shade of a tree there was a vendor selling red pistachios behind a brightly painted cart. He had a little monkey tied by an embroidered red and green leash that matched his teeny vest and cap. Once in a while the man would toss him a pistachio, which had stained his paws red. He bit them open, looking around nervously while eating the green meat inside. I'm not sure why I couldn't just enjoy watching him like everyone else, but I felt sad for the little fellow. Occasionally, he would glance upward like he would have rather been up in the leaves of that shade tree fending for himself than on a leash being fed expensive pistachios.

We followed Nana into Guys and Dolls, a children's clothing store. She sailed straight to the back of the store, where the shoes were sold.

"What're we doing here, Nana?"

"I want to have them check your toes while we're here to see if you need a bigger size shoe," said Nana as she smiled politely at the approaching salesman.

"Now, what could I help you with today, ma'am?"

Nana told him her concerns that my shoes were getting too small and would stunt the growth of my feet or give me corns, onions, or hammer toes, of all things. Why not carrot toes and stick with the other vegetables? How silly and embarrassing. The salesman didn't blink an eye. It was obvious he believed the customer is always right, so he didn't laugh or snicker or question her in any way.

"Okay, young lady. Step right up here on the Foot-o-scope and let's have a look," he said as he guided me in the direction of a tall wooden box.

Stepping up onto it, I placed my feet in the hole where he pointed. He leaned in close to my face, squinting down the hole of what looked like a periscope, finger on lips tapping while he pondered.

"Have a look-see for yourself," he invited Nana and me, pointing to the other two "periscopes."

Nana came over and looked down the metal tube.

"Now, isn't that something! Certainly takes the guesswork out of buying shoes for chil'ern," she said, amazed.

He joined us in looking again, pondering the picture of the bones in my feet inside the outline of my shoes. I wiggled them up and down for him. I couldn't believe it. I could actually see the bones in my feet and toes moving!

"Look, Grandy! You gotta see this. Look at my foot bones. Aren't they creepy? That's how skeletons look, isn't it, Grandy? Oooh, my skeleton's showing."

I reached for Grandy with wiggly fingers and leaned my head to the side to make room for him to see. He took my place at the center periscope-like tube, closed one eye, and looked down.

"Well, I never! What in the world will they think of next?"

"Hmm. Looks as though she still has plenty of room for now, but come back after the summer, and we'll be happy to fit you with a nice pair of new shoes. Children's feet tend to grow more in the summer when they're running around barefoot. My name's Harry. Ask for me when you come back." Harry extended his hand and shook with Grandy and then bowed his head slightly toward Nana.

"We surely will, and thank you kindly for your time," Nana answered as she turned and went right back out the way she came in, with us trailing along behind her.

We headed to Woolworth's while Nana finished shopping elsewhere. First we had to go to the hardware section to get a new plunger. Then we headed toward the back of the store to look at the red-eyed white mice and little green turtles in the pet department. Sure enough, just like always, when we walked past the aquariums flashing with bright-colored fish, there was one poor old fish, belly up, dead eyes staring at the colored rocks on the bottom. Copying the motions up and down and across my chest that I had seen a nun in her long, serious black-and-white dress on the television make, I paid my respects and kept on going.

Today they had a whole new flock of parakeets in a cage taller than I was. I surveyed the bottom of it, hoping to find a bright feather for my collection. Nothing. The birds were sporting a kaleidoscope of light green and blue shades, fluttering and twittering all around, and they were all real pretty. Their wings parted, and then there was the most beautiful one I had ever seen. It was like the fairy princess of birds! She was the loveliest shade of lavender, with white bands and dark purple tips on her wings and tail. She watched me admiring her, calmly from her perch. Instinctively, I called her a girl. She had to be a girl; no boy bird could look that gorgeous. It wouldn't be natural.

"Oh, Grandy, isn't she beautiful?" I whispered, not wanting to disturb her peacefulness.

"Sure is, sweetheart. God does make some pretty creatures for us to enjoy."

"Grandy, do you think we could get her? The sign says thirty-nine cents."

"She's pretty all right, Son. But I don't know about getting her. Your mother might not cater much to the idea of us getting you a pet that has to be kept in the house. We couldn't do that without her permission."

Smack! Reality hit me like an abrupt slap across the face. Only it hurt much worse and in a different place. Somewhere deep within my heart stung. I had almost forgotten, and it felt good to forget. I wanted to forget. I didn't live with Nana and Grandy anymore. I was only *visiting* them now. Tears sprang up and stung my eyes. My throat ached. I couldn't help it; a sob escaped from deep within my chest. Grandy quickly bent down and scooped me up in his arms.

"Now, now, Son. I know she's a very special bird. But we can't just go and . . ."

Suddenly the bird didn't matter at all. I didn't even want a bird anymore, not even a beautiful one that looked like a fairy. Tears stung my eyes and ran down my cheeks like a dam had plumb give way.

"No, it's not that, Grandy. I don't want to live away from you and Nana anymore," I sobbed. "I want to always be with you, not just visit sometimes and have to go back there every time. Sanctuary Oak is my real home! I love you and you love me. We should be together always, shouldn't we, Grandy?"

"Oh. Now, sweetheart, some things are beyond our control, and we have to make the very best out of it that we can. Life isn't always the way we would like it to be. That's when we have to trust the Lord that He's got a plan for us that we don't know about, something we can't see. That's when we learn to have faith."

"No, Grandy. I don't want faith. I want YOU. What happened to our wish? Why didn't it come true?"

"Son, don't you know that we got something better than being close distance-wise? We got heart-closeness, and that's a special gift from God. Nothing can ever separate us from each other in our hearts. If you were a million miles away, our hearts would be beating together." Grandy gently touched my chest and then his. "Deep in our hearts we'll always be close, and that's the best kind of close. It even goes from this world to the next, all the way to Heaven. Our hearts can never, ever be separated.

"And what about your new friend, Lyddie? I think God might have sent you there to be her special friend. You both look so happy when I see you together. I think she may have been a lonely girl until you moved in next door. And you needed a best friend to share things with too. Someone your own age. What'd ya think of that idea? You know God does move in mysterious ways."

"I know, Grandy. I do like Lyddie an awful lot. She's my best *girl* friend."

"There you go. See? Ever' cloud has its silver lining," Grandy said too cheerfully.

"I'm so glad we'll always be close in our hearts that way, Grandy."

"I am too. Now let's go see about that banana split. Nana must be done with her shopping by now. Come on," Grandy whispered close to my face as he gave me a big bunny kiss on the cheek. I could feel Grandy's heart hurting right along with mine. But if he could try and make the best of it, I guess I could too. Still, it was hard not to tell him I felt like a snake in the henhouse living there. I just didn't seem to belong.

Chapter Seven

The day of the grand family reunion arrived at last, ushered in on brilliant streaks of eager sunshine that found Nana already bustling around in the kitchen with last-minute preparations. Her calico apron looked as if it could have belonged to a famous artist with all of the drips, dabs, and smears decorating its front. Before long, she would pull on a fresh one from the hook inside the pantry door. Those smells from age-old secret recipes could have made the Statue of Liberty's mouth water.

Baked beans laced with rich dark molasses, brown sugar, bacon, onions, and our most special very secret ingredient bubbled in the oven. On the dining room table were shoo-fly, cherry, and apple pies, lined up carefully beside three-layer fresh coconut and chocolate cakes. Every inch in the Frigidaire was taken up with heaping bowls of yellow mustard and egg potato salad, cabbage apple slaw, and Nana's specialty—chicken salad made with sweet cooked-dressing, which happened to be everyone's favorite except for mine. I thought it was absolutely gaggy, a secret that I was positive was a sin and therefore was very careful to never let slip. There were Ball jars of spiced peaches, red beet eggs, and homemade three-bean salad. This alone would have provided a feast, but every single one of the relatives who came would bring their own specialty.

Aunt Tillie came, swinging a huge basket filled to overflowing with her homemade ham biscuits and deviled eggs. No doubt, she would swoop down for her kiss with lips puckered up like a cat's behind and smelling almost as bad. I always wondered what on earth could give her such terrible breath. It had to be a curse put on her by some wicked witch I decided, because putting that aside, she was one of the sweetest people alive on God's green earth.

Uncle Timothy brought his golden peanut brittle, safely stored in red King Syrup cans made from peanuts he grew himself and harvested alone on his old, arthritic hands and knees. We loved his brittle almost as much as we loved his gentle ways, and we greatly appreciated all the effort he put into making us this treat. Each year we knew it might be the very last taste we ever had of it, simply due to the undeniable fact that he was old as Methuselah and no one else on earth knew his recipe.

Aunt Edna Ruth and Uncle John arrived with a gigantic pan filled to the brim with her crispy-brown fried chicken. No doubt she had been killing and cooking chickens all week long, leaving her backyard gruesome and bloody like the scene of a mass murder until the next rainfall. She looked worn out as usual, with loose strings of white hair escaping from her bun at all angles and thick tan stockings held up by tight garters rolled unevenly below her knees, cutting off her circulation. Uncle John always looked the same, with his freshly pressed shirt and dark gray pants hiked up to his armpits with his red suspenders. He resembled a roly-poly egg in pants.

Junebug and Walter came dressed very stylishly, in matching colors no less, like they were on their way to a party rather than a family reunion. They were holding up and proudly presenting their noodle kugel topped with crushed and buttered golden cornflakes. Being quite elevated with the fact that they had been to the big city of New York, and what's more, they liked it there. This recipe they were able to beg from a city friend's grandmother who was Jewish. This was as close as we ever came to eating foreign food, and it was surprisingly yummy.

And Heavens above, let us not forget Cousin Donna Beth's coveted ambrosia salad. It seems everyone loved it and bragged on it endlessly, with the exception of me. Again, I was careful to conceal my feelings of yuck. She was so emotional and cried buckets over the silliest things. I didn't want to take a chance on upsetting her and ruining the family reunion. Bethie Lou, who was four years older than the twins, said that some days she cried over television commercials.

Leroy had the pity of all the men—how he had to tiptoe around on eggshells all the time to avoid setting her off. Everyone knew but was silent about the fact she had suffered a nervous breakdown shortly after Lisa and Teresa, the twins, were born. This did not occur *because* of them,

I had come to understand through eavesdropping—not on purpose, mind you, 'cause that would be considered rude, rather from listening around the corner as I brushed knots out of Martha's fur—but rather as a result of the terrible operation that followed immediately after their birth. It had rendered her unable to have any more children. Apparently, she would have bled to death if the good doctor had not been quick to do the unspeakable surgery. I think it involved sewing up all her private parts real tight to keep the blood from pouring out. Anyhow, it left her quite naturally in a complete and utter state of apoplexy, according to Aunt Tillie.

Uncle Emory and Aunt Dearest drove up in his shiny new dealer's car. Newly married, they didn't have any children yet but loved everybody else's. Rumor also had it that Aunt Dearest couldn't cook worth a lick. They were livin' on love. He greeted us kids with a great big hug and a swing 'round and 'round 'til our hair stuck out straight. As he hugged me hard, I smelled the Teaberry gum that he kept in his pocket, and though nearly being squeezed to death, I managed a "Mmmmm," to which he instantly offered me a piece.

They brought bags of store-bought penny candy for all of us kids to share after we ate. Each one of us had our favorites and more. We excitedly dumped out heaps of Tootsie Rolls, Fireballs, Mary Janes, Squirrel Nuts, Kits, jaw breakers, caramel Slap-Sticks, circus peanuts, and button candy. And let's not neglect to mention the various and sundry flavors of suckers. At least one of us would end up with either a toothache or a loose tooth being dislodged and swallowed. But that never stopped us from devouring every single piece.

Counted in with us kids was Louise. Even though she was almost nineteen, she was *slow*, which meant she would always have a childlike mind and never grow up. So we kids had better be certain to share with her and treat her nicely, or we would get the switch just as sure as we were living.

But the games that she liked to play were hated and dreaded by all of us littler kids. Last year she was obsessed with being a mother bird and insisted that we be the baby birds, peep, peep, peeping in our nest of hay in the hayloft, while she sat on us with pee-smelling bloomers. Every time one of us would try to come up for air, she would stuff us back under her skirt. That was voted the worst, hottest, smelliest, stickiest, and itchiest game ever. Finally, I decided that I'd rather face the music than stand one more minute of slow torture and suffocation. So, I pulled myself out from under her with mammoth effort and scrambled as fast as I could for the ladder. Half falling, half climbing, I made my escape to fresh air. I had a new appreciation for baby birds.

Later, we bribed her with extra candy so she wouldn't tell. Well, not really, because she couldn't count as good as us. But by giving her bigger pieces, like packs of Kits that we counted twice, her pile looked bigger than ours, and she was satisfied. We all agreed that she was definitely less fortunate than us and it was a bad thing to trick her. Nonetheless, we were able to justify ourselves with the idea that we had probably saved her from getting the sugar "bideetis" that we were all being constantly warned would happen if we ate too much candy. No one wanted to get stuck with those needles every day.

Aunt Ruthie and Uncle Melvin, and their son Travis, who was on leave from the Air Force, were walking up the lane. Travis looked some kind of handsome in his uniform. Someday I wanted to marry a man in a uniform, handsome and brave like a movie star. He was walking very straight and tall. Travis didn't appear to be worried about going to fight in Vietnam like other guys. He was proud to be in the service, and we were all very proud of him. We would sing "God Bless America" especially for him tonight. Nana and I had been practicing the words all week. They came with their arms loaded down with suitcases. He held his duffle bag with his name stenciled stiffly on the side. Coming from Atlantic City, New Jersey, they would be staying a few nights. Everyone ran to greet them, oohing and aahing over Travis' flashy uniform.

All of a sudden, Aunt Ruthie's brother, Uncle Earl, appeared. Never failed. He loved to get something going with Melvin, his brother-in-law.

He yelled out, "EEEUUUUUWW! What's that coming up the lane! Quick! Somebody get a stick and kill it!"

Uncle Melvin responded by dropping his suitcases in the dirt and running up and throwing Earl into a headlock and giving him some serious nubbin' pie. The perfect comeback because it was something that could not be reciprocated on his own glabrous head, polished to a blinding sheen. And so, the good-natured chiding that had been a part of their friendship for over twenty years began right where it left off.

I was partial to the Tradler cousins. Almost every year since I had been remembering, there was a new one of them.

I never recall seeing Brenda without her tent-like maternity smock and swollen feet. The wood-paneled station wagon being navigated by Ken finally turned down our lane, and I ran out to meet them. They were hanging out the windows yelling and waving. Doors flew open, and they jumped out before the automobile came to a full stop.

Sure enough, the excitement started as soon as they arrived. J. T. fell while leaping out, scraping his leg real deep on the gravel. Howling, he ran into the kitchen to Aunt Tillie, who was his grandmother. The cure, an ample coating of Mercurochrome, would be painful but sure to prevent imminent death from lockjaw. Little Kenny started showing off his new bullwhip, cracking it every which a way. Louise got a whelp on her arm, and off to get a switchin' he went. He came back whipless and red-faced. I was embarrassed for him.

Brenda, who never lost any of the weight she gained with each baby, was waddling up to the yard with the newest Tradler in her arms. Pink blanket, that's all I needed to know. Hurray! At long last, the girls outnumbered the boys. Charlotte, Roxanne, and I joined hands and danced around with glee, thanking goodness for the arrival of Deborah. Although for a couple more years, she'd be too little to add much except that she was indeed a girl.

We raced off to the side yard, where Charlotte showed me her latest moves in ballet and Roxanne talked a mile a minute and told the funniest jokes, nearly causing me to wet my pants. Well, actually I did and had to pull myself away long enough to run upstairs, change into a dry pair, and hide the soaked ones deep in the hamper. She told her jokes so well and made the funniest faces. Everyone said she was destined to be a comedian. This year she brought a bag full of chewing gum wrappers that she was making into a really neat chain. There was every kind imaginable: Juicy Fruit, Doublemint, Beemans, Peppermint, Black Jack, Sour Cherry, Clove, Teaberry and more. The smell of the Sour Cherry gave me a sharp twinge in my jaw and caused my mouth to fill with water.

She strutted around waving her hand in the air like she had seen Annette Funicello do in a movie on the television. She was obsessed with movie stars.

In her best movie star voice, she explained the makings of the chain. "Well, actually *dah-ling*, I don't like Black Jack in the least 'cause you see, *dah-ling*, I never did like licorice flavor; and of course, that's what it is, licorice, *dah-ling*. But the light blue color wrapper looks so ver-ry lovely *dah-ling*, you see, intertwined with the other colors, and it quite naturally reminds me of my dearest *dah-ling* boyfriend's eyes. Obviously, he's in Hollywood right now making his latest movie, *dah-ling*, so I'm here chewing all this gum, *dah-ling*, and making this abso-lutely lovely chain to wrap around his neck when he returns to show how much I missed him, *dah-ling*, and hoping that he doesn't notice that all of my pearly whites have now turned black and rotted out, *dah-ling*, from all the gum-chewing."

We were all doubled over in a hysterical giggling fit by the time she bowed deeply and finished. She was eager to teach me how to fold the wrappers just right so that I could help her.

She wanted to make the chain double as tall as her by the end of summer. To tell you the truth, I think I really did see a black speck, like the beginnings of a cavity on the tooth next to her big front tooth.

In all the excitement nobody saw Moldy Soul and Hyde pull up in his old black DeSoto. Now he wasn't actually real blood kin, more like adopted, because he needed family. He was thin and gray with shirt and pants that were thin and gray. The smoke that puffed from his pipe was thin and gray. Everything about him was gloomy, hence the name he bore. I don't believe anyone even remembered his real name. He slunk to the edge of the yard, shaking hands with all the men folk as he glanced out from under his old, crumpled-up hat. He didn't bring any dish food since he didn't cook much being all alone as he was, but he gave Nana a steady supply of black walnuts from the trees on his property. Every autumn he silently harvested, hulled, cracked, and picked them, putting them in jars to give away. In turn, everyone kept him in the milk, butter, and vegetables that he needed.

Hyde was his slow-moving hound dog that faithfully moped around behind him everywhere he went, even to church. He laid on the top church step, causing latecomers to have to step over him to enter. Punishment for being late.

Any ol' time, the two of them could be seen sitting on the little ridge where Anna Mae was buried. She had been engaged to him but died of the consumption before they had a chance to marry. Moldy Soul's heart was forever bound to her. And Hyde's heart was bound to him.

Soon family started coming faster than I could keep track of. Plate after plate of deviled eggs began appearing on the table, all variations. History had proved you could never have too many deviled eggs with this crowd. The lane all the way up past the cornfield was lined with automobiles and trucks. More and more cousins emerged and joined as we played.

Looking up, I saw John Lloyd. He had stretched about another foot tall and grown an Adam's apple since I saw him last. It stuck out sharp, like something stuck in his craw. He and I always did like each other, and we got along right good. No silly fights or spats had ever come between us. I was glad because he had a reputation for his hot temper.

There were the mean freckled cousins: two boys, Doug and Pete, and a girl, Laura. The boys said bad words, spit constantly, and liked to tell dirty jokes that made no sense at all. They were creepy. Their poor sister was a crybaby and continually had swollen red eyes. She was always feeling left out and would run to her momma and report us, and we'd get called down, which made us really want to leave her out or pinch her real hard. She caused much of her own misery, but having the brothers wasn't her fault.

Within minutes of their arrival, they began to taunt me. Dancing around just out of reach, they took turns singing, "Hey, it's Miss Lacey Fancy Panties. Racey Lacey was quite a disgracey." My throat got tight. I gritted my teeth and willed myself not to let one blasted tear leak out.

My name change was a subject that everyone else had undoubtedly been coached on ahead of time not to mention, instead to politely pretend it had always been Lacey. It wasn't that I hadn't noticed. I had *painfully* noticed that my name was avoided altogether—old name, new name, the whole shebang. It was as if I was nameless. Not wanting to admit that part of me was really, *really* gone, gone for good, I tried to push the idea down. It stung a little that when John Lloyd first saw me he had avoided saying my name, the same as everyone else.

His loyalty to me was quickly renewed just as I took a big swipe at Pete and missed. In the flash of a frog's eyelash, he stepped between me and the freckled terrors with clenched fists. The big vein in his temple was sticking out, which meant somebody had made him fightin' mad and he was glaring down the throats of the offenders. The freckled bullies, now freckled yella-bellies, turned bright red and looked like they wished they could slither away.

John Lloyd grabbed a hold of the back of each of their necks and squeezed real hard. His knuckles turned white. "Now, apologize and declare yourselves lower than pond scum and uglier too."

With high voices because of the pain, they squeaked their individual renditions of, "I'm lower than pond scum and uglier too." Pete said, "Sorry, Lacey." But Doug tried to get away without the apology.

"What else, stupid?" John Lloyd threatened, shaking him a little and squeezing harder.

"I'm sorry," he said begrudgingly.

"You surely are," I said, moving closer to John Lloyd.

Just about the time we all got back to playing real good, around the corner of the house came Great-uncle Ezra. He was senile, which was a disease that made you do crazy things. Big Mom would have said he was "titched in the head." I didn't want to think about anything from that life right now, so I pushed the thought away. He was also deaf as a post, which made everyone yell real loud and wave their arms when they talked to him. He still couldn't hear them. He weaved and tottered his way right over to Nana's goldfish pond, where he proceeded to pull his pants down and start to pee. At the sight of his wrinkly, old skin, all of us girls flew screaming into the kitchen, screen door slamming behind us. Under normal circumstances that would have been an offense. You NEVER let the screen door slam.

There was a flurry of multi-colored aprons as the women wiped their hands and ran out the door, yelling for the men as they went. Sure enough, they got there in time to see the splash. The men fished him out, and his daughter, Sarah, dried him off and dressed him in some of Grandy's clothes. She lovingly propped him up in a chair against the wall in the kitchen where she could keep an eye on him, planted a kiss on his forehead, and then pinned him in by pushing the table in front of him where he alternated between eating, sleeping, and yelling for freedom the rest of the afternoon.

Cling! Clang! Cling! Clang . . . ang . . . ang! The farm bell. Everyone knew the food was ready, and it was time to gather in the front yard, ask the blessing, and get down to the business of eating.

Grandy asked the blessing of the good Lord on all our family—present, past, and to come. He asked for blessing of the food and everyone who grew it, picked it, prepared it, and were about to eat it. And then he prayed silently for a few moments, as was his habit. When he said "Amen" and looked up, everyone flocked to the long table filled with food and began heaping it on their plates and chattering about how good it smelled and how hungry they were. Apparently, none of them had eaten since the last reunion.

After supper the men began to churn the ice cream. They lined up their wooden folding chairs along the lane so that the salt water that poured out the hole in the side of the ice cream freezer wouldn't kill the grass. Nana cooked the custard and added the fruit to create the best ice cream in the known world! We kids got to lick the paddles while the sweet stickiness dripped on our bare toes. This year's special flavor, along with the usual vanilla, was banana. Grandy's favorite. Most times it was something that we grew. We didn't grow bananas.

Shortly after all the cakes and pies were cut and everyone had consumed enough to sink a battleship, as my Aunt Lola liked to say, we began the entertainment phase of the reunion. There was singing, tap dancing, horn blowing, magic tricks, yodeling and whatever else anyone had learned in the past year and wanted to share. There was no bad entertainment. No need to feel self-conscious or shy. Everyone got big applause, seeing as we were family and all.

Even Henrietta, who recently entered into hippiedom and now wanted to be called "Rainbow," received loud handclaps all around. Ever since she became a teenager, a transistor radio had been permanently plastered to her ear. She hadn't been seen since wandering off earlier to pick wildflowers in the meadow. Now she emerged, blossoms woven around her head halo-style, dangling a flower necklace for her foggy-looking boyfriend, who chose to be called Peace. He gave everyone, young and old alike, the two-fingered peace sign. I thought it was very cool. They came forward holding a bongo drum, on which he patted out a hypnotic rhythm while "Rainbow" swayed to the beat, eyes closed as she gently twirled her long tie-dyed skirt. Right then and there, I vowed when I grew up and became a hippie I was going to be known as Gypsy Moth.

Great-uncle Ezra, who had been brought out for the entertainment, kept yelling, "Is all clear on the waterfront?" No one had the slightest clue what he was talking about. Neither did he. Sitting on the grass close to him, I patted his old, bony hand. He softly whispered, "Yvonnah." Smiling, he gazed off to another time and place. The remembrance slathered my heart like the Balm of Gilead.

As dusk closed in, the reunion was reaching its final stages. Chairs were pulled tighter in a circle so the storytelling could commence and everyone would be heard. The conversation invariably wound its way to ghost stories, true ghost stories. Although I was already known for being a scaredy-cat, I wouldn't have missed this part for Bluebeard's treasure. None of us kids would. Happily exhausted, mosquito bitten and sweaty from our games, we flopped down in the damp grass on the edge of the circle of chairs, and with each story we inched closer until we were in the center of the circle, safely surrounded by the grownups. I stayed pretty close to Grandy's feet. Even though we were scared "petrinoid," another one of Aunt Lola's terms, we didn't want to miss a single word.

They started out casually discussing mutual friends and neighbors, mixing in a few interesting current events. How their crops were doing with so little rain. What was the latest on that bridge tunnel they're thinking about building across the bay? (Crazy idear, never happen.) Little Tom had a promising heifer to take to the state fair. How their health had been. Who had another mouth to feed this year. Who died recently.

When we heard this last category mentioned, our ears pricked up and the shivers rippled down our backs. We shot one another wide-eyed glances. It had begun. Groping for Charlotte's hand, I held my breath and waited for the spell-binding words to follow. It didn't take long.

"Yeah, I hear Grissom's Funeral Parlor's been right occupied since April."

"What's good news for the widow Grissom is sure 'nuf bad news for 'er patrons." Chuckles rippled around the circle of chairs while we kids held our breath. The suspense was crushing us. Moldy Soul's pipe smoke hung eerily over our heads.

"Me and Effie stopped by to see Matthew's brother laid out. Now, I tell you one thing right now. He looked like he was just a layin' there a sleepin'. You could just imagine you saw him drawin' a breath."

Now, that was a horrifying thought. Although kids hardly ever spoke up for fear they'd be banished, I couldn't help it.

"What if he *was* breathing, Uncle Tom? How do they know if someone is good and dead before they bury them?" The words squeaked out of my fear-tightened throat.

"Well now, you got a point there. With this here formaldehyde stuff they use, nobody's gonna be a breathin' once they're put in that coffin. But, it wuddn't always so."

Here goes. His words tingled down my spine all the way to my toenails. Last chance to run for the porch, but I was already too scared to break away from the circle. Uncle Tom lowered his voice so we all had to lean in.

"No sirree. My great-aunt's family moved out Midwest somewhere, and while they was there their daughter, Marie, God rest her little soul, died from dysentery. Well, naturally, since the rest of the family was back east, they wanted to bring her back home to be buried on family ground. So, they loaded up her coffin on the train, and they all boarded broken-hearted, every one of them as you can imagine, for the long journey home. It was a few days. And they was a ridin' and a grievin', just 'bout to mourn themselves to death. Never suspectin' nothin' was goin' on back there in that baggage car where she lay. Oh Lord, if they had only known."

Shaking his head sadly back and forth, "If they had just known. But it wuddn't to be. When they got there and opened up that coffin, there was the silky casket linin' all ripped to shreds and some of it still gripped in her hands. On that long train ride, she had woke from a deep, ve-ry deep coma, found herself in that coffin, and suffocated! It's the God-awful truth."

Sad murmurs all around. Lots of head-wagging. We kids were speechless. Each of us were thinking about the horror of waking up in a coffin and not being able to get out, using up all the air inside, and slowly dying there all alone and confused. Most certainly her ghost was wandering out there somewhere wondering why, looking for answers. Glancing behind me and scooting tighter into the circle, I wondered anxiously if a ghost hangs around where they died, or where their body ends up. Looking over to the side of me, I was startled for a second as the light fell on J. T. squatting there, leaning forward. He looked just like a picture I had seen of a gargoyle.

For some odd reason, I clearly recall looking across at Moldy Soul, memorizing his silhouette against the porch light. It was like I knew what I couldn't have known—that by our next reunion, Moldy Soul would be the latest character in our ghost stories, as his thin gray smoke encircled us from his unseen pipe. His sad, old heart plumb gave out, unable to make it through another lonesome winter. He was buried up on the ridge next to Anna Mae, even though they were never married. No one thought it scandalous in the least.

Grandy later said that he had noticed last fall that Moldy's 'levens were up. This was a term used to describe the two bones on the back of the neck that stuck out like the number eleven when someone's health was getting poorly. Life's barometer. I felt the back of my own neck. Still fleshy. Whew!

Next summer, Uncle Tom told about how a few evenings after Moldy Soul (Lemuel Lee, his birth name according to the family tree in front of his Bible) had been buried, a star was seen rising up from the left of the ridge, and then another star rose up from the right of the ridge. They kept on rising until they met overhead and became one bright star. At long last, they were joined as one in Heaven. And finally, a smaller twinkling star rose up and came to a stop, slightly below the others. There was little doubt about it being the spirit of the ever faithful in death as well as life, Hyde, who had died within days of his best friend. Naturally, he was buried by friends in his rightful place at the feet of his master.

The last story at this year's reunion was told by Grandy.

"My father told me this story. When he was a boy, he went with his parents to a funeral. It was in the terrible heat of summer. In those days they had to pack ice around the insides of the coffin to keep the body from darkening. The preacher was telling about what a glorious morning it was for this good man who most assuredly was in Heaven, having been raised up from death to life to meet Jesus. And how they'd all be rejoicing to see him alive and well again someday when they too reached those crystal shores. Everybody was a noddin' and agreein'. When all of a sudden, right there, amid all of the amens, tears, and lilies, the *dead* man sat bolt upright in his coffin!" Grandy's voice raised at just the right moment. "He looked around the church in complete puzzlement and said, 'What's going on here?'

"There was a near stampede as even his closest friends ran screaming and pushing each other down the steps of the church. Leading the pack was the preacher, shoving the hardest of all. Only the man's poor shaky wife was left to help him out of the coffin. The ice musta' revived him from near death. So near in fact that his breath wasn't even visible on the mirror the doctor held under his nose. Honest truth." Grandy's father, just like Grandy, always told the unvarnished truth.

Shortly after the ghost stories ended, the grand reunion drew to a close for another year with everyone joining hands and singing, "When the Roll Is Called up Yonder." Then the hugging to beat all get out commenced. Everybody hugged everybody else. Young hugged old. Old hugged young. Farewells were bid, good-night and good year. Although most of our family we would see again tomorrow or next week, you would have thought they were going back home to Jupiter.

I silently watched and listened to the sounds of parting as they echoed through the meadow. Voices walking together down the lane in the dark. Car doors banging. Headlights snapping on, sending out long, narrow beams spotlighting other figures walking. Engines starting up and tires slowly crunching away. From somewhere in the woods an owl screeched. In my mind's eye I saw it swooping down to claim its prey. Moonlit Mom and Grandy shadows standing united at the end of the walk, calling out good-byes.

All of this was surveyed from their upstairs bedroom window, my nose pressed hard against the screen, leaving prickly crinkles on the tip of it. I sure didn't want to be one of those good-byes tonight. I listened to Mother and Khaki Dad's voices mingling with the other remaining kinfolk who were helping clean up down in the kitchen. I quickly slipped into Grandy's bed and pulled the coverlet up to my nose, grass-stained feet and all. Trying hard as I could to fall into deep, deep sleep, I only succeeded in keeping myself wide awake with the urgency of it.

I didn't have long to wait for the inevitable call from the foot of the stairs. It wasn't a surprise. I was expecting to be called. But *who* called my name *was* a surprise. It was Khaki Dad. Now, *that* caught me off guard. I was already too warm under the coverlet, but now I was smothering. With only a split second to decide whether or not to answer, I squeezed my eyes shut so tight there were twinkly, bright dots swimming around under my eyelids. Every muscle in my body was stiff as a poker. I held my breath for fear he could hear that I was awake.

"Lacey!" He called up a second time, impatient sounding. "C'mon down here. We gotta git goin'."

Mother, in the background, said, "I'll check the swing. She might be on the porch."

"Naw, she ain't on no swing. I saw her headin' up those stairs not ten minutes ago."

His tone was sounding awful irritated. I was just about to jump up and answer when I heard Nana's voice quickly ascending the stairs.

"I'll check. She might be in the bathroom."

I noticed she didn't turn into the bathroom first but came directly into her room and right on over to Grandy's bed. I felt her lean on the side of the bed and look close in my face. I was doing my best possum imitation. My eyeballs wouldn't keep still. I wondered if she could see them moving under my lids. She smelled safe. There was a little puff of her breath on my ear.

I wanted to reach up and hug my arms tight around her neck and say, "Please, please, please don't make me go." But

I didn't have to. As quickly as she came, she went, her voice this time going down the stairs.

"She's all played out, fast asleep. I'll tell you one thing right now, those chil'ern sure put in a full day of playing. Does my heart good to see all those cousins so happy to see each other year after year. I hope they'll always stay close and keep up the grand reunion tradition all their lives and pass it on to their chil'ern's chil'ern. You can look far and wide, and you'll never find nobody love you like your own kin. My father always used to say, 'Chil'ern, now God gave us five of you. Just like the fingers on your hand. They're close. They all work together and help each other out. That's the way I want you to be all of your lives. Be close and be there for each other.' And that's the way we've always been. Through thick and thin, we can always count on each other. Why, I remem—"

"The sooner she learns where her home is the better," Khaki Dad cut in sharply.

"That's right. You're just making things difficult. Interfering all the time!" added Mother with a familiar rise in her words.

Grandy's voice, like soothing ointment to a scrape. "I'm pretty sure she knows where she lives now, Howard, but she's just plumb worn out tonight."

I took special note that Grandy said where she lives and not where her home is. That made me feel somewhat better, although this conversation was making me feel yucky inside. I understood the difference. A home was a heart thing. Where you live was just a body thing.

"We're going up your way tomorrow to check on Adoette and take her some vegetables. We heard she's doing poorly lately. Why don't we just drop her by afterwards? It'd probably do Adoette good to see a young 'un's face. Hardly anybody goes to see her. Don't 'magine no children go at all."

The screen door slammed suddenly, causing me to wince. Shoe soles slapped hard on the cement of the walk, followed by an angry truck door shutting with *more* than enough force behind it. My stomach churned and I felt sick.

"Do what suits you this time. But some things are gonna change," Khaki Dad warned.

His footsteps quickly followed the angry path Mother's made. I pictured their footprints glowing hell red all the way to the truck.

The sound of his words made my throat and chest get achy tight. I wanted to scream down those stairs, *Go away, just go away, and never come back. You don't even like me!* But I knew that would only make matters worse for everybody. I could already feel Nana's silent disappointment at having this unpleasantness occur in front of the remaining family members. It was putting a damper on the memory of our grand reunion.

They sped away down the lane, engine roaring off into the night.

Grandy called after them, following out in the lane, "Be careful now. Lot of deer runnin' 'tween here and yon. I love you." His words fell unheard on the gravel somewhere between the Apostles.

Quiet murmurings from downstairs. Consoling kinds of sounds from Aunt Ruthie. I pictured her arm around Nana's shoulders. "Now, now, Beatrice, it'll all come out in the wash . . . still awful young . . . takes time. Don't get yourself all in a tither."

Quiet footsteps on the stairs and then Grandy was bedside, leaning over me.

"Hey, Grandy. They're pretty mad, huh?" I whispered.

"Oh, don't you worry none. That little fire'll burn itself out soon enough. Guess what?"

"What?" I could tell it was good.

"Misty had her babies."

"Oooh, Grandy, can I go see? Can I, Grandy? Please."

"Let's get the flashlight."

Out at the hutches we unhooked and slowly lifted the nesting box lid. Snuggled inside her fur-lined bed of hay was Misty and three teeny velvet bundles. I gently ran my finger down the tummy of one who was turned upside down nursing with his little feet wiggling happily. Misty gently nuzzled between my finger and her baby.

"Good momma, Misty. Night-night," I said softly and closed the lid.

"Mommas sure do love their babies," Grandy added quietly. Saying nothing, I contemplated the wider meaning of his words.

Grandy and I walked straight on past the kitchen door like we were being drawn. Drawn by an ineffable need to let the peaceable find us. Like a beeline, direct to our swing. Time passed as we sat, my head snuggled in the hollow of his shoulder, ear on his chest absorbing the reassuring beat of his heart, letting the solace of it soothe my spirit. Minutes melted away and slipped up into the midnight velvet sky as we sat, thinking, breathing, to the creak of the swing and the bullfrogs croaking. Calmness snuggled us in all around. Morning came. I didn't remember being tucked into bed.

Chapter Eight

A doette's small house was tucked away from all but those who knew her. The small dirt path winding into the woods was hardly noticeable in the summer. It could have easily been mistaken for a deer trail and probably had been just that when she first came here seeking peace and solitude. We had abandoned our automobile by the side of the narrow paved road. After crossing the ditch and wading through tall weeds, we found the path. A healthy patch of Queen Anne's Lace had sprung up masquerading as a gate, effectively obscuring it.

The walk deep into the forest was breathtaking as flora and fauna unhindered welcomed us. Beings of a more hostile nature would have been met as intruders. But we did not come with shotguns or chainsaws, destruction in our hearts. We came marveling at the gifts unfolding before us, our hands gripping only baskets heaped with vegetables, thick slices of cake, jars of summer's freshest preservations, and a bottle of rich cow's milk.

Fog was hanging in the treetops like sheer curtains as the morning rays filtered through to the forest floor. A beautiful spider web hung, dripping fresh dew like a string of pearls. Its occupant, a large, bulbous black and yellow spider, was busy taking down the old, fragile web, constructing a new one like a trapeze artist high overhead. At a bend in the path, a mother quail sounded out her familiar "bob WHITE" as her brood of seven identical chicks crossed with tiny quick steps in on orderly line behind her and disappeared into the pixie dust of camouflage.

Jack in the Pulpits stretched tall, up from the mossy dampness of their beds. The tickle of a breeze carried the scent of air so fresh I was sure it had been unbreathed by human or animal subsequent to its cleansing by the leaves of the canopy above. A fallen log was covered in green velveteen moss with large, floppy tan mushrooms growing up from the fertile earth surrounding it.

There was a pair of land snails with white spiral shells slipping along, leaving their glistening trail. Nana jokingly named them Hansel and Gretel Snail. We caught a sharp, musky whiff of an elusive skunk that passed by before us. Their thick black-and-white coat carried a strong scent even when they weren't riled up. They were so cute, the way they lumbered along. I wished we could have been a bit earlier to see them, even at the risk of being sprayed. Grandy said that having a skunk deliberately spray was unlikely if we didn't surprise them or make any threatening gestures. All of these sights and smells were set to a delightful chorus of birds singing their morning song.

I was so completely absorbed in the enchantment of the forest that I had all but forgotten our mission. Just then, as I looked straight ahead into a little clearing, intermingling with its backdrop was the unpainted wood of Adoette's house. You almost had to blink to realize there was indeed a tiny house in the middle of the forest and not your imagination playing tricks.

Intentional on the part of Adoette, she lived as close to Mother Earth as possible, taking only what she needed to survive, respectively replenishing what she took. This she had been taught by her ancestors before her, passed down generation to generation as was the Native American way. She had descended from the Nanticoke tribe, known as the Tidewater people. There were only a few left scattered along the peninsula and the old ways all but gone, but she remembered—remembered and treasured in her heart the days spent with her ancient great-grandfather listening to his stories in their native tongue.

She loved remembering even now that she was almost the age he was then, how her name spoken in their language sounded so rich and golden, full of promise. Al-do-AY-tuh— that's how it sounded as it flowed from her lips. To me, it was rhythmic and beautiful. It made me think of sweet amber honey dripping from a honeycomb. She told us that its meaning was, "strong as a large tree." It represented her spiritual kinship to nature. Of course, our Americanized way of saying it wasn't quite that lovely, even though we didn't pronounce the T's but made them A's instead to sound like, "Ado-a." Many of the Nanticokes had long since taken Christian names, but she had clung to her Indian name. She was attached to hers, as I had been to mine. I understood and held a special admiration for her.

As we drew closer, I could hear the tinkle of the shells and bits of colored glass that she had found and tied together with twine and feathers and hung from low branches of the trees near the eave of her house.

Nana called out in her cheerful, high voice. "Yoo-hoo, Adoette. You got comp'ny."

Almost instantly, from around the corner of the tiny porch popped Adoette, knobby walking stick in hand. She was very spry for being almost ninety. Old age had not diminished her hearing much. She had probably been aware of our coming since we got out of the car. I pictured the Indians I had seen in cowboy movies putting their ear on the ground and listening.

She was short and bent, very old, her face wizened with years and sun. When she saw us, a toothless smile stretched wide across her face. Her eyes were small and buried deep, almost hidden in the tan folds of her skin. Her white hair was long and pulled tight in a skinny braid that fell just shy of her waist. Other than that, she was dressed like any other woman of her age—I mean, no buckskin skirt with fringe or beaded headdress with feathers.

She also spoke our country-style language with no Indian accent, but sometimes her sayings told of her heritage. But I could tell, under her skin where she really lived, that she was full-blooded Indian, that deep in her heart and spirit she clung to what she knew and loved of her past. Her affection was evident in the stories she told us that her great-grandfather had told her. I could have listened to her all day sitting there at her feet, mesmerized as the buffalo roamed around the plains of my mind.

"Well, well, well. Welcome, my friends. If you ain't a sight for sore eyes."

"Good to see you too, Adoette. Heard you was feelin' poorly, so we brought you a few things," replied Nana, holding up a basket.

"Well, thank you kindly, I was. Felt lower than a snake's belly there for a while, but now I'm back up and kickin', not too much worse off for it. Took some sassafras root tea, weak, with Uneeda biscuits for a few days. That settled me."

Looking from one to the other of us and then at the baskets we held, she turned back toward the porch.

"Come on in and put 'em down 'ere in the kitchen."

We followed her around the corner to the kitchen door. There were banty roosters and hens, as well as some guinea hens scratching around the clearing. They provided her with more than enough eggs. She tenderly gathered them up each night in chicken wire pens to save them from the wild things that roamed at night looking for a meal. All in all she had done a good job of eking out a living for herself here.

Behind her house I caught a glimpse of her garden. Amid various flowering herbs that I was not acquainted with, she had butterbeans coming on. The corn and tobacco plants were tall, racing each other to the sky. She enjoyed her pipeful of tobacco once in a while as she rocked on her porch. The first time I saw her light up a pipe, I was thunderstruck. I had never seen a woman smoke a pipe. There was something almost scary about it, but thrilling at the same time. She made no excuses, just puffed away happy as a clam, slowly rocking her chair.

Inside Adoette's kitchen was so confined. A smoky kind of haze hung in the air, probably from the continual use of her wood stove for cooking and fireplace for heat in the winter. There was one four-paned window, very dingy, that gave everything outside a blue-gray tinge. As our eyes adjusted, I saw assorted varieties of herbs hung around the wooden rafters, drying. Some I recognized, some I didn't. There was a very decrepit-looking "ice box," as she called it, which Grandy opened up and put the bottle of milk in.

Large and small woven baskets hung on rusty nails that were driven unceremoniously into the beams. They were old, sacred to her, woven by the hands of her family way back when, and passed down to her. On one occasion, she told Nana her wish for her to have those baskets after she herself had gone on to join the rest of her family with the Great Spirit in the sky. She still referred to Him as that, even though she knew and believed that the one and only true Great Spirit was Jesus. I don't know for sure how she came to believe, but I suspected Nana had a hand in it.

"You'd be the only one I know who'd treasure the story of love and family that these baskets carry. There's value in the rememberin'," she had said softly as her gaze fell on them.

On shelves along the wall, a few old aqua Mason jars held tightly shut with metal fasteners were filled with tired-looking vegetables, fruits, and some kind of meat. I couldn't bear to think about what kind. I had seen her box traps hid in the woods. Not many, just enough to meet her needs. More than enough, she would set free.

No one knew any more details about how she had come to live here other than that she had once been married and had two sons. Now they were all gone. She alone had been here in the woods for many years practicing contentment. I wondered if there might be a family plot in the woods somewhere with three stones marking graves where she knelt down on occasion. She never said, and no one ever asked, out of respect for her feelings.

"Sit down. Sit down. That cake sure do look good. I'll have me a piece after supper, and I sure do thank you for all you bret," Adotte said, as she poured a glass of water into the top of the pump to prime it.

She pumped up and down vigorously to get the flow of ice-cold, irony-tasting water started, catching the sudden gush of it in a big kettle to put on the stove for tea. As the gentleman Grandy was, it was hard for him to watch her work the pump handle so hard and not offer a hand, but past experience had taught him that she preferred to do it for her guests. She considered it her privilege to serve us.

"Up come so much meadow grass this season. It's runnin' rampant out back and on this side of the house. 'Fore you leave I wanna pull you up some to take home. Makes some mighty good meadow grass tea. I know you got a likin' for it, and it's good for what ails you. How all your folks been gettin' along?"

They shared news back and forth and then talked some more about the way things used to be, like older people enjoyed doing. Their conversation usually wound down with them shaking their heads in agreement, "I don't know what this world's coming to!"

I sat down on the braided rug in front of the quaint wooden table. Nana and Grandy had taken seats on either side of it. Adoette sat in the rocker facing them and waited for the pot to boil. When I plopped down, there was a sharp stab in my thigh, reminding me of the arrowhead I had stuck in my pocket to give to Adoette. As I pushed my hand down in my pocket and fingered it, I wondered if it had been flung by one of her ancestors. Waiting for a break in conversation so that I could speak and offer it to her, I turned it over in my hand, marveling at the possibility of her feeling the connection of their spirit through it. Finally, a pause occurred as Adoette got up to attend the boiling pot and make tea. Jumping up, I grabbed the chance to present it to her.

"Miss Adoette, I brought you a surprise." I offered it to her on my outstretched palm.

"Ohhh," she whispered as she gently cupped the bottom of my hand with her left and covered my palm containing the arrowhead with her right hand. She drew me closer to her and looked me deep in the eyes for a moment. Her eyes were cloudy, the shade of stirred-up creek mud, with a bright ring around the colored part. But I had the feeling they could see very well, deep down into me.

She then lifted her top hand and gingerly withdrew the arrowhead from mine, saying, "Much obliged to you, my dear young friend. You have a thoughtful and kind heart." Turning it over in her small wrinkled hand and running her finger along the edge, she continued in a reminiscent tone, "It's a fine one and still has some bite. Quartz. Extremely sharp, good at making its mark in its day. My great-grandfather told me stories of searching for particular stones that would make the best arrowheads. Where has it lain all these years?"

"I found it on the back hill of Sanctuary Oak, sticking out of a furrow."

"Well, I certainly 'preciate you thinkin' of me. I will treasure it as I do our friendship."

The visit ended shortly after we shared a cup of meadow grass tea and ate some sweet corn pone that Adoette had in the ice box. It was sweet and grainy, darker than the kind Nana made. Dipping it in the little dish of molasses, I was still licking the stickiness from my fingers as we said our good-byes and headed back through the forest. Adoette stood in the clearing, waving until we disappeared into the woods. Perhaps she was savoring the sight of the three of us, or perhaps she had a presentiment.

The first person I was looking for and found as we pulled into the driveway at my new house was Lyddie. She was propped in the crook of her favorite tree dangling a string in the air in front of Misty Maple, who was alternating between batting her paws in the air and leaping up trying to catch it. Both Lyddie and Misty Maple appeared to be enjoying the game, so much so that they didn't even notice our car as it pulled up.

I was jittery to run and join them. Throwing my arms over the front seat from my perch where I was standing behind it, I gave Nana and Grandy's necks a tight hug and planted a kiss on each of their cheeks, lips still a little sticky from molasses. I could hardly wait for the car to coast to a complete stop so I could jump out and run to see her.

"There's your friend, sweetheart," said Nana.

"'Spect she'll be right happy to see you're back. Love you. See you later, alligator," said Grandy.

When the car finally came to a complete stop, I threw open the door, and ran across the yard yelling behind me, "Love you too. After while, crocodile."

"Hey, Lyddie! Hey, I'm back!" I exclaimed, running toward her. She looked up, abandoning her game at once, and ran to meet me. Misty Maple pounced on the string she had dropped and ran across the yard with it in her mouth. I heard Nana and Grandy's car doors shutting as they got out of the car and went on in the house to see Mother.

"Hey, you're back! You're back!" We joined hands and danced around and around in a circle. "Quick! I been waiting to show you the paper dolls my auntie in Philadelphia sent back for me with Tony. Although it took me forever to get them from him." Lyddie narrowed her eyes. "He was being a jerk, holding them up so I couldn't reach and making me jump. I finally had to kick him you know where." Lyddie pointed, and we both giggled. "While he was bent over, I grabbed them."

I had all but forgotten Lyddie had a brother.

"They're so pretty, and the dresses are made of the shiny kind of paper. Momma helped me cut them out real neat like.

I did one, but I cut the tabs off by mistake. So Momma had to tape them back on. Good as new. And guess what?"

Not waiting for an answer, she continued on excitedly as we ran into her house and up to her room. She got there first and held up the cardboard dolls, one in each hand facing me. They were glamorous in their permanent bathing suits.

"There's two of them and they're both girls. One's blonde like me and one's got brown hair, JUST LIKE YOU!" she shrieked happily.

We played with them the rest of the afternoon on the floor of her room, trying on all the different outfits and acting out scenarios for each one. They had some really groovy-looking outfits. "Groovy," a cool new word, compliments of Tony.

Tony. I was a little leery of him at first when he stuck his head around the door, startling us out of our wits. He looked so different from Lyddie, chubby with curly woodchuck-colored hair and dirty toenails. He seemed menacing, sneaking around to see what we were up to, butting in our conversations, tapping us on the shoulders and when we turned around, pretending he didn't. But as time went on, I got used to him and realized he was fairly harmless. Just a typical pesky older brother vying for attention, maybe even showing off a bit for my benefit.

Much later I heard Nana and Grandy's car engine start up. I ran to Lyddie's screened window. In my haste, I almost upset the lamp on the nightstand there. It was the one that she used to signal me at night after we were supposed to be in bed. I settled the globe quickly back on its base and peered out just in time to see them pull slowly away. Waving and throwing kisses, I hollered frantically for them to see me, totally forgetting that Lyddie's father worked night shift and slept during the day; therefore, we shouldn't be loud in the house.

At the last possible moment before they turned out onto the road, Grandy in the passenger seat looked up at Lyddie's window, saw me, and blew a big kiss. The lump in my throat was choking. I felt as though my heart would burst. Tears immediately sprung up and stung my eyes.

Right then, Lyddie, who was at my side, gently took my hand and pulled me back to the paper dolls, saying simply, "It's gonna be okay. I just know it."

I didn't question how she just knew it. I chose to believe her. What choice did I have? I was so grateful for having Lyddie as my new friend. And really and truly, a lot of my new family was becoming very special to me also. I only wished we could all be in one place and get along together real good. Then life would be ideal. Maybe there would be an earthquake, and Burleyville and Cedarton would slide closer together. Yeah, that would solve my little problem real quick. Not big enough to knock down any buildings or hurt anyone, just enough to remedy the situation.

Reverend Gladding said nothing was too hard for God, and I believed that with all my heart; so tonight I would pray for a weensy little earthquake to move us closer together. In the morning I would wake up, look out my window, and there would be Mom and Grandy working in the garden, which would now be in my new front yard!

Without either of us realizing it, our summer was slipping away like the moon on that first night back. It hung in the early night sky, illuminated by just enough light to reveal the gray outline of its sphere and bright crescent below, silently shedding its dark skin like a shiny silver coin slipping out of a purse.

That evening Mother left for work, and it wasn't as weird as it had been the first few times when Khaki Dad told me to go and get my bath. I had since learned the trick to filling the tub. I just had to climb in first so that I could reach the spigot and then fill the tub while I was already standing there. Sometimes I still got it too hot or too cold, but I was getting better at it. And sometimes when I didn't feel particularly grimy, I just ran the water and sang real loud.

He never seemed to notice, and then I'd go upstairs alone and turn both lights on in my room while I checked everything out for ghosts and other equally creepy imaginations. Next I'd pull out the Treasure Trove box that held my wishbone, press it over my heart and against my lips, and carefully put it back. That done, I would turn out the overhead light and flicker the lamp in front of my window on and off a few times to see if Lyddie was in bed yet. If she wasn't or if she had already fallen asleep, I'd look at my books awhile and try to remember the words.

Looking at those books was my favorite thing to do at night, especially the fairy tales. The pictures of Princess Aurora encircled with those brightly colored tiny fairies and little stars helped me think peaceful, dreamy thoughts. I was positive that Lyddie would look exactly like her when she grew up. Of course, I had to carefully avoid the pages with the bad fairy, witches, or that terrible fire-breathing dragon. I would always end with my favorite Little Golden Book, "Gay Purr-ee," and keep it under my pillow. I missed having Martha close by to rub.

The sun rose strong the next morning, promising another hot and steamy day. First thing after jumping out of bed, I looked expectantly out my window for Nana and Grandy or any sign that Sanctuary Oak had been earthquaked closer. Disappointed, I vowed to pray the same prayer tonight but a little bit louder this time.

After dressing in a pair of purple-striped shorts decorated with pink rickrack and a matching crop-top that Nana had made for me at the beginning of summer, I remembered my cherished wishbone and decided to share its preciousness with Lyddie. Carefully taking it out of the gold box, I stuck it in my shorts pocket, giving it a pat for safekeeping.

After breakfast Lyddie and I met in between our two yards to decide upon what adventure we should embark today. While we were pondering, suddenly there it was again. Someone was whistling a strange tune. It was the very same dirge I had heard in the dead of night. Shaking off a shiver, I saw Lyddie's eyes automatically begin to follow a peculiar old man wearing a battered hat and railroad-striped overalls walking on the dirt side of the road. He was obviously the midnight whistler who had left me frozen with fear. His eerie tune made me want to cover my ears and run.

Lyddie must have seen my alarm. Almost immediately, she offered, "That's Hickman. He lives down the stone road a ways, on past your house, in that Halloween house."

I knew precisely which house she meant and was quick to blurt out, "I know which one you're talking about. It's the one that looks like a scary face when you drive by, and it has a cemetery on the side of it."

This time I was careful not to say *bone yard*, even though the avoidance of the word caused it to whisper in my mind, which concerned me briefly. It had been labeled mightily fearsome to me the very first time I saw it. Halloween house certainly described it to a T.

"Yep. That's where he lives all right. Everybody else calls him Hick, but I'm not allowed to. For some reason, Momma don't like that name." Lyddie shrugged. "She says it's hurtful. He's a mystery, though, just walks up and down this road. Don't bother nobody, whistling along, always nods his head if you wave and keeps right on trudging. I can't say as I've ever heard his voice. He might have lost it or something."

For a brief moment I entertained the thought of telling Lyddie about the nighttime whistling, but decided to wait for fear she would think I was silly.

"Wonder who's buried inside that fence on the other side of his place," I offered instead.

"Yeah, me too. Oooh!" Lyddie suddenly rubbed her arms up and down so hard I thought she was trying to shed her skin. "I just got chicken bumps! Wanna go over while he's off in the other direction and look at the tombstones to see if there's any writing on them?"

Now, why we would have wanted to do that was beyond me, considering neither one of us could read more than our own name (and now *that* had even been made difficult *for me*). I was scared, but sorta intrigued by the thought of this shared adventure with Lyddie.

"I don't know if we should. It might be trespassing or something. I don't wanna have to go to jail."

"Aww, I never seen a sign or anything, and besides, I don't think they put kids in the slammer, do they?"

"No, but there's special places for bad kids, like reform school. Mother said it one day when I didn't listen to her. She said I better 'walk the chalk line ginger blue' or I might have to go to one."

"Wow," said Lyddie, eyes round as dinner plates. "What in the world did you do?"

"I started behaving, I tell you that much."

"No. I mean, what did you do so bad that she would say such a thing?"

"Oh, I don't really remember, but I think it was about Old Maid cards I left on the bedroom floor after she told me to pick them up. But honestly and truly, Lyddie, I wasn't being bad on purpose. I just forgot to do it."

"I know that. I couldn't picture you robbing a bank or something like that." She giggled and pointed her fingers at me like she was holding guns. We both erupted into waves of relieved laughter.

But now back to the matter at hand: Did we dare or did we not go investigate? Soap operas would be starting soon, and that would be a good time for me not to be bothered with. Not that anybody really worried about not seeing us all day once we went out to play—as long as we showed up for meals and no neighbor called saying we were up to no good.

It was pretty well assumed we were just out playing in the fresh air, wearing ourselves out so we'd go to bed early and leave the grownups to their evening chores and television programs.

"Well, do you wanna sneak over there and see? We can make believe we're spies on a secret assignment." Lyddie hopped up and down from one foot to the other.

"I guess so. But aren't you a little scared?"

"Nope. Well, maybe a tad, but it's daylight." Lyddie raised her eyebrows and shoulders simultaneously and let them drop.

"Okay, let's go by way of the field, behind the houses, along the ditch, just like we're on a secret mission. That way we aren't near the road. I'm not allowed on the road."

"Suits me. That's what a real spy would do." Lyddie put her finger to her lips. "Try to be invisible."

So off we went, sneaking around the corners of the garage, squatting along the fence, running toward the two walnut trees on tiptoes as fast as our legs would carry us. Then, hiding behind them until the coast was clear to run, we took off and plastered ourselves against the side of the abandoned barn. Crawling on our bellies across the pasture proved a challenge because we had to look out for bees in the clover and avoid sheep poop. Somehow I kept scooping up dirt and grass pieces in the elastic of my shorts. Suddenly, Lyddie sprang up, ruining our invisibility screen.

"Oww-wee!" She yanked up her shirt and plucked at a sharp piece of straw that had gotten lodged and stuck right in her belly button! "Look quick, is it bleeding?" She bent her head way down. Straining her neck, she pulled up on the skin of her tummy trying to see in, without success.

"Here, let me see," I said, inspecting it. "Nope. Don't see any blood. Just a teensy red dot where it pricked."

For the first time in a long time, I saw the scar on her chest. It didn't look as bright pink and sore as it had been, and blowing up the balloon was easier for her now.

"Sure stings."

"You wanna go get some methiolate to put on it? There's some in the medicine cabinet at my house."

"Maybe later. That would sting just as bad."

"Yeah, you're right."

"Quick, get down. Invisible, remember?"

And down we went, flat as pancakes while making our way across the last quarter of the pasture, weaving back and forth, east and west, like two crooked-backed snakes.

Chapter Nine

Reaching the edge, we laid there without words, staring through the puff balls of dandelions already gone to seed over at Hickman's ramshackle house. Close up it was no more than a shanty. Out back there was a pile of burnt garbage with some more recent cans thrown on top.

The outhouse was dilapidated as well. Its door hung slightly askew and was ajar. On the ground in front of it was a catalogue with torn-up pages. Big black flies buzzed in and out. Its contents left a pungent stain in the air. Lyddie and I looked each other in the face and pinched our noses tightly closed. I started to gag and had to spit on the ground, unable to swallow. Yuck above all yucks! But I reckon everybody has to go. I just didn't like to breathe it in.

Lyddie plucked a dandelion and blew hard, sending dozens of itty-bitty parachutes into the air. We both watched as they caught a draft and drifted up, up, and over the field.

A few were carried around the other side of the house out of sight, in the direction of the cemetery. Easy for them.

"All right, let's go. Around the back," ordered Lyddie. She sounded raspy and serious, like a sergeant leading his troops. She took off, bent over double trying to stay out of sight. She cut a wide circle around the perimeter of the outhouse. I was hot on her heels. As we ran past the outhouse, the pitiful little fence surrounding the graveyard came into view. Even more weeds had sprung up since I saw it from the road, and some had flowers now.

We inched along the side of the fence until we came to a broken-down place where a small gate had lost the battle and fallen over. Weeds (pretty ones, though), blue bachelor's buttons, and some white Queen Anne's Lace mingled and grew up between the pickets as if to console it.

At this point we forgot about being invisible. Quietly, almost reverently, we stepped through the opening—Lyddie first, and then me. We stopped and stood there, hushed in the presence of the humble tombstones before us. They were patched with lichens and looked to have been there for hundreds of years. A pale-yellow butterfly landed on a clump of buttercups nearby. It didn't look all that scary now, actually.

We were still cautious. Slowly, we ventured forward to get a better look, but not close enough to be standing on the grave where we might go crashing through to the coffin or get grabbed and pulled in by something.

One ancient-looking stone was off to itself more. It must have been there long before the others because the old-fashioned letters and numbers were very faint, hardly readable, even if you *could* read. Time had all but erased them. It leaned toward the others. I wished so much that I could read.

There were two of them, closer together. The larger of the two had a rosebud engraved above the name, leaving us to deduce that it must have been a lady. Then our eyes fell on the smallest of them all. It was also leaning, sorta sideways and backwards. On the top was a little lamb peacefully laying on its side, sleeping. I could see the cement curls of its fleece.

Whispering to Lyddie, I broke our silence. "This one must have been a baby or maybe even a little kid."

"Yeah, or maybe a pet sheep," whispered Lyddie back. "I wish I could read."

"Hey, that's what I was just thinking, too."

We inched closer as if distance could be hindering us from making out the letters.

"Look, Lyddie, there's only one set of numbers on this little one, and they're the same numbers as this one next to it," I said pointing, but careful not to touch the stone.

"One, nine, one, four," we both recited together in a sing-song way. Luckily we had both learned a few numbers—me from *Jack Rabbit's Counting Book* that Nana read to me and Lyddie from having to count the deep breaths needed to blow up her balloon to exercise her lungs.

"Wow, bet that's a long time ago," I said.

"Yeah, bet so, but why are the numbers the same, and why's there only one set on this one?" Lyddie wondered out loud.

"That's really weird, I dunno. Big Mom would know, though. She knows ever'thing about ever'body around here. We could ask her."

"No way. Then she'd know we were over here."

"Yeah, we might get in trouble, big time. We better get outta here while the getting's good!" I whispered sorta loud.

Just then, we froze in our tracks as we heard whistling close enough to raise the hair on the back of our necks. It stopped abruptly, directly behind us. We both spun around simultaneously to see Hickman looking hard, right at us, fists pushed down in his dirty overall pockets. He opened his mouth to say something, but before a word escaped, we flew out the back of the little graveyard through another break in the fence and off across the field. We were no longer invisible. We were just a blur of arms and legs churning through the weeds.

"Go, Lyddie! Go!" I yelled.

Behind us we heard Hickman yell, "Hey, come on back here, you two scallywags. I'm wantin' a word with you!"

Just as we were rounding the corner of the garage, we ran right smack into Tony.

"Whoa! Whatza heck's going on?" asked Tony as he stopped Lyddie up short, hands on her shoulders. "You twos look like the devil himselfs after yous." His newly acquired Philadelphia accent was apparent. "What's yous two been up to?"

In a tone I had never heard from Lyddie before, she growled, "None of your beeswax, Tony." She shrugged his hands off her shoulders and skirted around him. I followed quickly behind her.

"I'm tellin' Ma," threatened Tony.

"Oh yeah? What're gonna tell? That you were pestering us again? Then Momma'll be mad at *you*. You know what she said about bothering us."

Tony looked deflated and slunk off around the garage, probably looking for some kind of evidence of our transgressions that he could present to Mrs. Magistorm. But for now he was out of our hair.

Not having any brothers or sisters to sharpen my wits against, I was amazed at how easily Lyddie handled our situation. I had never heard her speak so fierce and plucky.

"Whew, that was a close one!" I said, turning to Lyddie.

"Yeah, but he don't wanna get in trouble with Momma again, so he'll leave us alone for a while. C'mon. Let's go see if Momma's made any Kool-Aid. I'm thirsty."

"Yeah, me too."

Shooing off fat black flies from the screen door of Lyddie's kitchen, we hurried in, hot and sweaty from running. Flies stuck to the screen door like that usually meant a storm was coming. The air felt close.

Lyddie called out as we went in, "Momma, Lacey and I are thirsty. May we have some Kool-Aid, please?" using her best manners, I noticed. Smart.

Mrs. Magistorm emerged from the little side porch where the wringer washer sat. Her reddened hands gripped a wicker basket full of clothes that had been squeezed stiff and flat.

"No. Sorry, honey. We're all out of Kool-Aid, but I have some orange Fizzies if you want them."

"Oh boy! Yeah, Fizzies! I love Fizzies!" We waited with tongues hanging out, pretending to pant as Lyddie's mom cracked open a metal tray of ice, sending a stray shard skittering across the linoleum. After retrieving it and throwing it out the screen door, she dropped the cubes into our glasses with a clink.

Truth is, Fizzies didn't taste all that good, and they left scum around the top of the glass. Just the same, it was fun dropping them in the water and watching them fizz—lifting up and down like they were alive, turning the water into drink. Before we dropped the tablet in the glass, it was impossible to resist sticking it on our tongues to feel the sizzle. If you held it on too long, though, it might burn a hole clean through.

The grass and dirt collected around my waistband was beginning to itch. Just then I remembered my wishbone. Reaching hastily into my pocket to show Lyddie, I was instantly distraught to find the pocket empty. Frantically I searched my other pocket, anxiety building.

"What's wrong, Lacey?" asked Lyddie.

"I put my wishbone in this pocket to show you, and now it's gone." Wringing the hem of my shirt, I said, "It's really important. Grandy and I made a special wish on it." The back of my eyeballs started to ache like tears were pushing to get out.

"Well, you two will just have to trace your steps backwards and try to find it," said Mrs. Magistorm. Easy for her to say.

We gulped the rest of our drinks, thanked Lyddie's mom, and then ran out into the backyard. We headed straight to Lyddie's tree to discuss our dilemma.

"All right," whispered Lyddie when we were safely out of earshot. "We just got to mull around here in the yard awhile and then sneak back over toward Hickman's, following our same tracks as close as we can."

"Oh, Lyddie, I'm scared. You heard him. He'll be on the lookout for us now. What if he catches us and throws us in his cellar?"

"Do you want your wishbone back or not?"

"Well, course I do, but . . ."

"There's only one way to find it, and that's to look for it. So let's get going. We'll never give up till we find it."

I was beginning to see a side of Lyddie that I never knew existed. The side that loved the thrill of real honest-to-goodness adventure and challenge. The side that relished the idea of having the pejeezes scared out of you. The same side in me that was seriously malnourished and just wanted to go home, crawl in bed, and cry myself to sleep.

We circled the yard twice, looking here and there in the grass and then cautiously glancing around for Tony. Once we were sure he must be occupied elsewhere, we struck off in the direction of our original spy route. Keeping our eyes down, we scanned the area back and forth for my wishbone. It was a lot more fun the first time. This time I had a sense of impending doom.

On the way we decided to pretend we had just wandered over while chasing butterflies and picking wildflowers in case someone saw us there. The closer we got to the pasture beside Hickman's, the harder my heart pounded. I felt like the Cowardly Lion with Dorothy. Lyddie was busily picking flowers and seemed to be lost in the moment, while I, on the other hand, was so nervous that I just randomly snatched up any old kind of weed, squeezing the clump in my fist.

Closer and closer we meandered, heads down searching, looking for the tiny bone. The pasture felt airless and muggy. The sickening stink of the outhouse surrounded us as the wind picked up and shifted in our direction. Feeling a little dizzy, I realized I had been practically holding my breath.

Closer still we ventured. Desperate now, I prayed in my head, *Please, Jesus, help us find my wishbone and don't let Hickman kill us.* Lyddie was humming, oblivious to my fear. The sky darkened as a thunderhead obscured the sun. It looked like someone had spilled a bottle of black ink in the sky as it slowly spread out, covering the light blue. In the distance I heard the rumble of thunder. I could smell the rain. The air felt electric.

We had to go back. Go back empty-handed. I'd never find it. It was gone forever. How could I stand it?

I dropped my head down, weeping. A gigantic tear dripped off the end of my nose and splashed close by my foot into a tall patch of red clover. Wait a minute. Could it be? Could it really be? Yes!

"Lyddie, I found it! I found it! I can't believe it!" Pressing it against my heart, I took a deep breath of relief.

"There. I knew we'd find it! Let me see," exclaimed Lyddie.

Holding it out for Lyddie to behold, I totally forgot about being scared. She carefully took it from my hand. Twirling it slowly between her thumb and forefinger, she examined it carefully. Our eyes met on either side of it.

"I'm sure glad you found it, Lacey. I really am. It don't look like much, but I know how much it means to you."

A stifled sob floated across the pasture. We were not alone. We both swung around in the direction of the sound to see Hickman on his knees in the little graveyard. His head was bent down and his shoulders were drooped forward, shaking in great spasms. We heard the sound of grief cutting through his old heart as fresh as if it were yesterday those graves had been dug. The age on the stones had not lessened his pain. Hickman was no longer terrifying. He was just a lonely old man who had loved somebody. Someone who had been gone a long time, leaving him to miss them ever since.

Before I had time to realize what was taking place, Lyddie was already halfway to the fence. I followed and then stopped, not having a clue what was about to happen. The rain started to fall in big, hard drops as Lyddie came to stand beside Hickman, her bouquet of flowers extended.

Startled, he looked up, angry like. I thought for sure he was going to yell or grab her or maybe throw a rock. But as he looked from her to the flowers, I saw his expression soften.

She said simply, "Hickman, these are for you. I'm sorry."

He looked up, studied her face with deep, sad eyes for a moment, and then gently took the flowers. Lyddie turned and walked back toward me.

It was my turn. I looked at the scraggly bunch of weeds in my hand and dropped them. Walking slowly, I gave the wishbone one last kiss and pressed it against my heart. Stopping in front of Hickman, I held out my hand, tears mingled with rain.

"Hickman, this wishbone has a promise in it that someday people who love each other will be together forever. It's for you."

He carefully lifted it out of my palm with his arthritic gnarled fingers. His old eyes were brimming over with tears as he looked at me knowingly and held it tightly against his heart.

Running back to Lyddie, I felt light as a feather. We grabbed hands and began skipping back across the pasture. All fear was gone.

Gigantic drops of rain began to fall even harder, washing all of us thoroughly. Now, I could never know for sure, but I will always believe it was God crying happy tears. His words about perfect love casting out all fear, lived out by two little girls in a pasture.

The rain didn't last long, though, you know. God being God and all, I imagine He had a ton of important things to attend to. By the time we reached Lyddie's yard, I could see a bright rim peeking out around the edges of that dark cloud. Grandy said every cloud had a silver lining, and sure enough, there it was for all to see. And me? I felt like it was God smiling down on Lyddie and me, pleased as punch. I looked up, smiled back, and waved.

Chapter Ten

The following weeks weaved me more and more intricately into the fabric of my new family and neighborhood. Turns out, Uncle Donnie *did* ask Helene out on a date. That one having gone so fine, he asked her out again and again after that. And now they were dating "hot and heavy," according to Big Mom. Whenever they drove up in his car, she was sitting so tight up against him that it was hard to tell who was actually doing the driving. Some evenings, they sat in his car under the shade tree a long time, just listening to music real loud and smooching.

I took note that she did not write Helene and Donnie, Donnie and Helene, and draw hearts all over her new pocketbook. It could have been because this one was made of woven straw-like material, making it hard to write on, or it could have been a more practical reason, like she didn't want to have to throw out a perfectly good pocketbook every time she got a new boyfriend. Just the same, she seemed awfully smitten with Uncle Donnie.

Whenever they looked at each other, it was real dreamy-like, and they called each other "Sweetie" and "Honey" a lot. She was always running her fingers up the back of his hair when they were in the living room watching television. Big Mom said they had been bitten by the love bug. They spent every day together when Uncle Donnie wasn't working. Even then, sometimes she came and hung around, watching him and reading movie magazines. She drank Cokes and ate Reese's Cups, sharing them with me.

Then she carefully reapplied her Mocha Rose lipstick, making kisses in her compact mirror. Once when I was there watching her, she offered to put some lipstick on me. It tasted good. I couldn't stop licking my lips, so it didn't last too long, which is just as well because I don't think Mother would have approved much.

She didn't want me growing up too fast, so she said when she threw out my treasured pocketbook I found on my excursion to the dump with Uncle Donnie. But it felt like she was just plain being mean. At least I still had my spectacles to play secretary.

Helene was nice to be around. She smelled good and said "groovy" a lot. Uncle Donnie was right, she was *sure* pretty. Sometimes she wore a scarf around her neck that matched her blouse.

Big Mom seemed half aggravated when she stated, "That scarf don't fool me none. I wuddn't born yesterday! It's because of those hickeys."

"Well, she should try drinking a glass of water holding her breath instead," I suggested. "'Course, that doesn't always work on me, but it's worth a try."

Snorting a laugh and causing a hot blush to flood my face, Big Mom said, "Not hiccups, 'Tunia. Hickeys. Love bites. That's what comes from too much kissin'. One thing leads to another, and next thing you know there's trouble."

I had just about all of that kind of education I could stand for one day, so I didn't ask what kind of trouble. Instead I crinked my neck hard to see out the window, up at a yellow jacket's nest under the eaves of the house.

Lyddie and I played each day. We never tired of being together. Some days we played store and let Tony be one of our customers. Cutting rectangles out of old catalogues to use for dollars and bottle caps for coins, we took turns pretending to know how to make change. Tony kept swapping hats borrowed from his dad and trying to change his voice or use an accent to be new people.

"Podden me, ma-ams. Woulds you all happen to hay-ave ainy baiked bains 'round heah?"

Giggling, we'd look around and hand him a can of something, charging him a terrible amount and so on and so on.

Other days we roamed the fields, often ending up lying flat on the cement embankment under the bridge and counting the cars and trucks that went over. It was a little scary at first when the feed trucks went over. We watched their shadow in the river. I had the terrible thought that they might be too heavy and collapse the bridge on us. We'd be squashed like bugs. Nobody'd ever know what became of us. No idea in the world how just cement with nothing under it could hold up all that weight.

But much to our relief, every time a truck rattled over, it held. Sometimes it was exciting to be scared, and we screamed as it crossed, looking at each other with mouths wide open and veins straining in our necks.

One afternoon when I went home for lunch, Mother said, "You better stop that screamin' unless somethin's really wrong. I could hear you two all the way upstairs. You cry wolf, and someday you'll be tough outta luck!" After that we screamed as loud as we could with our mouths shut.

Sometimes we tied string on long sticks, added a freshly dug worm without a hook, and went fishing. We never caught anything, but once a snapping turtle swam by and looked up at us like he was as big as God's dog. That's how Big Mom described someone who felt too important for their own good.

Once in a while, when Lyddie's dad was home from his trucking job, he would give us some money to go over to the store and buy penny candy or orange popsicles. We took our good old time picking out the candy and visiting with Virgie the storekeeper, who was right pleasant to be around. Her eyebrows were the same shade of red as her hair. She smiled at us a lot and wore striped or polka-dotted smock tops over skinny pants. We took lessons as she rang up sales on the real cash register and lifted the heavy wheel of cheddar cheese from the round wooden box to slice off wedges, wrapping them in freezer paper for her customers. She gave Lyddie and me a sliver now and then. It was oily and delicious.

She had a baby boy named Dale. *His* hair was not red. She brought him to work with her every day, and sometimes we played with him, getting him to laugh at our silly faces. During naptime he slept in the front display window of the store, which she filled with soft blue baby blankets and his terrycloth toys.

Everyone that came by admired him sleeping peacefully and monitored his day-to-day growth. The older ladies freely offered Virgie advice on everything from diaper rash to teething. So many people asked how much he was that Virgie taped a sign on the window that said, "Not for Sale." The window crib worked out real good until one day when he rolled right through the plate glass window, landing on the porch floor in front. He was unhurt, mostly just surprised, with a few scratches on his legs.

That was big news around town for a while. Advice was offered once again, and disagreements broke out among the ladies about how best to treat his wounds. Virgie treated them with kisses, and they healed quick enough. After that he had to be corralled in a playpen like a duck.

Saturday evenings were still filled with sounds of frantic preaching, wild music, and commotions of healings from God's Church. Most people had come to accept their different ways since no harm seemed to come of it. Every once in a while, Lyddie and I snuck over, hid under the church, and listened. We memorized some of their songs and on occasion sang them as we hung over the sides of the bridge, listening to our voices float down river.

As Elzie put it, "So long as they don't come 'round knocking on my door and trying to preach at me and acting all high and mighty, things'll be just fine," to which Iris and Big Mom agreed.

Just so happened that Sid and Ella Belle Farnsley had started attending there the very next Saturday after the doctor told Ella Belle that she was going to need surgery on the big goiter in her neck. Ella Belle was terrified of hospitals, more afraid of them than she was of being the object of Burleyville's scorn. And doggone if that old goiter began to shrink away, making lifetime members of Sid and Ella Belle. A couple other families that lived on farms on the outskirts of Burleyville started coming to worship with them for one reason or another. And so, little by little their congregation grew.

Mother had given me a great privilege. She had taught me how to cross the stone road safely to go over to Big Mom's whenever I wanted to. Standing back off the road, I was instructed to bend forward at the waist looking left, then right, then left again and right again, turning my head each time to be sure no cars were coming. After completing this ritual satisfactorily, I was then to run straight across—fast as a bullet.

Not only was I near 'bout busting my buttons with pride at being able to accomplish this dangerous feat on my own, what's more, it expanded my field of inquiry in another direction. Lyddie and I fairly quivered at the possibilities that lay waiting on the other side of the stone road. Before the day was out, Lyddie asked her momma for permission to cross with me. After a few trial runs, she was okayed to cross as well.

This is when I got to know Pop Jazz better, Big Mom's husband. He was a quiet, small man who rose before the sun every day and went to bed before the birds sang their evensong. He was very sparing with his words. In place of conversation, he listened to jazz music through the static on his radio while he worked in his shed behind the house, hammering and sanding away on the cabinets he made to order. The wholesome smell of fresh sawdust surrounded him.

I liked him, but I wasn't sure how he felt about me. He never said. Sometimes he gazed at me sorta squinty-like, but he didn't smile. He drank beer, causing me some initial anxiety. Having heard about the evils of drink, but never having the circumstance to observe someone actually partake, I fully expected him to be staggering around, cussing, and fighting by the second gulp. Much to my amazement and relief, nothing about his demeanor changed. He just kept right on smoothing the wood with his piece of sandpaper and listening to his music. Big Mom said he drank beer because he was from the old country where they didn't drink water, only beer. And if he didn't drink something, he'd dry up like a human prune. He smoked cigarettes too, one right after the other, leaving more than enough opportunity for me to sneak a lick from his overflowing ashtrays left about. He never appeared to notice—me or the spit-streaked ashtrays.

On Sundays he got all cleaned up, shaved and donned a starched shirt, and smelled of Old Spice. He put on a gigantic pot of chicken soup with sprigs of parsley, carrots, parsnips, and onions from his garden. He made homemade noodles, adding loads of black pepper and sneezing all the while, and simmered it for hours.

It smelled wonderful, but there was one BIG problem. He put the chicken in, FEET AND ALL. Every time he lifted the lid to stir, there they were, chicken feet spread-eagle, bobbing around in the pot. He seemed to particularly enjoy chewing on them, especially the toes. Well, *old country* way or not, the sight of it made me feel like throwing up. I had to high-tail it back across the stone road when he got ready to dip them out into his bowl.

Uncle Donnie brought home a German shepherd puppy one afternoon. Said he found him wandering the edge of Stillway's field. After asking around, it was apparent that he had no owners, so Uncle Donnie claimed him and named him Chief. He took to his name right away. When I held his face between my hands and looked deep into his sad brown eyes, I wondered if *he* had ever had another name.

He was very thin, but after a few days of home-cooked table scraps mixed with his dog chow, he started to lose the pitiful look. Chief was also gun-shy. Every time you pointed a finger at him, he would drop to his belly and crawl away, whimpering piteously. Everyone but me found that comical. I thought it was sad.

Uncle Donnie gave him a bath, which he tolerated long enough to get the soap rinsed, and then he shook like crazy, spraying droplets in all directions to cool us off. Then he took off running back and forth across the yard, rolling and sliding along on his sides, drying off in the grass. For the first time, he seemed truly happy and full of energy.

He liked me and followed at my heels, nudging me in the rear end for attention. He liked to be chased. Boy, was he fast! I never even came close to catching him. Once, I saw Pop Jazz smile as he watched. I'm pretty sure the smile was for Chief.

Hickman carried on his walking ritual much the same as he had before, except Lyddie and I noticed that he whistled a lighter tune nowadays. It didn't seem as though I heard him quite as often whistlin' in the night either. I wondered if in his shirt pocket he carried the wishbone close to his heart.

I thought I'd miss it a whole lot, but I didn't. My gold treasure box with the green rubber band around it was in its usual place. Sometimes I pulled it out and held it. The essence of the bone still lingered there, perhaps more powerful for the sharing.

Things seemed to be rolling along pretty smoothly for the most part. I didn't get to stay with Nana and Grandy as much as I would have liked to, but I had been given a phone privilege and could call them once in a while if I asked permission. It wasn't as good as being there, but it helped some when I got down in the mulligrubs with missing them.

I have to admit, I felt pretty grown-up picking up the phone and saying, "Miss Marge, would you please give me Cedarton-five-five-four-zero?" I even sat at the phone table and crossed my legs, jiggling the top one up and down just like a grownup while I waited for the familiar musical, "Ye-llo" on the other end. All I needed to complete the picture was a cigarette and I would have officially looked all grown up. But Nana would not have liked seeing that, so x out the cigarette part.

As life would have it, nothing stays the same for too long.

There came the day I went across to Big Mom's early one morning. It was baking day, but the smell of fresh-baked rolls was curiously missing as I came near the screen door to the kitchen and was no less absent when I stood inside, sniffing. Big Mom was not in the kitchen. I stood there in front of the cold stove disconcerted, knowing that something was terribly wrong.

That's when I heard it. Bawling coming from the bedroom. Alarmed, I went to the door and saw through the crack Big Mom in her nightgown, standing in front of the marble-topped dresser. She had her hands over her face, sobbing her heart out.

It frightened me to see her this way. For the first time, she seemed not to be indomitable. Something sharp and mean had penetrated her tough veneer and crumpled her, leaving behind someone raw and hurting I hardly recognized—in *her* nightgown, no less.

I crept quietly across the room to stand close beside her. Touching her arm lightly, I asked in a whisper, "What's wrong, Big Mom?"

She uncovered her face and sat down on the end of the bed, flopping her hands into her lap helplessly. Pulling me closer, she looked at me through tear-burned eyes. It was obvious to me that she did not consider my being there an intrusion, but a comfort.

"It's your Uncle Donnie, 'Tunia," she sobbed. "He's been drafted, and he's got to go off and fight in that durned Vietnam War. He's just a boy, hadn't even had a chance to vote yet. I can't stand it! I tell you, I can't stand it! It'll be the death of me."

I suddenly had a lump in my throat the size of a cannonball. Not my new Uncle Donnie. How would Helene take the news? I had been hearing about this war for a while now and seen pictures on the front page of the newspapers occasionally. I had even heard of some fella nearby being killed, but I never thought it could touch someone in my family.

"Big Mom, maybe the war will be over soon and he won't have to go. Maybe they'll call a truce or something," I offered hopefully.

"Maybe, but it don't seem likely. It's been going on too long already." She got up and pulled a dress out of the closet and headed toward the bathroom. "We got no business over there in the first place. It ain't our war to be fightin'. Sending our boys off to die in the jungle won't change one thing over there. It don't make no sense a' tall."

I followed her and sat outside the bathroom door on the rug while she washed her face and rinsed her teeth and put them in. She'd look much more like herself now, even if she didn't feel any better.

She was barely out of the bathroom when the screen door flung open and the troops arrived to console her. It was amazing how fast news traveled in this little town. Iris went straight to the pot and got the coffee started. Elzie plopped down at the kitchen table with a pan of some sweet-smelling bread she had baked and began cutting it in squares. It was still hot from her oven. The phone rang. It was Margie telling Big Mom she had just heard. It was the news that every mother with a son feared.

Beulah went straight to Big Mom and took her by the arms, looked long into her face, and said, "Now, honey, I know it's hard, but you're gonna have to get a hold on yourself for Donnie's sake. You don't want him worrying about you with everything else weighin' on his mind right now. We'll just have to pray to the good Lord to get him there and back safely. Ain't nothin' else we can do 'less you want to go up to Canada, and you know how Donnie and the boys feel 'bout them draft dodgers."

"I know. I know. It's just that you're fearin' for it day after day and hopin' and prayin' that his number don't come up, and then it does. It's just such a shock to the nerves," said Big Mom, shaking her head. "Come on now and sit down. Elzie baked some of her sweet dill bread this morning."

After Big Mom sat down to the table and helped herself to a piece, Iris brought her coffee over, and placing it in front of her, said, "Where is he this morning? I saw his car was gone when we pulled up."

"He's off to try and tell Helene 'fore she hears it from somebody else. She's gonna be heart-broke, that's all there is to it, plain heart-broke like the rest of us," answered Big Mom.

"I figured that's exactly where he was off to," Iris said with a knowing nod of her head.

Well, Big Mom was in good hands now, but I felt immobilized like I should be nearby, so I hung around out back and rubbed Chief and talked to him, explaining all about Uncle Donnie having to go away to the war. His eyes sympathized, but his tail wanted to play. So I found a stick and threw it a few times for him to fetch. Throwing it with all of my might, I still couldn't get it to go half as far as Uncle Donnie. Each time, he brought it back and looked up at me with anticipation like he was waiting for the real fetch game to begin.

After a couple more throws, I abandoned that game and flung myself down on top of him. Grabbing the scruff of his neck and growling as ferociously as I could, I began rolling back and forth in sort of a new wrestling match with Chief. That got him going. He instantly loved this new game and joined me in growling savagely and playfully snapping and nipping at my hands and arms.

We rolled all over the backyard until I was itchy from the grass, sweat, and dog drool. I wanted to stop playing, but Chief was just getting started. Every time I tried to get up, he jumped up, put his big paws on my shoulders, and knocked me down again. Finally, I had to play dead a long time for him to stop wrestling.

Later, he became known as the official wrestling champ in these parts. He could outlast anyone when it came to wrestling. He wrestled men and beasts alike. He wrestled with other dogs, hogs, and one day a man named Sewell even brought his pet monkey over to wrestle with Chief. He was wiry, but Chief was still declared the winner due to the unfortunate fact that the monkey was a sore sport and bit Chief on the hot dog.

Rinsing my arms and legs off with the garden hose, I saw Lyddie across the road and decided to go over and tell her about my Uncle Donnie having to go fight in the Vietnam War.

It wasn't until that moment, crunching my way across the fallen leaves in Lyddie's yard, when it occurred to me that summer had been quietly drawing its curtain. Looking up for what seemed like the first time since autumn had stealthily begun, I saw with new eyes the brilliant orange and yellow of the maples and oaks surrounding our houses. My mind's eye saw the ridge at Sanctuary Oak—colors spread over the hills like a new fall coat woven of vivid red, orange, yellow, and rust.

A wave of homesickness swept over me as I stood in stillness, thinking of the pumpkins that had been growing fat and round while I was gone. I saw the funny-shaped gourds, Mexican Hats, Indian corn, and the like that Nana always grew just for decorating.

Yes, nuts would have fallen by now, and the squirrels would be scurrying back and forth under the black walnut trees, storing them up in their tree hollows for the approaching winter. Grandy would be gathering them up in baskets to hull and dry out for Nana's Christmas baking. Last year I had been there to help as we gathered six baskets. My hands had been brown for almost a week from the sticky ripe hulls of the walnuts despite Nana's lye soap and scrub brush. Eyes closed, I could almost smell their acrid odor.

"Hey, what're you doing? Playing statue?" Lyddie's voice snatched me back to her yard.

Startled, my eyes snapped open to see Lyddie almost standing on my toes. I hadn't even heard her traipse across the leaves. "Naw, just thinking," I answered.

"'Bout what?"

"Aww, nothing I guess," I said. I didn't really want to risk bruising her feelings by telling her that right now I'd rather be with Nana and Grandy.

"C'mon, tell me. Penny for your thoughts," Lyddie persisted.

That did it. I burst into tears at hearing Grandy's words come from Lyddie's lips. He always said, "Penny for your thoughts" when he caught me daydreaming.

"What? Lacey, what's happened? C'mon." She pulled me by the hand over to her favorite tree. It was the tree where our friendship began with our very first conversation not so long ago.

Funny thing is, it felt like we had known each other forever. I couldn't imagine living without seeing Lyddie every day, just like I couldn't imagine continuing to live apart from Nana and Grandy. It felt like two people were living under my one skin, and there just wasn't enough of me to be everywhere I wanted to be. So, that's just what I told her as we sat with crispy leaves falling all around us in the shrinking shade of her tree.

To my surprise, Lyddie understood exactly what I was saying. She said that one time when she had been super sick with her breathing problem, she had a dream that was so much like real life that she had never forgotten it. In the dream she could hear her mother's voice and see her reaching out to hug her, and she wanted to go to her and hug her back. But on the other side of the room there was a very bright, warm light that seemed to draw her near to it, and the nearer she got to it, the easier her breathing became. She had wanted to be held by her mother, but she had also wanted to be warm and breathe in lungfuls of air, free of pain or struggle. Just like I described now, she too had felt torn, wanting to be in two places at the same time.

"Gosh, Lyddie, how did you ever decide?" I asked.

"I didn't. The next thing I knew, I woke up and I was breathing better. Momma said I'd been asleep for a long time inside that plastic tent at the hospital."

"I know! We should put you in a tent, and maybe you'll come up with an answer. We could call it the Magic Think Tent!"

At that, we both started laughing, real belly laughs, and then rolled over in the grass and giggled until our stomachs ached. Every time we almost stopped, we'd look at each other and start all over again.

Finally the giggles subsided, and Lyddie said, "Wanna go over to the pond off back field and look for turtles?"

"Yeah, that'd be fun. There's probably lots of them today."

So, that's how we whiled away our afternoon, keeping company with each other and a few fortunate turtles that had the privilege of being turned into living masterpieces as we painted their shells with swirling designs of leftover blue and yellow paint. They were returned to the pond at the end of the day transformed creatures. Actually, transformed, *tired* creatures since we couldn't resist *encouraging* them to compete in a few races after they were painted.

On the walk back from the pond, we found a dead hummingbird just lying in the weeds. I picked it up, and we reverently examined it, looking for clues as to why it had died. It was tiny and perfect, iridescent green with its little black bead of an eye staring but not seeing us. Sadness hung heavy between us that something so precious had died.

"Why do you think God lets little birds die?" said Lyddie quietly.

"Dunno. But I think they're not really, *really* dead."

"Whadaya mean, not really dead? How many kinds of dead are there?"

"Well, like, I think everything has a spirit living inside, and the spirit goes to Heaven. That is, if they're good and love Jesus. Nothing bad gets into Heaven. That's what Grandy says."

"So where do the bad things go?"

"They go straight to hell, you know, way, way down there somewhere." I pointed to the ground.

"Man-o-man, that must be a scary place."

"Yep. It's burning all the time there and has a lot of worms, and everybody's screaming for a drink of water, 'cept there isn't any. That's what a preacher who was visiting our church one time said. I had the willies just thinkin' 'bout it that night."

"Sure hope I go to Heaven when I die."

"Oh, Lyddie, of course you will." I turned to look her right in the face and took her hands in mine. "You're good and Jesus loves you. All you have to say is, 'Jesus, here's my heart. Come on in. I'm sorry for all the wrong I've done.' It's easy as pie!"

"Jesus, here's my heart. C'mon in. I'm sorry for when I've been bad." Lyddie giggled and breathed a sigh of relief dramatically. I could tell she really felt good about it.

"So, should we bury this hummingbird and say a prayer for it? Maybe even have a little funeral," I said.

"Aww, it's too pretty to cover up with dirt. Don't you think?"

"Yeah, but what else could we do? We can't just leave it here all alone."

"Let's just take it with us until we think of something."

"Good idea," I agreed as we headed off toward home.

Chapter Eleven

Autumn days slipped into autumn nights. The air stayed warm with an extra-long Indian summer that year.

There were a few short but precious visits with Nana and Grandy. During those times we did all the usual fall activities together, making the most of every moment. Packing each day full.

Grandy and I picked out the perfect pumpkin for our Jack-o'-Lantern. He cut a lid in the top, leaving the stem for a handle, and hollowed it out, careful to deposit the seeds in the bowl I was holding. Later we separated some of them out for roasting with butter and salt, saving the rest to dry out on newspaper for next year's planting. Nana put the orange flesh in a pot to cook for pie.

While it simmered, we discussed what kind of face our pumpkin should have this year as Nana drew out the options on a piece of paper. We decided on a Cheshire cat face with a huge smile. After carefully drawing it on the pumpkin, Nana carved it out and as the final touch, placed a candle in the middle and put the lid on. It was perfect. I mean *really* perfect because after staring at the big fiery grin on the cat's face, when you looked away with your eyes closed, the big smile was still there shining brightly on the inside of your eyelids, just like in *Alice in Wonderland*. It was completely wonderful.

Especially 'cause Nana had the idea to take it back with me to share with Lyddie. She was always thinking of things for me to share with Lyddie. I think she really liked that I had a special friend my own age to play with.

On my most recent trip to Nana and Grandy's house, we made really neat scarecrows. This time I didn't have to beg to go or anything. For some reason unknown to me (and believe me, I wasn't asking any questions), they just showed up after lunch and said I was going home with them for a little while. I hardly had time to say 'bye to Lyddie. I was overjoyed at such an unexpected surprise. It musta been talked over ahead of time 'cause Mother knew all about it and didn't act perturbed. She had stuffed a few of my things in a bag to send with me. I could tell she had other things on her mind that afternoon.

Anyhow, after we got back to Sanctuary Oak, we took old jeans, flannel shirts, and straw hats and made a scarecrow family to sit atop bales of hay that were loaded on the wooden wagon behind Grandy's tractor. There was a definite bite in the air. Nana and I needed a sweater. We had noticed thousands upon thousands of birds taking wing to fly south.

"Filling the sky like celestial pepper," Nana observed.

When I asked, she said that means pepper from Heaven. The sky had begun to take on that gray-blue wintry color. Flocks of snow geese were landing in the fields hoping to glean any corn that had been missed during harvest. The farm animals were beginning to look shaggy as they grew their winter coats.

The following morning on the way out to the barn to feed the animals with Grandy, I saw the breath of Naysayer the horse, frosty in the air as he snorted a greeting to us and tossed his head. We bedded down the rabbit hutches with more of the sweet timothy hay they liked so much. Misty's babies had grown nearly 'bout big as her since I saw them last.

Winter was most definitely coming again this year. Grandy was rubbing his hands together like he did when the change in weather caused his arthritis to act up.

Upon returning to Burleyville, I was greeted with an unexpected surprise. Actually, it was two in one.

The first being a kitten. Well, it wasn't a teeny kitten. It was probably three or four months old, but it was still small. Probably the runt of the litter. She was the cutest thing I had ever laid my eyes on. Big green eyes looked up at me from a delicate little face of white fluff. Her nose was the shade of the palest pink rosebud. She looked like a snowball, so fresh and white, except she was warm.

The second surprise came when Mother said that *Khaki Dad* had brought it home for me. Some lady who had a leaky pipe he had been trying to repair gave it to him. So he brought it home for me. That news was surprising for two reasons. One, that he thought of me; and two, that he would let me have a cat. Another mouth to feed, as I had so often heard him describe kids and animals alike. This seemed to be an unlikely thing to take place, but it had, and I was happy for whatever had brought it about. I named her Snowball. I couldn't wait to take her over to show Lyddie.

Not long after that, there came the ominous day when I hung around outside for a long time without Lyddie coming out to join me. In my jacket pocket, I had stowed away the cream sachet jar that held my quicksilver. Having recently remembered it again, I wanted to show Lyddie. She would be as fascinated with its mysterious ways as I was, of this I was certain. I could hardly wait.

Of course, I wanted to show her my armpit that was red and swollen where I had pulled a tick off last night, too. Mother had promptly snatched it out of my fingers with a piece of toilet paper and flushed it down the toilet with disgust. It swirled 'round and 'round with its legs outstretched, still gripping the pale piece of skin that had pulled off with it. I watched 'til it was sucked down with a satisfying gurgle. Gone.

Mother had to get out the blue bottle of ST37 and douse it good to kill any infection that might have been brewing. She declared it way too late in the season for ticks. But to this particular tick that fact didn't matter one iota, not even if

Mother said it. He was hungry and latched onto me just the same. Probably one last bloody meal before he hibernated or did whatever ticks do in the wintertime.

Right now it was itching like crazy, and I had almost dug it raw. It needed a dab of toothpaste. Lyddie used that on mosquito bites to help take away the itch.

After occupying myself for as long as I could watching Snowball and Misty Maple trounce each other while nipping good-naturedly at each other's neck, I bent down and rubbed Snowball's belly as she purred like a furry little motor.

Finally, I decided to go knock on Lyddie's back door to see what was keeping her. Mrs. Magistorm opened the door, inviting me in. She attempted a smile, but the easy cheerfulness was not there. Looking closer, I saw worry lines etched across her forehead, and she held her lips kinda tight.

Something was wrong, bad wrong.

The kitchen clock on the wall ticked away the seconds loudly as I stood there. Tick . . . tick . . . tick. My heart started to pound in my temples. Tick . . . tick. Funny, tick in my armpit. Tick on the wall. If Lyddie had been standing there with me, we would have laughed about it. Without her it didn't seem so funny.

"Where's Lyddie, Mrs. Magistorm?" my voice squeaked out of my tight throat.

"Lacey, I hate to have to tell you this. I wish it wasn't so, but I'm afraid Lyddie's not feelin' well today," said Mrs. Magistorm, flopping down in the kitchen chair, hands helplessly dropped in her lap. I didn't recall having seen her like this. It was scary.

"It came on her sorta sudden-like last evenin' after her bath. I shoulda seen it comin'. Shoulda made her keeping blowin' on that balloon, but she's been actin' healthy as a horse lately. I thought the operation had cured her. Her breath just isn't comin' easy, and that cough is startin' back up. She's feelin' real tired out."

"Oh," I said, suddenly feeling deflated and worried myself. "Can I go up and see her? I brought something special to show her," holding out the jar I held clutched tightly in my hand.

"Sure, honey. I know she wants to see you. Probably perk her up a little. Go on up."

Starting to go, I turned back. The strain I saw on Lyddie's mother's face and the helpless droop of her shoulders caused me to suddenly throw my arms around her waist, hugging her tight. She hugged me back real hard, like she was in the ocean clinging onto a rock to keep from drowning.

"Lyddie's going to be all right, Mrs. Magistorm. Don't worry. I'll ask my Nana and Grandy to pray for her with me. We always pray when somebody's sick or hurt and other times just 'cause we think of them. Prayer is real powerful, you know."

"That would be real nice, honey. Yes, you do that. We'd sure 'preciate it."

With that, I started up the stairs to see Lyddie. Halfway up, I heard her rattling cough, and fear gripped me. This was not the usual cold cough. I knew that much.

Peeking around the corner of her door, I saw her lying on her back propped up on two pillows. Her face was pale, and her blonde hair was spread out on her pillow, giving the impression of a halo floating around her head again, just like the very first time I saw her. The menthol smell of Vick's salve was strong in the air, causing my eyes to water up a little.

Her eyes fluttered open and she smiled. "Hey, there," she said weakly as she pushed up some on her pillow. The effort triggered another bout of coughing. Her face suddenly got bright pink, except around her mouth, which stayed white.

"Hey," I whispered.

"What're you whispering about?"

"Don't know. Just felt right."

"Well, it don't feel right to me," whispered Lyddie loudly, mocking me with a smile spreading across her face. "That is, unless you got a secret to tell me."

We both giggled, and Lyddie coughed hard some more. As her cough died down, I suddenly remembered the jar in my hand.

"Oh yeah. I brought a surprise to show you, and I didn't even know you were sick when I thought of it."

I sat on the side of her bed, slowly unscrewing the lid as she leaned closer to see.

"What is it, a bead?" Lyddie asked, looking puzzled.

"Nope. It's quicksilver. It's really neat. Look what it does," I said. I reached for a bobby pin on her night stand to stir it up.

"Wow!" Lyddie watched wide-eyed as the big bead broke into smaller beads and then magically disappeared back into the big bead again.

We took turns trying to pick it up, but it eluded our fingers, slipping to the side at the slightest touch. We rolled it back and forth in the jar and then turned it loose on Lyddie's hand mirror that had a narrow braiding around the edge, just perfect for hemming it in.

"Where'd you get it?"

"One day I accidently broke a thermometer, and it just rolled out on the floor," I said, digging at my itchy armpit. "I had to scoop it up with a piece of paper to get it in this jar. It's impossible to pick up. It's so weird."

Another unexpected spasm of coughing sent the silver balls flying off the mirror onto the floor.

"Oh no!" said Lyddie between coughs. "Look what I've done."

"Don't worry. I see them. I'll just use this paper-doll dress to scoop them up."

After several tries the elusive quicksilver was safely back in the jar, with the lid screwed on tightly.

As if on cue, Mrs. Magistorm appeared in the doorway with two steaming bowls of soup and a pile of crackers on a tray. "Lunch time, ladies." She sounded more like her old self now.

"Lacey, can you stay and have a bite of lunch with Lyddie? I thought it would be fun for you two to have an indoor picnic."

"Sure, that'd be great!" I replied, although I didn't feel the least bit like eating anything right now. I was just practicing being polite.

She set the tray down and took off her flowered apron, spreading it on the floor for us to sit on while we ate. "I've got some sugar cookies in the oven for after lunch. I better get them out before they burn," she said over her shoulder as she quickly disappeared back down the stairs.

Lyddie seemed very shaky getting out of bed onto the floor.

"Lyddie, be sure you wrap up good in your robe and put some socks on your feet, you hear, " Mrs. Magistorm called up the stairs.

"Yes, Momma," Lyddie called back, rolling her eyes a little. "Now she's gonna fret over every little thing again, just like when I was in the hospital before."

"I know. That's what they do," I agreed.

We ate our soup. The dry crackers made Lyddie cough some more, so she didn't eat them. I licked the salt off first and then dipped them in my soup before eating them. A ritual I had been performing as long as I could remember. I usually got full on the crackers before I could eat the soup, so Mother limited my crackers.

The cookies smelled yummy. They made my mouth water. It smelled like Christmas time in Nana's kitchen.

After we had eaten a few cookies, we played a round of Chinese Checkers. Lyddie picked the blue marbles. They were her favorite. She said they reminded her of ocean waves. I chose the green ones for no particular reason. I won, but only by one turn. Somehow I felt guilty about that. I wished she had won, honestly I did.

After our game, Lyddie started looking more peaked. She could hardly say anything without a hacking cough interrupting her. She winced every time like it was hurting real bad, deep in her chest. My tick bite felt like nothing now. In some strange way, I was glad I had it, like somehow I was sharing in Lyddie's discomfort.

Her mother came up with the brown bottle, gave her a teaspoonful of medicine, and said she better get back in bed to rest awhile. I said good-bye and promised to come back bright and early tomorrow.

When I pushed the door open and stepped out into the yard, the rush of cold air felt so good on my face. I sucked it down deep into my lungs as if breathing for Lyddie. With the exhale that followed, my lungs felt fresh and purified. It didn't seem right that Lyddie wasn't out here with me breathing in this healing air.

Looking across the stone road toward Big Mom's house, I saw that Uncle Donnie's car was in the driveway. Helene was probably with him crying and carrying on about him having to leave. That's all she had done since she heard. Her eyes were permanently red and swollen, and her nose was pretty red too. I don't think it would have cheered her up any to tell her that she looked like Rudolph.

There were several other cars pulled up in the driveway that I recognized. Big Mom and Beulah would be hashing it out. This time they were most likely on the same side. A real manifestation. Most everyone agreed that our boys shouldn't be going off to Vietnam. Every direction I looked seemed to be full of its own kind of misery.

So, I took off across the field behind our house in the direction of the woods. It was farther away than it looked, I recalled from trekking out there shortly after I had come here to live. That day, the corn was tender and green and only about a foot high. A lot had taken place while the corn grew tranquilly toward its gathering. "High as an elephant's eye," Grandy said one time as we drove past.

Now, the closer I got to the trees, the better I felt. I stepped over row after row of dried nubs of harvested corn stalks and made my way, anxious to be surrounded by the woods. Trees. That's why I picked the green marbles. Trees, a part of God's creation where I always found peace. Quiet, steady strength. No matter what came or went, they just stood, changing only for the seasons, and that was expected. Predictable.

A light wind picked up as I approached. The dried leaves in the tops of the trees sang gently, welcoming me. There were crows cawing sassily back and forth to each other from the upper branches of a tall oak. Not entering immediately but walking along the boundary of the trees, I spied a wooden box trap with the door dropped down.

That meant either of two things: one, it had been sprung; or two, there was a creature inside waiting for the hunter who had laid the trap to return and finish him off.

If the creature was a skunk and I shook him out, I might get sprayed for my trouble. If it was a snake, I might get bit. If it was a porcupine, I'd probably get quilled. But whatever it was, I couldn't let it stay in there to meet certain death. I decided to slide open the trap door while standing behind it, and hopefully whatever it was would just run off in the opposite direction, happy to be free. So, that's just what I did and then ran a couple steps away to watch.

As I stood there expectantly, nothing happened. I waited for what seemed a long time more. Maybe it was empty and had just been sprung shut. I crept forward, trying not to make a sound, but still leaves scrunched under my feet.

Just as I almost got to the trap, two brown ears poked up, followed by the rest of the rabbit. It hopped a couple hops away from the trap, blinking in the bright sunlight, eyes sensitive from being in darkness for who knows how long. It turned and looked in my direction, sniffed the air, and nodded as if to say thanks.

"Go, bunny, go! Run home to your family as fast as you can!" I called after it as it quickly scampered toward a thicket, white cottontail bobbing 'til it was out of sight.

After that, I was on a mission to find as many box traps as I could and free the animals. I knew a hunter rarely put out just one trap. The edge where the cornfield and forest met was his hunting ground.

Losing track of time while searching, I found three more traps, all empty. Springing each one with a stick, I took out the cut-up apple that had been left inside for bait and placed it outside as a free meal. Satisfied that I had found all that I could, I looked up to realize the sun was sinking fast, painting up the sky with great orange strokes, its last hurrah before saying good night. Supper would be on the table.

The days were getting shorter now. As I hurried back across the field, a large "V" of geese flew overhead, honking back and forth to each other. Their chests were glowing bright orange, with the reflection of the setting sun blazing on their feathers. Fireballs with wings.

Facing the sun, I suddenly stopped and yanked open my shirt to bare my chest and let the sun rest on my naked skin, stretching my arms out as far as I could. "As far as the east is from the west," I whispered.

"God," I prayed, "Please let this sun You sent shine through my chest just as if it was Lyddie's and make her well. Please, God, I'm afraid my best friend is really sick. You said you sent your Son to heal the sick."

Waiting to feel something happen while standing still, eyes squeezed tightly shut and seeing bright red oozing inside my eyelids, I felt the warmth and light penetrate deeply inside my chest. Reaching my heart, it spread out to the tips of my fingers and tingled there.

It seemed as if I could feel the earth spinning and the movement of the clouds overhead. From the sheltering trees I could hear the sap trickling toward their heartwood. I felt the earthworms hidden underground churning, churning the earth. The warmth seeped down into my legs and settled briefly in my feet and then passed on through my toenails and into the rich soil where I stood.

Timidly, I opened my eyes and looked down. I truly expected to see my legs as well as the ground at my feet all lit up, glowing brightly. Instead, it was just dry brown dirt. It might not have been for my eyes to see, but I had most *definitely* felt it. Why, my fingertips even still prickled a bit. Turning around slowly, arms still outstretched, I looked.

There! Starting at my feet—stretching over the bumpy rows—plain as anything was the shadow of a long, slender cross. I stared at God's answer. Knowing that indeed it was an answer though not quite understanding *what* answer.

A little shaky, I looked around to see if anyone else might have seen. Only the slightest movement of a branch near the thicket, probably an animal. I buttoned my shirt and started running toward the house. No time to ponder. The geese were far out of sight now, long gone. I would be late for supper.

Lying in my bed that night, I tried blinking my night light on and off a few times with high hopes that Lyddie would see it and blink back. Looking for any sign that life had returned to normal and that Lyddie was all well or that the bad cough had just been a fluke or maybe even a bad dream.

But no. Eyes glued to her window, I saw shadows walking back and forth across the room, tall worried shadows like grownups bending over Lyddie's bed and then straightening back up again. Once, one of them—I'm pretty sure it was her mom—came and stood directly in front of the window, looking out into the night. I wondered if she sensed me watching in the dark, if she could see my outline. I waved a little fluttery wave. She could not see me. After a bit, she turned slowly back toward the room, bent over as if to kiss Lyddie good night, and then reached over and turned out the light.

Staring into the dark where the light had been, I tried not to bat an eyelid, afraid of missing a blink from Lyddie's light. Eyes turning scratchy and dry, despite my efforts I *did* blink and saw the leftover square flash bright yellow inside my eyelids. Still holding out hope that Lyddie would flicker her light as a beacon to me that all was well, I struggled to keep watch. No blink came.

As I was getting drowsy, my mind went back to the cornfield. The memory of the shadow cross was still mysterious and a little scary. God had never answered me directly before. Tomorrow I would call Nana and Grandy and ask them to pray for Lyddie to get well. Maybe they would know what the shadow cross meant.

Early the next morning after I had eaten a few bites of buttered toast and jelly and attempted a few gulps of milk, I asked to call Nana.

"You don't eat enough to keep a cat alive. Do you know there's children in China who would just love to have that breakfast? And here you are wastin' it," Mother reminded me as she picked up a piece and took a bite. "Go ahead. But don't be tying up that line for too long. You never know when there's gonna be an important call, and I don't want to miss it."

"I won't, Momma," I said very softly, trying out Lyddie's name for *her* mother. Mother turned with a puzzled look, opened her mouth to say something, and then didn't. Lately, I just felt the need to feel closer to Mother.

Ever since I was allowed to have Snowball, things seemed to be friendlier. I don't know why. It was like maybe they really *did* want me here. And they knew something about me, and that was I loved cats—well, all critters actually, but especially cats and bunnies.

I still could hardly believe I had a cat of my own and that *Khaki Dad* had actually brought her home for me. I still couldn't picture him driving his truck home with her on the seat beside him or maybe even curled up in his lap. I wonder what that would feel like. He and Mother both liked to watch her funny antics when she played with a piece of ribbon. Once, I saw the corners of his mouth go up a wee little bit. I think that was his way of smiling.

"Hello, Miss Marge. Can I have Cedarton five-five-four-zero, please?"

"Yes, you certainly may. Say hello to Mizz Beatrice for me."

"I will."

Rrringing once. *Rrringing* twice. *Rrringing* . . .

"Yel-lo," Nana answered with a cheery note.

"Hi, Nana. It's me."

"Well. What a sweet voice to hear this morning. I was just going up to the sewing room. I got a real pretty little dress I'm working on."

"Oh, you are?"

"I sure am, and guess who it's for."

"Is it for Martha?" I giggled.

"Wouldn't that be cute?" Nana laughed. "Martha hunting a mouse in a little red plaid dress with a big bow in back."

"Yeah, and you could make a little suit for the mouse, too."

Suddenly, I remembered the urgency of my call.

"Nana, you know what?" I said in a serious tone.

"What, honey?"

"Lyddie is bad sick with a cough. Her momma is worried about her—a lot, I can tell. I am too. She couldn't come out to play yesterday, and she didn't even blink her night light back at me last night. Remember about her operation on her chest? I think her mother is thinking about that. I told her I would ask you and Grandy to pray for her, and she said that would be nice."

"Well, we most assuredly will do that," said Nana quietly as if she had already begun to pray.

"But, Nana?"

"Yes."

"They don't go to church or nothing."

"Oh, sweetheart, you know that don't mean anything to God. He loves them anyhow."

"I know. And you know what, Nana? Lyddie asked Jesus in her heart when we found the dead hummingbird."

"Well, that's good to hear."

"Oh, and you know what else?"

"What else?"

"After I played with Lyddie in her room yesterday, I went out in the field close to the trees and prayed for God to heal her. I felt warm all over, and when I turned around there was a great big ol' shadow of a cross on the ground in front of me. I think it was an answer somehow, but what could it mean, Nana?"

"Well now, that does seem very special. Maybe it means to do just what you're doing. To pray for Lyddie and to get others to pray for her too. You know we have to take all our burdens and worries to the foot of the cross and leave them there for the good Lord to do as He sees fit."

"I want Him to make Lyddie well."

"I know you do, sweetheart. So, let's say a prayer together right now. Grandy just came in. C'mon, Grandy, and let's pray for Lyddie. She's down with a bad cough, and it's got Lacey awful worried about her."

Closing my eyes, I could see both of them standing side by side, bowing their heads together. I bowed mine too and clutched the telephone tighter as if to shorten the distance between us.

"Dear Lord, this little girl is sick with a bad cough. You already know that, so we're just asking You to touch her and make her well as You see fit. And also, Lord Jesus, please give peace of mind to all of those who love her. Amen."

We all three said amen just before Mother came around the corner with a basket of wash on her hip and said, "Are you still on that phone?"

"Just finished, Momma." I could hear Nana thinking over the new name I had just used in place of "Mother." I knew she would like it.

Out in the cool sunshine of the yard, I spun and leaped this way and that, leaf-catching as yellow and orange leaves fell from the sleepy trees. Drifting down just as I was about to grab one, it would suddenly change direction, spinning out of my reach on a current of crisp air. The game was to catch them before they hit the ground.

Twirling around and facing Lyddie's house, I caught a glimpse of her looking out the window, laughing, then coughing hard and turning bright pink. I stopped and waved.

She waved back and pointed excitedly behind me at a new batch of leaves that the wind had scattered about.

I jumped and twisted, grabbing after them. At last, catching two of them, I held them up and motioned, one for me and one for you. Lyddie smiled, coughed some more, and slowly turned away from the window.

Knocking on the kitchen door, I could smell warm banana bread baking as I handed a bright orange leaf to Mrs. Magistorm. "I caught this one for Lyddie. Would you give it to her?"

"Well, well. I surely will do. We can tape it on her window and let the light shine through it."

"That'll be real pretty," I said. Not knowing what else to say, I turned to go.

"Lacey, here, have one of these banana muffins I just took out of the oven. Tony always loves them hot out of the oven like this."

"Mmm, okay," I answered, thinking how muffins and bread smelled exactly the same.

It was hot in my hand, not the burning kind of hot, just the yummy kind of hot.

"Thanks a lot," I said, taking a nibble off the top and thinking how Tony really missed out on a bunch of good things by having to go to school.

Sitting in the crook of Lyddie's favorite tree, I took a few more bites and stuffed the rest of it in my jacket pocket. Sure wish she could come out and play. Loneliness settled in and around me. Gingerly, I picked at a fingernail I had been chewing on. Now it was down to the quick, starting to bleed a little and smarting. Sticking it in my mouth to suck away the pain, I thought, *What to do.* I looked up and down the road and decided to go in the direction of the God's Church. Adoette's house was way down that road somewhere. Maybe I could find it and pay her a visit. She would be surprised to see me all by myself.

Chapter Twelve

Walking close to the ditch bank so as not to step on the stone road, I heard a meow and turned to see Snowball bouncing along behind me. Scooping her up in my arms, I kissed her right between the eyes, and then I took her along until she wiggled to get free and ran back toward the house. She sure did have a mind of her own for a little fluffy-pie.

Coming up on the front of the church, I wondered if the doors were locked. I sorta wanted to go in there for some reason. I resisted the urge and kept on walking.

There were a lot of potholes in this old winding road. Some of them had been patched darker than the rest of the gray stone. *If I just kept following it, I could probably make my way all the way around the world and back*, I thought as I kicked an empty oil can. It would most likely take a whole year though, and I'd probably wear out my shoes. Everyone would be worried about where I was and if I had enough to eat.

Hearing whistling behind me, I looked around. There was Hickman leaning over in the field cutting greens and stuffing them in a burlap sack. As he straightened his back and turned, I waved. He nodded in my direction and touched the brim of his hat, whistling a nice tune the whole time.

Passing a yellow house with white shutters on my left, I saw a lady hanging out her wash and noted that she was what we called *in a family way*. Even thinking it I whispered in my mind because that's the way it was always said—real quiet, like it was a special secret. Her flowing maternity top was lifting high up in the gusty wind. I watched closely for a glimpse of her stomach, curious about how things looked under there. The white sheets filled like a sail and blew up around her, shielding her from my gaze. I had seen lots of animals that were going to have babies, but they didn't act all mysterious about it like people did.

As I was coming up on a white-shingled house farther down the road, a huge black dog came running furiously at me, snarling and barking. I froze in my tracks, knowing he did not mean to be friendly. The fur was standing up on the back of his neck, a sure-fire sign that he was good and mad—biting and fighting mad.

I closed my eyes, cringing to the core, bracing to feel the lunge against me and whatever dreadful that followed. Instead, all of a sudden-like there was a sharp "yip" as he came to the end of his long chain. With a thud his body flew back in the air and landed on the ground. For a second or two, he was stunned as I put it in high gear and ran past. Fierce barking soon started back up again behind me. I didn't look back for fear that he had broken free.

Finally, I had to stop. My side felt like it was splitting open with a sharp pain. As I bent over with my hands on my knees, my lungs ached from gasping in air. He was still barking, only in the distance now. I'd have to remember to cut way out in the field going home.

I walked on past soybean fields and a farm that had pigs rooting around practically in the front yard. P.U.! They stunk to high heavens! It made me want to hold my nose, but I was afraid the farmer's wife might see me. So I held my breath instead and walked faster to get past before I had to breathe again. Nana would never let pigs that close to the front door.

There were black-and-white dairy cows gathered around a big clawfoot bathtub in the pasture taking long drinks. Feeling parched myself after all that running to escape the devil dog, I realized I was starting to get a bit tired of all this walking. It seemed like I had been gone for hours and musta walked miles and miles. Maybe Adoette didn't live down this road after all.

Trudging on past the forest on my right, I kept looking carefully for the almost hidden path. No path, but lots of gray squirrels scurrying about gathering acorns for the winter. My lands a' mercy! They kicked up such a ruckus in those dry leaves. It sounded like a great big animal coming through.

After the hardwoods there was a spicy-smelling pine thicket. Going in there and taking a rest on some nice cushiony moss was enticing, but instead I tromped on down the road like I was on a mission. 'Cause I was.

Thinking to myself along the way, I remembered that Adoette grew all kinds of plants that helped sicknesses. She knew medicine passed down from her ancestors. One time when Jerimiah had been laying-out sick for almost a week with fevers from infected tonsils, she gave Nana special roots and leaves to be boiled up into a tea for him to drink. He could hardly even get down sips of it, his throat was so swollen. Next thing you know he was fit as a fiddle again. On Nana and Grandy's next visit, Mrs. Rhodie sent a basket full of canned tomatoes, country ham, homemade biscuits, and fig preserves, but most of all gratitude for curing her boy.

Adoette even collected cobwebs from her dilapidated shed, storing them in jars. Old people used to put them in big cuts to help stop the bleeding. 'Course, they probably died later of infection. Nana held to the idea cuts needed to be washed out good and kept clean, but she respected Adoette's beliefs.

Noticing a faint trail on the other side of the ditch, I crossed over. Sure enough, this looked like the path to Adoette's house. Rushing now deeper into the forest and turning the bend, I could see it. Running the rest of the way, I called excitedly, "Adoette, Adoette!"

My excitement was more than a small part because I had found her house all by myself. Moreover, to see an old friend. I guess it should have been the other way around, but this was a big accomplishment for me and proved I was growing up.

"Adoette!"

"Well, howdy-doo!" Her piercing aged voice came from behind me, causing me to be startled with surprise. Whirling around, I saw Adoette just emerging from the woods with a worn shovel and a basket half full of fresh dug roots.

"What takes you in this part of the woods? Yer grand mammy and pappy comin' down yon way?"

"Nope, just me today," I announced proudly.

"Well, glory be! You be comin' all this ways by yerself?"

"That's right, Miss Adoette. It's a right far walk down the stone road, and I had to outrun a mean dog."

"I know the one. He's contrary, won't let a soul near that house without them havin' to come out and hold him. He's got a bad moon-eye."

"What's a moon-eye?"

"One eye's a differ'nt keller, whitish, sometimes blue. Shows meanness in 'is spirit, can't trust 'im."

"I can believe that! When I go home, I'm cutting a wide circle in the field around him, I'll tell you that much!"

"That'd be best if you be valuin' your parts. C'mon, let's draw a cool drink a' water. You look like you could use it."

"Sure could."

That's when I remembered my manners. Nana always said you never go to visit someone empty-handed, and I hadn't brought anything. With relief I recalled the slightly nibbled muffin that I had stuffed in my pocket. Pulling it out, it was lopsided from being smooshed. Still, it was a gift just the same.

"Here's a banana muffin for you. It was warm when I got it."

"Well, thank ya. I sure enough like 'nannas when I git 'em."

By now we were walking side by side down the path to her house like long-lost friends. She wasn't much taller than me, really. When we reached the porch, I stayed outside and sat on a stump under a twisted old apple tree, waiting for her to return. There were still a few apples left, clinging in the top branches. As we sat there sipping our water and enjoying each other's company, I told her all about Lyddie's sickness and asked if there was any kind of medicine she had that might help her.

Adoette thought for a bit and drew deeply on her pipe 'til her cheeks hollowed in and then puffed it out as she spoke.

"You say she's got a scar from bein' cut there by the doctor?"

"Uh-huh."

"That'd call for somethin' a bit differ'nt. She'll be needin' a poultice, somethin' to draw it outta her."

"We've been praying for her, Nana and Grandy and me, that is."

"Well, that'd be the most important. Soul medicine. No poultice'll do what the Great Spirit can, but He gives these here roots and herbs to ease us along, I believe."

"I'm believing that too, Adoette," I said, glancing over at her hopefully.

She looked mighty wise. After a short time had passed, she got up. I noticed that her knees didn't straighten all the way when she stood anymore and she sorta hobbled side to side when she walked. She must be getting a touch of the rheumatism I heard old folks talking about, making their joints stiff and bent. *Wasn't there any root cures for that?* I wondered to myself.

Following her into the kitchen, I watched as she went from one jar to the other, from one bunch of dried herbs to the next, pinching off just the right amounts of each one and carefully depositing them into an empty Sir Walter Raleigh tobacco can. As she snapped the tin lid down securely and handed it to me, she gave the instructions.

"Tell the sick 'un's mother to boll this together with just enough water to barely cover it 'til it thickens and turns bracky-green. Then tell her to ca'm down the bollin' and leave it sit in the pot so it's just tolerable on the skin. Spread it on a piece a' cheesecloth and lay it cross the sick 'un's chest. Cover it up with strips of soft flannel to keep the heat in long as you can."

"I'll tell her. Oh, thank you, Adoette. Thank you so much. Hope it works."

"Hope so myself."

"'Bye, Adoette," I said as I started down the path toward home.

"Don't forget to leave a wide space 'tween you and that moon-eye."

"I won't." Glancing back over my shoulder, I saw her bending to pick up the basket of roots she had left in the clearing.

As is often the case when you're not looking for something, the walk home seemed to go a whole lot quicker. I shifted the can from one arm crook to the other, it being too big around for me to hold with one hand. Contemplating its precious contents and hoping Lyddie's cure lay captured inside the walls of tin made the journey go even faster. I hardly even noticed the pig smell or the blister rubbing on my heel. So lost in thought was I that I nearly forgot to take to the field to miss the moon-eye. Lucky for me I did. As soon as he caught sight of me from way across the field, I saw him barking and yanking at his chain. That moon-eye of his must be telescopic 'cause from where I was he looked the size of a cricket hopping around.

Approaching the edge of the woods, I walked close to the thicket hemming in a stand of poplars on the far edge of the field. The warning Khaki Dad had given me on the day of my name change was the last thing on my mind as I hummed my way along. Suddenly, a pair of rough hands grabbed me from behind, stopping me dead in my tracks. A cut-off shriek was barely able to escape my lips before a dirty hand, smelling like dried blood, clapped over my mouth.

"No need drawin' no attention, missy," a gravelly voice said right next to my ear, causing the hairs on the back of my neck to stand straight up. Hot breath that stunk seeped around my face.

"I see ever'thang. I see'd you in this here field wid your shirt open wide. Tha'd be right af'er you let my supper outta dat dare trap. Now lessen, you want to end up like dat rabbit in a box, you best be a' leavin' my traps alone, ya heah? I know'd where you sleep."

With a sudden push from behind, I was released as I FLEW back across that field toward home. Now, I *do* mean *flew*. I'm pretty sure I actually flew, being lifted up by something unseen from behind because I could see the ground passing by under my feet as I crossed the field at an amazing speed.

Then, just as quickly, I found myself standing still on the grassy side of the road in front of the God's Church. It had all happened so fast that the actual terror I'd felt hadn't registered until now when I realized with embarrassment that my pants were wet.

Looking down as I gathered my wits about me, still clutching the tin in my hands, my eyes focused on the shadow of a cross on the road in front of me. Already spooked, whipping around, I saw that this time it was being cast from the top of the church steeple.

Yes, I understood. That's what it had meant. Of course, a healing. Lyddie was in need of a healing!

Excitement took precedence over the terrifying ordeal I had just been through. Forgotten, fear died right there on the side of the road at the foot of the cross.

Lyddie could be healed. Just like the people we had seen in the church. Reverend Whitecap did healings all the time. We just had to figure out how to get her up to that altar, her being so sick and all. Then there was the other small issue— we were forbidden to go near there. Man, oh man. So many things to think about, my head was swimming.

First things first. I knocked on the kitchen door with the can of cure, giving it and the instructions to Mrs. Magistorm. Pulling my jacket down, I hoped she wouldn't notice my pants. As I told her how to boil up the poultice, she looked a bit doubtful, smiling grimly to try and hide it. I couldn't tell if she doubted it would work or doubted she would try it or doubted that it had come from an old Indian woman who lived in the woods.

Her doubt left me deflated, and I was plumb worn out. I just hoped she would make the stupid poultice, at least give it a try. She said Lyddie was about the same—no better, no worse. She had just a few minutes ago fallen asleep after another exhausting fit of coughing, so I didn't get to see her.

In bed that night I laid awake going over all the possibilities of getting Lyddie to the church for a healing. We could dress up like two little old ladies. One of us would carry a cane. If we wore hats with the veils pulled down, maybe Reverend Whitecap wouldn't notice. But how to get Lyddie out of the house was the hard part. Her momma never left her alone. She was too weak to go out the window and shimmy from the porch roof to the railing below. Plus, any activity got her coughing started up again. Even laughing, which is supposed to be the best medicine of all.

Pondering these things over in my mind, I felt drowsiness closing in. As it settled about me like a warm blanket, I recalled the frightening incident that had occurred earlier. This time I distinctly remembered having heard the flapping of strong wings behind me on my flight across the field. I remembered the shadow cross as peace poured over me. For the first time since I had come to live in this house, I turned over on my right side, my back to the closet door. Unafraid. Totally at ease, I fell asleep saying my prayers.

". . . if I should die before I wake, I pray the Lord my soul to take."

Days slowly drug by as Lyddie struggled to get better. Nothing seemed to be helping. Not a trip to the doctor or the expensive medicine he ordered. Blowing up her balloon was forgotten. A vaporizer at her bedside blew mentholated warm air into the room over her bed. Out of desperation Mrs. Magistorm finally tried the poultice, only after her sister recalled a time when their grandmother had cooked one up and put it on their cousin, making him well right away. It had offered some short-lived relief from the pain in Lyddie's poor chest.

Looking pale as a ghost, she could hardly lift her head when I visited. She still had the sweetest smile, and I knew she was glad I was there. Pushing away the frightening idea of how her hair-halo made her look like an angel, I tried to remember some of Nana's stories to tell her. She liked hearing them but often fell asleep before I finished. I'd sit there a few more minutes watching her chest move noisily up and down. Then I'd slip out heavy-hearted, as quiet as a snowflake.

There was talk that Lyddie might have to get another operation, a very dangerous operation. Tony overheard his parents whispering their fears to each other in the night. We had to get Lyddie over to that church for a healing service, but there didn't seem to be a way.

Her momma seemed to grow thinner every day. Her dad slept less and less during the day after he got home from his night job. When Tony got home from school, he didn't feel much like playing and to tell the truth, neither did I. He took to wandering the fields.

It seemed to me that there were an awful lot of dark, rainy days. The wind got colder and blew hard against our house one night, causing the boards to creak and groan as it howled past. Thunder rumbled and shook all the windows. There was one particularly horrifying crack of thunder, followed by lightning so bright it lit everything up like it had set the world on fire.

Nana called to say there had been a ferocious wind storm on the farm, too. It had blown the tin roof off the barn, and one of the Apostles down the lane had been badly broken. It was doubtful that it could be saved. Grandy was out with some men fixing the roof. They had been able to salvage some of the tin they found blown way up on the hill.

Immediately, there was that old feeling again. I hadn't felt it in quite a while until now. That feeling of needing to be in two places at once. I wanted to see the damage for myself. I couldn't imagine the hole that would be left if one of the Apostles had to be cut down. The twelve had always been there, six on each side as long as I could remember, safely guarding the lane.

Rushing out into the chilly air, I crossed the stone road over to Big Mom's house. It wasn't baking day, but there was always some delicious aroma to welcome me. Today it smelled like pumpkin pie. Sure enough, there were already two out of the oven cooling on the rack.

Flopping down at the kitchen table, I must have looked as miserable as I felt, 'cause Big Mom said right off the bat, "What in the world ails you, 'Tunia? You sick or somethin'?"

"No," I answered gloomily and then blubbered out the whole mess, about the storm breaking the tree and Lyddie getting sicker and sicker and me wanting to be both places at once.

Big Mom just sat at the table and listened intently with her hands folded in front of her. When I was finished, she took my hands in hers and said, "Heaven's sake. That's a whole bunch a misery for one little girl to be totin'."

As I looked down at our hands together and felt the warm comfort of a listening heart, she continued, "Things like this ain't in our hands. It's up to the good Lord Himself. After we done all we can do with the gifts He's given us, the rest is in His hands. You know that song?" Singing swelled up from deep in her bosoms.

"He's got the whooole wor-ald in His hands. He's got the whooole . . ."

Hearing it only served to make me feel more urgent about getting back to Sanctuary Oak. Aidleen often sang that song as she worked. She said a great woman from the South named Mahalia sang it one time for a king. It was her gift from God, Aidleen said.

That's when it hit me. All this talk about hands and gifts perked up my memory of being out in the field and the strange tingling I had felt in the tips of my fingers right before I saw the shadow cross the first time. That was a gift God gave *me*. All I had to do was figure out how to use it.

"Thanks, Big Mom. I feel a whole bunch better now. Like your singing. Gotta go see Lyddie," I yelled behind me as I jumped over a sleeping Chief on my way out the door.

Being so excited caused me to be careless as I ran straight across the road without looking. Instantly, I was caught in my mistake with a flash of chrome, alarming *screeeech* of brakes and sliding of tires as a passing car hit the loose gravel on the roadside, barely able to avoid hitting me. The sound of flapping wings was blotted out by a loud horn blare. Oh, shoot! If mother heard that horn, my crossing-the-road days would be over! Running hard past the front of the house, I kept on going. I wanted to be safe out of danger if she looked out the front windows, preferably out of sight completely.

Leaning against the back fence to let my breath catch up with me, my arms and legs felt like rubber. Whew! That was a close call. I pictured myself on the side of the road. Arms and legs stuck straight up in the air and tongue hanging out like that poor old possum I saw the other day. As my breathing returned to normal, it was apparent that Mother had not heard or she would be yelling for me by now.

Then I remembered my hurry. Lyddie. First, I had to think over the words Reverend Whitecap used when he went about healing someone. Inspecting my hands palms up, I noted that they looked exactly the same as they did every day. I believed the healing was in my hands. I had felt it. But it was God who put it there, so He'd have to tell me what to do. Believe. Believe God can do anything. That's it. We just had to believe really hard.

"Be healed in the name of Jesus," was what he had yelled when he knocked down the lady in the pink dress. I sure wasn't going to push Lyddie down like that. She was way too sick for that rough kind of healing. I don't think Jesus knocked people down either.

At the kitchen door, I saw Mrs. Magistorm stirring a pot on the stove. Her drooping shoulders told of her sagging spirits. She looked worn out. Turning around, she saw me and came to the door.

"Come on in. You look like you been running like a deer," she greeted me. I had the sneaky feeling she had heard the horn. I didn't know what to say, so I ignored her comment.

"Is Lyddie feeling any better today?" I asked hopefully.

"Not really, I'm afraid. Just now waiting on the doctor to call back. He's thinking she might need to be in the hospital." Her voice broke as she said the word.

Just in the nick of time, I thought as I headed up the stairs to Lyddie.

Her room felt warm and steamy. She looked over and said, "Hey" very weakly.

"Hey, Lyddie," I replied, crossing the room to her bed. Standing there beside her, for the first time since we'd known each other I was at a loss for words. I stood there awkwardly, looking down at her face. She barely resembled the Lyddie I knew.

On the window were droplets from the vaporizer. They had loosened the tape holding the orange leaf, causing it to hang sideways. The drops ran together, forming rivulets that streamed down the window like tears. My only best friend in the whole wide world was slipping away. That distressing thought snapped me back to what I must do. It gave me the courage. I didn't care if it did seem weird.

"Lyddie, remember when we saw Reverend Whitecap do those healings?"

"Yeah."

"Well, you need a healing. You been sick too long now."

"I know, I been thinking about . . ."

Her words were cut off short by coughs and wheezes as she desperately tried to draw another breath.

"Don't try to talk. Just listen. Something strange happened in the field when I was asking God to make you well. I can't really explain it, but I think I got the healing power."

"What're you"—she struggled to get words out between chest-shredding spasms—"waiting for then? Do it." Another soggy-sounding cough rattled up from deep within her chest.

"You have to pray and believe," I said, gently placing my hands on each side of Lyddie's chest.

"I do believe," she whispered and coughed immediately.

"God, please heal Lyddie in Jesus' precious name," I said meekly with my eyes squeezed shut. Opening them slowly, peeking through my eyelashes, I saw Lyddie looking straight at me the same as she was before. Once more for good measure.

"Lyddie, be healed in the name of Jesus!" I said more confidently this time, knowing she was counting on me.

"Do you feel any better?" I slowly lifted my hands from her chest.

"Not sure exactly just yet."

"That's okay. It might take a few minutes 'cause you've been so sick. Just rest some more and I'll come back soon." Walking toward the door, I added, "I might be going to Nana and Grandy's for a little while."

"Okay. Lacey?"

"Yeah?"

"You're the best friend there ever was."

"You too. 'Bye. I *mean,* see you later, alligator," I blurted out quickly. I hated the sound of 'bye as it landed on the air.

"After while, crocodile," grinned Lyddie.

Taking special note of the fact that her last few sentences were not punctuated by jagged, raw coughing, my heart felt lighter. Could it be? Hope against hope. Thank You, God.

Snowball, all huddled up in the corner of the step, scooted in past me as I went into the house. Mother had changed from her housecoat into blue slacks with a matching blouse printed with teapots sprouting blue flowers. She had just finished the last few dishes and was wiping off the counter.

"Get ready in a hurry. We're going over to Mother and Dad's and help clean up some of the mess left from the storm."

Relieved at not having to beg to go to Nana and Grandy's, I didn't have to be told twice.

"I'm ready already," I said, heading for the door.

"Put that cat outdoors. I don't want her doing her business in here while we're gone."

"Okay, Momma," I said behind a poof of fur as I grabbed her up for a quick snuggle on the way out.

As we drove closer to Sanctuary Oak, I saw evidence scattered about from the storm. There were branches and debris blown about from nearby farms. The ditches on the side of the road were full of muddy water. A piece of curved roof was missing from the top of Brentford's silo. The wind had definitely been stronger out this way.

The radio played a song we could barely hear for all of the static. Just when the ride seemed that it would take forever, the cannery loomed up on the horizon. With tomato season over, it was vacant and eerily still.

Over the railroad tracks and now wide open fields for a bit farther. Right turn and then another. Here at last. Because the clouds still lingered, there were no blue reflections in the pond. It had taken on a dreary, dark color.

As we drove up the lane, I scanned the row of trees on either side. There it was. Second from the end, on the left-hand side. The old tree's branches lay sprawled out pitifully in the meadow. The trunk was split halfway down with a huge bough broken, still pitched precariously in the top. Dread swept over me like a dark cloud as we passed slowly by.

Trucks of neighboring farmers were parked up by the barn. As we got out of the car, hammering could be heard echoing in the cold air as men worked on the damaged roof. Spotting Grandy near the top, I ran and climbed up the ladder nearest him. I yelled to get his attention.

He paused for a moment, looked up, and smiled. Motioning with his hammer, he called over to me, "Hey, there, Son. Good to see you. Now go on to the house and help Nana. It's too dangerous for you up here."

"Okay, Grandy. Loove you." I dragged the words out mournfully, trying to show how much I wanted to stay.

"Love you, too. Back down real careful now. Go on."

Reluctantly, I backed down the rungs and went to the house. Inside Nana's kitchen was a bustle of activity as the women prepared dinner for the men to eat before they moved on to the next farm to repair more havoc wreaked by the storm. The homey smell of ham and cabbage enveloped me as I came in.

Going to Nana, I tugged on her apron saying, "What can I do? Grandy said I had to come in."

Nana bent down and gave me a quick peck on the cheek. "Well, I'm glad he did. I can use your help to make these biscuits."

She handed me a basin, heavy with a smooth lump of dough. She cleared a spot on the counter and pulled up a stool for me. I proceeded to roll the dough between my hands, forming small, round biscuits and lining them up on the pan. When that task was completed, Nana gave me the next job of setting the tables with plates, cups, silverware, and napkins.

From the kitchen window I saw Khaki Dad's truck pull up. As he got out, I was surprised that he headed toward the house rather than straight out to the barn to help. It didn't take long to find out the reason.

"Big commotion going on 'fore I left home," said Khaki Dad as he came in.

"What?" said Mother with a look of alarm.

"Seems Tony was out wandering the field looking for something to get into and got more'n he bargained for. He come up on Bad Otis dead as a doornail, laying on the edge of them woods there."

"Oh my heavens," said Aunt Ruthie. There were other exclamations, some blessing his soul throughout the kitchen.

"Fat rabbit nibbling clover sitting right next to him," Khaki Dad continued. "Tony said that hare didn't so much as flick a whisker when he came up on it. Sat there calm as a dove chewing. The whole scene was other-worldly."

"That poor dear boy. That must have been quite a shock to his messatabulism," added Aunt Lola.

"I 'spect it was," said Khaki Dad glancing in her direction. "Tony was right spooked all right. He said it looked like ol' Otis done got struck by lightning. Split him right down the middle."

"Oh my Lord, have mercy," said Nana.

That put a terrifying picture in my mind's eye of his ghost wandering around the back field wondering what happened. Then I remembered my scary encounter. A Bible verse came to mind, the one about how children are precious to God and how He sent angels to look over them. I could almost hear those flapping wings behind me again. Could it have been? My thoughts were interrupted with more grisly details.

"He was a' laying there flat on his back, eyes staring, arms stretched out straight, skinning knife gripped in his hand. Knocked his shoes clean off like it was hallowed ground or something. It's strange enough. I'll say that much," said Khaki Dad as he put his hat back on and turned to leave.

"Looks like the Lord had plumb had enough of his meanness. Not to pass judgment or anything," said Aunt Tillie, coming closer as she dried her hands on her apron.

"Of course not," added Aunt Ruthie quickly.

I really can't remember a lot of details from the early part of that day after this point. I know that the food was cooked, the table set with the leaves put in to accommodate all of the men and their wives who had come to help. I remember sitting on Grandy's lap eating bread pudding topped with Nana's delicious vanilla sauce. The men left, going back out to cut up the broken branches and take down the rest of the tree. Grandy said once again I had to stay in. It was too dangerous for me out there. Reluctantly, I slid off his lap and clung to his leg until he bent down and gave me a big bunny kiss. Then he went back outside.

Chapter Thirteen

A trio of chainsaws whined away as they worked. Looking out the window, I was sad as I watched Grandy put the ladder against the trunk and start to climb with his chainsaw in hand. Not wanting to see the final moments of the old Apostle, I turned away and found Martha asleep in a basket of yarn by the stairs. With a loose end from a stormy-blue skein, I tickled her nose, inciting a silly game of "chase the string."

There was a loud cracking sound. That's when the chainsaws stopped abruptly, followed by frantic shouts and an equally frantic, almost immediate booming on the kitchen door. Alarm swept over me as I jumped up and ran to see. Loud, excited voices and Nana wailing.

"Oh Lord, help us! Nooo! Rayford. Dear Jesus! Aaahhhh!"

I was caught by someone who covered my face with her apron as I struggled desperately to get free. Nana's wails pierced my heart. Mother was sobbing. Fear for what

I couldn't see gripped me. Instinctively, I began screaming, ripping, and pushing myself away from the handcuffs of flesh that held me.

As I pulled free, running to the window, I was just in time to see the flash of a green pick-up truck tearing down the lane on the way to the emergency room in Salsten. The remaining men stood staring after it, frozen in their tracks. The large bough of the tree lay across the ladder, and both were on the ground beside the massive trunk. Grandy's chainsaw was propped crooked, blade up against the trunk. It struck me that he would have never left his chainsaw in such a careless position.

Reeling, I turned back to the room and the hysterical commotion of women around Nana trying to calm her and Mother. Everything else after that is practically a blank in my memory, mysterious gray nothingness as days disappeared into nights. Murmurs of prayers like bright flashes of light were all that penetrated the darkness. Until suddenly one afternoon from upstairs I heard the telephone ringing.

I recall Nana saying as she hung up the phone, "I'll be right there."

"Nana, I want to go with you to see Grandy," I yelled hoarsely, running down the stairs. I looked around at the surprised faces of Mother, aunts, and other relatives and neighbors who had apparently been coming and going since the accident. The table was covered with a collage of pies, cakes, and dishes brought by the church ladies, not knowing what else to do. One of the ladies stood ironing one of Grandy's shirts.

"Sweetheart, I know you want to go, but they don't allow chil'ern in the hospital. That's just the rules."

"I *have* to go. Nana, please! I have to see my Grandy. Please, please," I pleaded with desperation building in my voice. "You took me to see your friend one time, remember?"

"I know, but that wasn't the intensive care unit."

"You are *not* allowed," Mother added firmly, taking hold of my arm but more gently than I expected.

"Wait now, just wait a minute. Let me think," said Nana as she put on her long coat. "Come here and stand close behind me a minute."

Mother's lips tightened, but she didn't object any further as she let go of my arm.

Rushing to Nana's side, I snuggled tight against her as she buttoned her coat over the two of us. "Now, walk," she ordered.

We took a few steps moving forward together. I squeezed her waist tightly with my arms. She could not pry me loose with a tire iron. Wherever she went, I was going to follow no matter what, no matter where.

On the way to the hospital, I sat as close to Nana on the front seat as I possibly could. Mother sat next to me. In the back was Aunt Lola, along with Aunt Ruthie and Uncle Melvin, who had come from New Jersey as soon as they got word.

The ride was unusually quiet except for Aunt Lola, of course. She was trying her best to ease the apprehensive atmosphere by relaying the weather report she had heard on the television last evening.

"Well, we should have brought umbreldas because Peggy Ivie said that the astrobarominater indicated it was going to rain heavy again sometime soon."

Ordinarily, there would have been some chuckles at her daffy rendition of the English language. Today the mood was somber. No one smiled or laughed.

While staring out the windshield as farm after farm whirred by, everyday scenes appeared more graphic to me. A corn crib by the barn was full with this year's harvest—a season passed. Slender, leafless birches bent over a pasture stream could have been etched with white chalk against the blue sky. Slowing down to take a sharp curve, we passed a barbed-wire fence that had stretched around an old tree and became one with it over the years as the bark slowly enveloped it. An abandoned shed, wood silvery with age, leaned hard to one side. Still, there was beauty in the leaning.

Everything spoke of the merit of time. Time that I wanted a lot more of with my Grandy. My throat tightened painfully, squeezing out a little sob. Mother gently patted my leg.

As I entered the hospital elevator tucked tightly next to Nana, hidden underneath her coat, the rest of the family encircled us closely. Passing unnoticed by the elevator operator gave us confidence as we made our way down the shiny linoleum hallway. Nauseating hospital smells seeped into Nana's coat and found their way to my nose, making me queasy. I pushed the feeling away. I had to be strong.

"Mrs. Grason?" a lady's voice asked.

"Yes, that's me," Nana answered quickly. I could feel the tension in her back as our entourage moved closer. For a fleeting moment, a picture of Dorothy, followed by a quivering lion, a tin man, and a scarecrow crossed my mind.

"I'm Nurse Wells. We spoke on the telephone."

"Yes, thank you for your call."

"Mr. Grason roused briefly since we spoke. He asked for his son."

"Oh, I'm afraid we don't have a son."

Immediately without thinking, I shot out from under the coat and stood before the nurse, who appeared unruffled by my sudden emergence.

"That's me! I'm the son he wants to see. That's what he calls me! Doesn't he, Nana?" I said excitedly, looking back at my now sheepish family.

"Yes, Son, he does," Nana confirmed.

"Shhh!" The nurse quickly put a finger up to her lips as a sharp warning.

She whisked Nana and me away so fast, I was sure she was going to toss us down a chute, out of the intensive care unit, and into the street below for breaking the rules. Instead, we were taken to a room where she quickly swooshed curtains around us. She then pulled up a little stool for me to stand on so that I could see over the side of the bed. I stepped up.

There he was, my Grandy. Though it was a bandaged, frail rendering of the robust Grandy I knew. No band-aid or kiss could heal this. My heart found ease just being next to him, all the same. He just *had* to know I was there. While the nurse explained that he may or may not be able to hear me, I whispered, "Grandy. Grandy, it's me. I'm here. I love you, Grandy. Whole big bunches."

I stretched hard to reach his cheek and give him a big bunny kiss. No response. His breathing was hard. But, he *was* breathing. Putting my hand gently on the only part of his arm that wasn't wrapped up or had a tube coming out, through tears I prayed real hard.

"Dear Jesus, please heal my Grandy. Please, please make him well. I love him so much."

Grandy's eyelids flickered slightly and then opened.

"Beatrice. Son . . . love you." His eyes closed again. Long pause that seemed to stretch into eternity, and then, once more his blue eyes opened. I will never forget their twinkly crystal blue. They were happy eyes.

"Son," he said softly, looking from Nana's eyes to mine. He paused between labored breaths. "The trees . . . are clapping." And then he smiled and closed his eyes.

Uncle Melvin drove home from the hospital with Aunt Ruthie and Aunt Lola in the front seat, weeping and blowing their noses. Nana, Mother, and I were huddled together on the back seat sobbing and trying to console each other. How would we ever live without him? I felt sad for my mother and how bad she must feel having to say good-bye to her one and only dad. Her tears seemed to match the pain in my heart. I felt a new and awful kind of bond. He was my one and only Grandy. It was the saddest, longest car ride. The sky grieved with us as heavy gray clouds formed and hung low over the treetops.

One picture stuck in my mind from the ride home, a harvested field where an ancient springhouse sat resting over a brook. Its old stone walls were beginning to crumble and fall, reuniting once again with the earth. Nevertheless, the brook running through it kept right on flowing past, carrying in its midst the reflection of the springhouse.

As we pulled slowly into the lane at Sanctuary Oak, no one dared look to the left. It would have been unbearable. Finding myself unable to go into the house with everyone else, I wandered around outside feeling lost and miserable. I missed Snowball. A melancholy thought of Lyddie came to mind. Maybe I didn't have the healing power after all. I pushed the thought away, unable to take in anything else distressing.

Martha was standing on the wheelbarrow, purring happily to see me. She had no idea. Picking her up in my arms, I wept huge, salty tears into her fur, matting it to her side. I remembered how once I cried over losing her, but she had come back. Grandy would not be coming back.

Eventually, Mother and I went home to gather our best dresses for the services. As our car pulled into the driveway, I glanced over sadly at Lyddie's house, wondering if she was in the hospital. Obviously, I had been mistaken about my gift of healing. I had let her down, too. Miserably, I got out of the car and turned to go into the house.

"Lacey! Lacey! You're here. You're finally home."

I heard footsteps running across the driveway and was immediately tackled from behind. Turning around, I was nose to nose with Lyddie! As she laughed and talked, her words spilled out, incomprehensible to me at first.

"Lyddie," I whispered.

"Lacey, you're never gonna believe what hap—"

And then she stopped mid-sentence and hugged me hard.

"Lacey, I'm real sorry about your Grandy. Your dad told Momma, and I been saying prayers for you."

Tears clogged my throat, keeping me from saying anything.

Lyddie continued, "I loved on Snowball and played with her while you were gone. I think she missed you a lot. I know I sure did."

Finally, able to talk past the lump in my throat, I said, "Lyddie, you're all well! You're really all better?"

"Yep, no cough, no pain, no nothing bad left. Momma even took the vaporizer out of my room. It was amazing, Lacey! After you left, I fell asleep for a long time and slept so sound, no coughing or anything. Momma was getting real worried. She kept checking on me. When I woke up, I didn't feel weak and shaky anymore. I went downstairs to the kitchen. Momma, Dad, and Tony were eating breakfast. You should have seen the look on their faces when I said, 'What's for breakfast?' Tony almost choked on his scrambled eggs."

Lyddie's laughter was contagious. We grabbed each other's hands and danced around in a circle. Finding Snowball and Misty Maple, we took them over to Lyddie's favorite tree, squeezed into the crook of it together, and cuddled them. I could hardly get over how healthy Lyddie looked.

My heart finally felt lighter, though our time together was over too quickly because Mother and I had to return to Sanctuary Oak for Grandy's *funeral*.

Oh, that awful word; how it clutched at my throat every time. It made me feel as though I had been punched in the stomach.

Right then she called for me to come and get in the car, and Lyddie said, "Don't worry. I'll take extra-special good care of Snowball until you come back home."

"Thanks, Lyddie. I know you will. See you later, alligator."

"Yeah. After while, crocodile."

I felt tears well up and start to burn my eyes. Lyddie saw them, too.

"Lacey, I'm gonna keep praying for you. I bet God can heal a broken heart. He can do anything!"

"Thanks, Lyddie."

We said our good-byes and kept waving until the car was out of sight.

For the entire car ride I pondered why God healed Lyddie and why He didn't heal Grandy. Mother was grieving also. I saw a tear slip down her cheek as she listened to the radio, lost in her own thoughts. Feeling confused and sad, I needed to talk to Nana. She knew a lot about God.

When we arrived, Nana was hanging some clothes on the line. She always kept busy, especially if something heavy was on her heart. I ran across the yard and gave her a hug.

"Hey, Son," she lisped around a clothespin sticking out of her mouth. I noticed how she had started calling me "Son," and I cherished it. She pulled the clothespin free and stuck it on a pillow case.

"Nana, guess what?" I told her before she had time to ask. "Lyddie is all well. She doesn't have a cough or anything."

"Well now, that *is* a good piece of news. Lord knows we could use it."

"Yeah, it is, real good. But Nana, I don't understand why God healed Lyddie and not Grandy." My voice wavered as tears began to fall. "Why didn't He heal both of them? I prayed for *both* of them the best I could."

"I know you did, Son. And I did too." Nana's eyes reddened and brimmed over with tears as she pulled me close, continuing as her voice caught with a little sob. "God's ways aren't our ways. His plans are far and above anything we could begin to decipher. But there's one thing we *can* be sure of, and that is, even when we don't understand Him, we can trust Him just the same. That's where faith comes in. If we could tell God what to do, then He wouldn't be a very big God at all, would he?" She pulled a hanky with a yellow-crocheted edge from her apron pocket and blew her nose. "We just need to lean on Father God. No matter how much it hurts, we know He loves us more through the hurts—and He loves Grandy, too."

"I know, Nana. But I just want him back. I miss him so much," I said, scrubbing my eyes with the edge of my shirt. "I don't know how to live without him. He's always been here."

"It'll be tough, and we'll miss him every day. But we'll get through each day as it comes. When we're too weak or the sadness is too strong, God will shore us up." Nana looked up as a bright ray of sunshine fell across her cheek.

"We'll remember all the love, and He will start to heal our hearts. And someday we'll see Grandy again in his new body in heaven. What a grand reunion that will be! All those trees clapping—welcoming us home!" We stood and held each other tightly for a few more minutes, each of us crying softly.

Then Nana gently loosened my arms from around her, and she turned to continue hanging clothes.

Out in the shed I picked up Grandy's tools one by one, trying to remember the last time I saw him use each one. I could see his strong hands holding it. The tears dripped from my face, soaking my shirt. I needed a handkerchief. Grandy always had a handkerchief in his pocket when I needed one. That thought caused my throat to tighten. The misery in my heart was the worst I had ever felt. It seeped to the very edges of my soul and throbbed there. I couldn't stand it.

Howling, I ran out of the shed straight down the lane to the stump, kicking it as hard as I could, first with one foot and then the other.

"So, *you* are the one. *You're* the Judas tree! Stupid, stupid tree! You caused this! I hate you! I *hate* you, Judas! I'm glad you're nothing but a stump! That's what you deserve!"

Flinging myself down on the stump, I sobbed heart-wrenching cries of anger and pain until I was finally exhausted. Lying there sniffling, chest heaving, I opened my swollen eyes and traced tears that mingled with tree sap. They ran down the bark into the sawdust and dirt. I stared unseeing at the ground, hiccupping with sobs.

As my eyes focused on what was in front of me, my heart took a leap. I couldn't believe what I was seeing! There, lying beside the trunk like a precious jewel cushioned in velvety moss, was Grandy's half of the wishbone. Grabbing it, I kissed it and pressed it against my heart. I wanted to hold it there forever, treasuring the memory of the hands that held it last.

"Thank You, God," I said looking up into the sky, suddenly feeling the immense depth of His love for me.

That's when I heard the faintest of whispers as a gentle breeze caressed my cheek.

People that love each other will be together again someday. I promise.

Getting up, I wiped my tear-streaked face on the sleeve of my jacket and found a bright face full of joy. I ran to the house as fast as I could to share my good news. The healing had begun.

Questions for Discussion

1. What is your favorite scene in the book? How does it resonate with you?

2. Explore the different types of healing that you see happening throughout the story.

3. Do you think Lacey saw Grandy as a God-like figure?

   a. What role did the Apostles have in that correlation?

   b. How did Lacey's memory of Grandy saving her from the copperhead further suggest that notion?

4. The story took place in the early '60s. How is Lacey's situation even more prevalent in households today?

5. What are your feelings regarding Khaki Dad? Was he typical of fathers during the '60s?

6. Have you ever struggled with the same question as Lacey regarding why God seems to answer some prayers and not others?

7. Discuss Lacey's relationship with her mother.

8. How do you think Lyddie's healing affected her belief in God?

9. Think about the "trail" of the wishbone throughout the story. In your own life, what symbols has God employed to speak to you?

10. This story is written from an adult perspective looking back through the eyes of a child. Are there places in the story where Lacey's fond memories may have been embellished by the nostalgia of time?

11. Take some time to reminisce over your own life. Can you see God's hand orchestrating events, bringing you to where you are today?

12. What social conflicts were taking place during the time of this story?
    a. How did Nana and Grandy respond to the issue of racial tension?

b. How did Big Mom and Uncle Donnie respond to the draft during the Vietnam War?

13. Lacey was often comforted by nature. Are there things in nature that bring you peace and comfort? Why do you think that is?

14. The story of God working in the lives of ordinary people always has a ripple effect. With that in mind, project five years into the future. What changes do you think might have taken place? How do you think God may be working in the lives of Uncle Donnie, Lyddie's family, Khaki Dad, and Mother?

Acknowledgements

irst and foremost, I thank my God for all the majestic trees, woodland creatures, beautiful skies, family heritage, loving friends, the moon and stars, and all of nature that inspires me. Without His love and care, none would exist.

To you, the reader, thank you for choosing my book. We only get so many minutes in life. I am honored you would spend some of yours reading my book. I pray it will bless your heart.

To my hubbin' Bill of 42 years, who understood my need to be surrounded by nature and said, "This is the year we make our dreams come true."

Special thanks to my son, Will, and friend, Trevor, who struggled with my antique desk up the stairs and maneuvered it through a doorway too small to place it in front of the perfect window. It was here that I first saw Lacey among the trees.

Grateful thanks to my daughter, Hillary, for looking over and writing contracts.

Many thanks to both Hillary and Will for answering my panicked calls for help with flash drives and other technical aspects that remain in my mind as mysterious and dangerous to the preservation of my manuscript as a black hole.

To Frankie and Nicky, my beloved kitties and faithful desktop companions, who kept me company throughout the writing of this book.

My dear family and friends, who continue to enrich my life with their love, encouragement, and prayers.

To my parents, who taught me to appreciate the simple things in life.

To my grandparents, whom I miss every day.

To the members of my writers group at Mountain Christian Church who have become dear friends and prayer partners as we have shared, encouraged one another, and learned together.

Great appreciation to Candy Abbott and all of the vinedressers at Fruitbearer Publishing for the blessing of working with amazing, God-centered staff. It has been an uplifting, joyful privilege to share this leg of my journey with you. God's timing is always perfect.

Much gratitude to Nancy Rue, who put my heart at ease by beginning her edit with a special prayer for me. Your edits encouraged me with grace, kindness, and honesty. Your insights into my story were incredible. It has been an honor.

Special thanks to our amazing artist, Jessica Bastidas, who caught the vision for the cover and perfectly captured Lacey.

Meet the Author

Bonnie Mae Evans is a registered nurse and writer. She and her husband of 42 years reside with their many beloved pets in their Maryland home surrounded by trees, the inspiration for her book. They are blessed with a daughter, Hillary Grace, and son, Will.

Bonnie is a member of Mountain Christian Writers Group, where she is a regular contributor to their devotional blog, "Portions of Grace." She is a contributing author to several books, entitled *God Stories 7, God Stories 8,* and *Blessed Are You*. Her short story, *Iris Blessing*, was included in the book, *It's a God Thing*, published by Freeman-Smith. Several of her devotions were included in a devotional called *A Daily Walk with God*, published in Kenya for WGM missionaries to share with new converts. She is also a contributor to *Christmas Moments Book #3*. Proceeds will benefit Samaritan's Purse.

Serving the Lord and sharing His great love through stories is the true joy of her heart. You can follow her on Twitter @ BonnieMaeEvans.

Order Info

Available on Amazon.com,
from your favorite bookstore,
or www.fruitbearer.com

For autographed copies
or to schedule speaking engagements,
contact the author at
bonniemaeevans@icloud.com

Facebook.com/TheTreesWillClap
Twitter @BonnieMaeEvans
bonniefiedbybonnie.blogspot.com

For quantity discounts,
contact Candy Abbott
Fruitbearer Publishing LLC
www.fruitbearer.com
302.856.6649

info@fruitbearer.com

Made in the USA
Middletown, DE
07 December 2016